Best Regards

Donna R. McGrew

Wildfire

by

Donna R. McGrew

Bloomington, IN Milton Keynes, UK

AuthorHouse™
1663 Liberty Drive, Suite 200
Bloomington, IN 47403
www.authorhouse.com
Phone: 1-800-839-8640

AuthorHouse™ UK Ltd.
500 Avebury Boulevard
Central Milton Keynes, MK9 2BE
www.authorhouse.co.uk
Phone: 08001974150

© 2007 Donna R. McGrew. All rights reserved.

No part of this book may be reproduced, stored in a retrieval system, or transmitted by any means without the written permission of the author.

First published by AuthorHouse 7/12/2007

ISBN: 978-1-4259-8207-2 (e)
ISBN: 978-1-4259-8206-5 (sc)

Library of Congress Control Number: 2006910958

Printed in the United States of America
Bloomington, Indiana

This book is printed on acid-free paper.

Table of Contents

1: Nebraska Territory 1

2: Thanksgiving in the Plains................................... 12

3: The Sleigh Ride To Town 24

4: Mattie Kelly's Dilemma.. 44

5: Mattie and Ambrose.. 56

6: Loup River Mystery 64

7: Cynci, Sauk Slave Woman 75

8: Medicine Bow Country 90

9: A Letter From Ambrose 115

10: Back Home in Indiana 125

11: The Runaway Coach 145

12: Rose and Jesse 153

13: Rose's Music Lessons 166

14: Obediah Riddle 177

15: The Ravenna Incident 191

16: Death in the Afternoon...................................... 199

17: Hessie Riddle 216

18: A Day To Remember 224

19: The Summer Of Regret 234

20: Hessie's Mission 242

21: Rose Goes to Colorado 261

22: Hannah Ahrens 283

23: Home in the Teton Mountains 297

Author's Note

Wildfire is a work of fiction. Wildfire is defined as a fire that spreads rapidly and is impossible to put out. Any relationship to actual events, places, and persons is purely coincidental. It is based on the life of the families who homesteaded in the Great Plains. Actual events are referenced from the texts: *America*, Brief Fifth Edition by Tindall and Shi, W. W. Norton, Inc. New York, NY 10110; and the *Omaha Sentinel*, (Omaha Bee), Omaha, NE, and *The Oregonian*, Portland, OR. The artwork is by Nona Pool Goodrich.

Foreword

During the 1890's, Grover Cleveland was President of the United States when the stock market crashed. Unemployment was rampant. Times were hard and Coxey's Army of the unemployed descended on Washington where Cleveland dispersed them forcibly. In 1894, William McKinley ran against William Jennings Bryan from the plains for the presidency. Bryan was touted as an evangelist, capable of bringing a roomful of people to their knees. A Republican, McKinley's mantra was "every man must have a full dinner pail" which appealed to the working poor. McKinley became the next President.

There was a Wildfire burning in the plains, bright and strong and forcefully. Jesse Peers and Rose Sikes were young. They were the hope of the next generation that resided in Nebraska.

This story is based on the life of young Jesse Peers after his journey to the Great Plains from Valparaiso, Indiana. Jesse brings his good friend, Pearl Lux, Hannah, the love of Pearl's life; B.J., the wild Apache cowboy, three drovers: Hank, Del, and Ephraim; the Joe Lone Bear family from the Red Cliff nations of Wisconsin, along with 200 dairy cows to Nebraska.

Wildfire is the Gold Coin Arabian stallion with a blaze face who belongs to Jesse. Wildfire bursts with strength, energy, spirit, and temperament. This is the heroic account of the settler of the plains who battled blizzards, droughts, hardships, and violence. The time when lawlessness prevailed. William Butler, aka Wild Bill Hockok noted: "If a man is assailed and challenged by someone with a gun, and you were quicker and the bullet was before you, you could get away with almost anything." Lawlessness was the code that men lived by and protected themselves against. It is a love story of the adventurous people of the plains, the wonderful folks who live there even now. It is the struggle of the families who foraged a place in the plains with hard work and integrity to build a life for themselves.

Dedication

I dedicate this story to my sisters:
Ella, Viola, Jessie, Helena, and Sara Ann without whom this story could not be told.

Acknowledement

I want to thank my daughter, Jacquelyn Ellenz, who gave so generously of her time and talents, to peruse and edit this work. The many hours she spent made the book possible. Thanks to Steve Snyder, whose analytical capability helped me to complete the illustrations and technical work. I want to thank Cheri and Patrick Kelly whose consultation and advice helped me accomplish this work. I also thank Dillard Gates and the Friday Writers who listened so patiently while I read this story through to the end. Without their tenacity and support I would not have achieved this work.

Preface

The plight of women who lived in the mid-western states, is one of hard work and struggle. Though they saw some benefits it took years to bring about a way of life that was rewarding. One of the assets of large families was the hired hand. Often relatives or friends earned their way in the homesteader environment. Large families were accepted as the woman's role. The American couple averaged 5.42 children. They often died from their attempt to thrive in the harsh environment of the 'steaders wife. Diseases such as smallpox, typhoid, malaria compounded with drowning, shootings, and accidents plagued the early settlers. Doctor's became adept at diagnosing coma and fear of premature burial led to bizarre funeral customs. Shovels and pickaxes were buried in coffins allowing the dead to dig themselves out. Bateson's Revival Device consisted of a bell above ground with a pull cord attached to the hand of the deceased. Often the homesteaders choice of a place to settle required their assessment that the location was healthy.

Chapter 1

Farmers and The Land Among the legendary figures of the West, the sodbusters had an unromantic image in contrast to the cowboys, cavalry, and Indians. After 1860, the federal land laws offered favorable terms to the farmer. Under the Homestead Act of 1862: A farmer could realize the old dream of free land simply by staking out a claim and living on it for five years, or by buying the land at $1.25 an acre after six months. --Where farming was impossible, the ranchers simply established dominance by control of the water, regardless of the laws. America, "The New West. New Frontiers South and West," (Ch.18) Pp.667

Nebraska Territory

Time moves so slowly. Like the windmill on the homestead, it goes around from sunup to sun set. There is so much to do and so much more to be done. Dawn broke this morning with storm clouds shot with gray and purple thunder heads. It crested the flat horizon with searching scribbles of light through the flat clouds. The light through the trees spun spirals of green and gold. Somewhere morning doves sang their gentle song.

I've been here four months now; Thanksgiving approaches, and not one word from Mattie. Maybe she's one of those people that don't feel the need to write. Some folks are not born letter writers. My presence in Mattie's life will easily be filled. Ambrose will be there as ample as summer sun and spring rain, while I sit here with empty arms. My heart yearns to reach out, but my head tells me there's more to it than just Mattie's silence.

I ponder why I came to this barren flat land that blows sand as gritty as salt into your very pores. Driving a man a little daft at times wondering why you ever came here at all. Discount the weather, the work was a day's torture morning till night and then not always a success. The risk between sewing seed and harvest was a stretch even to the most experienced landman. You needed more grit in your spine to realize it is a losing game at times no matter how hard you try.

You'd not heard this carnage in Indiana for the weather was kinder all around. Not having to prepare each winter for frost bite or worse. Losing your cows to blizzards that buried everything so deep even fence lines disappeared. I can't fault the likes of Pearl wanting to return to Indiana. Only the anchor of Hannah keeps him in the plains.

Ma watches, her eyes full of questions. I'm sure she's been filled in on my consuming attention to Mattie. The women workin' in the kitchen are full of talk on matters that don't stray far from the truth. Their speculation stretches my limit of surprise and confound me at times.

"You need to let yourself enjoy life, Jesse. Let the rest go," she told me.

Pa confided, "Sara Ann is what her peers call your Mother. She is a wise woman who's done an overwhelming job of settling in here in the Platte valley."

She walks with a crutch for her knee. It's a special one built by Pa after the tornado set our cabin down on her leg early in their marriage when my brother Ray was a baby. The doctor wanted to amputate the lower leg, but she wouldn't allow it. Pa thought for sometime the damaged leg would claim her life. Instead, she bathed the leg in herbs from the river bed. She wrapped it in finest wool that kept the limb warm and clean. After six months, the foot began to look some better, Pa built this special stool that got her about her house, making it possible to go outside and around the homestead. Ma celebrated her 55th birthday this year. A little heavier than the last time I saw her, she still has her youthful face. Dresses she makes cover the leg and her infirmity has never held her down. She carries herself with dignity, the quiet calm of a woman who knows what the homesteader's life is all about.

"Are Maudie and Ethel doing all they can?" I inquired knowing this move was a job for five women the likes of Ma.

"It seems they're doin' their best. Of course, they're not getting any younger. You know how it sets with them that there isn't ne'r a sign of a man who's interested," Pa responded, a hint of regret there.

"All the entertaining Ma does seems to me those girls would get courted regular by someone looking for a strong wife," I was trying to grasp how this could be.

"Even the most eligible men don't seem to work out," Pa chuckled. "Ethel's head strong and set in her ways, and Maude is not the most insightful where men are concerned. What's more, Sara and I agreed we're not marryin' them girls off just so they could be married to someone."

"What you're saying I believe is, if it suits you, it doesn't suit them. Now that's about what I thought. Am I right?" I had discovered for both of us what the real dilemma was.

Pa looked down at the ground and examined his shoes like he was turning some new idea around in his thoughts. Now I may be daydreaming on this but I believe I solved a problem here. Pa replied, "Well, you'll see as you spend more and more time here." He patted my shoulder like he'd finally figured out something that was bothering him.

"You missed the Spring plantin' of crops. You were a great help when you were here for our harvest, though. The split rail fences you fella's built will withstand wind and rain. The Sweet Creek that borders along the homestead feeds the sapling fruit trees--cherry, apple, peach and plum. They're the ones I brought from the Indiana homestead in sod wagons during our long trek to Nebraska. They were dug from the ground and placed in wooden buckets. I picked our best Winesap and McIntosh, North Star Cherry, Cling Free Peach, along with selected Damson plum trees. Brought all the way from Indiana in sod wagons to this here place. Uncovered by day to the warm sun and covered at night with canvas against the early spring frosts, they came through just fine. Now they grow beside the bank of the creek. Under your Ma's close supervision, garden plants and all them pumpkins and squash were planted."

Since she only has two sons to provide the needed labor, it's with a heavy heart I resign myself to remain here in the plains. My thoughts flee to Indiana and the boarding house where Mattie lives out her life. There are others with dreams of traveling East.

Sweet Water already laments the need to see her Red Cliff clan and her family there. She feels the need to flee once again to Wisconsin and the Apostle Islands where she can live as free as the wind that blows. Morning Star and Ishtapa fill some of this need, but Lone Bear has begun to plan to take them once again through the plains and home again. Cynci, the slave woman, has bonded completely with Lone Bear's little family and plans to return with them. Perhaps B. J. Rivera will have something to say about that.

Cynci is a slender tall woman that we guess to be in her early twenty's. Her memories are short, so I could be wrong on this. Her buttery chocolate eyes and dark brown hair blend with the dark beauty of Sweet Water. Even though she has white blood, she blends well with Lone Bear's family because of the early years she spent with the Kiowa's. B. J. believes she will become a second wife to Lone Bear, if she continues to follow them. You can see it bothers him, and he has had heated arguments with Cynci about her plans to return to Wisconsin. His black eyes reflect silent messages as well as his concerns. There is lots of feeling and his Apache blood boils hot and fierce when he talks of this.

Cynci's slight of hand has me wondering about things that have disappeared around here. I could be wrong as I haven't had occasion to convince me it could be true. It seems to be a coincidence that wherever the women are, something is always amiss. Most of the time they write off a missing item being lost on the way to town or in the garden or creek somehow. This winter will turn up some interesting facts unless I'm wool gathering on this. Every time I ponder on this woman, I come out lacking some real facts. Her background is too murky. Her lack of memories is a guarded secret.

Pearl has been a never-ending source of wonder to my Pa, who respects Pearl's wisdom with horses. Hannah continues to show a real affection for Pearl. We see some improvement in her health, although there are still nightmares and the terror of her childhood. Ma sees to Hannah's welfare and needs her help with the constant stream of work in the garden and kitchen to keep this bunch of sod busters fed.

Pearl told me he will return to Ambrose in Indiana. Pa listens with interest, but all the same hopes he'll change his mind. Mostly Pa wants to encourage Hannah to stay with us and make her home here.

My sisters, Maudie and Ethel, have taken to Hannah like bees to honey. Her willing spirit and her desire to please are welcome and appreciated by all of us. Maudie studies on Hannah, since she has no experience with the trauma this young woman had seen, "There seems to be a big effort for Hannah to remain calm at times. We will see her through this no matter. "

Maudie and Ethel have lots of plans. Their suspicions run rampant about Hannah's past, but it will come out in time. I feel this is Hannah's affair and don't think it wise to be an informer until Hannah decides to share on her own accord. Each time I ponder on this, I come out a week short and a lot sorry. There are no compromises. We all learned a painful lesson with Benny Ahrens.

Before Thanksgiving neighbors and friends came to the house for a party. "I invited the Millers and the Sikes for an old fashioned taffy pull come Sunday," Ma quickly added. "I've ask Maudie and Ethel to entertain us with the flute and harpsichord and you too, Jesse, if you're willin'. I'd like you to play the violin."

We rolled up the Persian rug in the parlor and set the harpsichord in that room. Everyone spent the day cleaning and scrubbing the whole house.

On Sunday, everyone dressed in their very best clothes. Ma spent about an hour trying to find a favorite silver broach. She looked so puzzled. We all searched but never did find it. This was the gol' durndest thing. A little mystery we couldn't solve.

We were a real three piece trio, Maudie, Ethel and me. I brought out my old violin and people sat around that day sipping hot cider and tapping their toes. We slid into "The Old Sod Shanty on the Plains," and "The Strawberry Roan," followed by "The Prisoner's Song." Hannah wore the green velvet dress that Ma and the girls had made for her. It set off her dark hair and those beautiful smoky gray eyes just fine. Pearl wore his usual tight denim pants and vest with a silk shirt. He'd bought snakeskin boots with part of the reward money paid out by the courier service for returning the rider's possibles bag and the mail he carried to the Post in Fort Kearney. We came upon a young courier scalped and mutilated by the Oglala Sioux not far from Omaha just before we arrived at my parent's place in Nebraska.

Greta and Hans Sikes brought their son, August. Hans Sikes, a huge man over six feet tall, appears to be nearly bald and completely white haired. A weekly tonsorial keeps him looking quite trim and impressive. He wears a fur cap that makes his huge head look even bigger. His eyes reflect a stern nature, where emotions dance with a fiery depth. His face always seems to be pondering some dark thoughts, his mouth turned down with impassive eyes. The classic brooding man seems to embrace adversity as his destiny. Pa says Hans has a shrewd condescending personality. People around this country avoid dealing with him.

Greta, on the other hand, is her husband's complete opposite. She is a spry witty person, whose face reflects her challenging nature. Her eyes sparkle as if she knows some special secret. I believe she somehow manages to manipulate this stern serious man with her wit and keen intelligence. Mama tells me Greta is a veteran match maker and will be here today looking for prospective husbands for single females she knows. Greta and Hans have born ten children, and eight of them have survived.

Their daughter, Maggie Sikes, arrived with John Miller in his buckboard. John was a local farmer who was very taken with her. In fact, so taken that he overlooked any of her faults. I don't believe I will ever grow old enough or smart enough to fathom what goes on with some men and the women they chose. Maggie recently turned fifteen and was lovely to look upon. A great brown bow was tied around her head. A feisty nature was reflected in her glittering iridescent-green eyes. She wore a floor length dress of yellow plaid, and her tiny feet were encased in high-buttoned shoes. Every man in the room became the focus of her flirting. A sparkling smile and quick laughter made her the center of attention.

Ma noticed that Maudie and Ethel shared private jokes, whispers, glances and giggling as they observed Maggie Sikes from across the room. Their obvious jealousy brought them the attention of Ma who threatened both of them, "See that you behave when Maggie is here. No nonsense now, you hear, or we will not have the Sikes back again!"

Today, Ma stirred up huge batches of molasses taffy on our kitchen range. Going about this task from practice, knowing exactly when it was ready to pour. While the platters of molasses syrup cooled, she made sure everyone washed their hands in brown soap and hot water. Then she instructed, "Everybody grab a handful of taffy. Be sure it's cool enough to handle. Don't want any burnt fingers."

Everyone pulled until the taffy turned lighter and began to set. Ma and Maudie used huge kitchen shears and clipped the thick strips, twisted in swirling pattern on buttered trays. Afterward we carried the pans to the pantry where they cooled and hardened.

When Ethel brought cocoa for our guests Maggie bumped her arm and spilled hot cocoa on her. She covered the stain on her spoiled dress with an apron that suddenly fell to the floor revealing the ugly splotch of cocoa. Ethel was so embarrassed I could see she was about to cry. I held the cocoa pitcher while she replaced the apron and regained some composure. Later, Hannah and Mama served the chewy strips and cookies and black coffee. Maggie's eyes danced with liquid glee as she glanced at them with meaning looks. You knew something was going to happen with these three women. I sat and sipped cocoa but left the taffy to the others. Maudie's last pass around the room with the cocoa pitcher found her near John Miller. I noticed Maggie stretch out a foot and trip Maudie with a lightning quick move. Maudie tumbled down in a torrent of cotton petticoats and lace bloomers. Maudie was so befuddled she didn't know what to make of it. If either of my sisters did anything to retaliate, I did not see it. By the time the party broke up, most of the taffy was gone. It would be the last of our visiting for awhile, no doubt. John Miller looked relieved as he escorted Maggie to his buckboard. Her words floated back as she complained about the cold sitting in an open buckboard. Maggie's childishness leaves a trail of mischief wherever she goes it seems.

Mama told us she'd be more careful in the future having Maggie Sikes over since it seemed to result in one calamity after the other. Maudie and Ethel seemed unable to cope with the likes of Maggie. At the ages of fifteen and sixteen, my sisters are still more child than adult. Pa informed them they were still not to old to be to be taken over his knee. They recovered quickly letting the incident and any threat made drift off them as ashes off a dead fire. The rumpus with Maggie

Sikes continued to befuddle me. The topic rode into the months ahead with me.

Nebraska winters are severe and our guests were bundled in winter woolen clothing. Pa, Pearl and I brought up horses hitched to buggies we'd put in the barn to protect them against the cold. The jingle of harness bells and the squeak of leather accompanied our guests as they rode off down the country road toward home.

Chapter 2

The lands of the new West, as on previous frontiers, passed to their ultimate owners more often from private hands than directly from the government. Many of the 274 million acres claimed under the Homestead Act passed quickly to cattle ranchers or speculators, and thence to settlers. The land-grant railroads got some 200 million acres of the public domain in the twenty years from 1851 to 1871, and sold much of this land to build population centers and traffic along the lines. The New West of ranchers and farmers was in fact largely the product of the railroads. The first arrivals on the sodhouse frontier faced a grim struggle against danger, adversity, and monotony. Though land was relatively cheap, horses, livestock, wagons, wells, fencing, seed and fertilizer were not. Freight rates and interest rates on loans seemed criminally high. –As time passed and farmers were able to lay aside some money from their labor, farm families could leave their dugouts or sodhouses and build frame houses with lumber carried by the railroads arriving from Chicago. <u>America:</u> "New Frontiers South and West." (Chap. 18) pp. 668-669

Thanksgiving in the Plains

Thanksgiving marked a time of remembrance. Lone Bear snared a wild turkey and Sweet Water brought out dried cranberries. Shyly she told Ma, "My sister brought them from the Red Cliff village in northern Wisconsin where they are grown in bogs. There is a small bag of them and I think it will be enough for our dinner. I soak them in warm water and sweeten them with raw sugar."

Ma had no experience with this and left Sweet Water to do her cooking in the way of her clan. You could see Ma was a little concerned with some of Sweet Water's ideas. She listened intently to the story of the growing of these berries in bogs where they were harvested somehow by the Red Cliff nation. She accepted most of Sweet Water's ways, even though they were foreign to her own way of doing things. When I ponder on it, I'm surprised at the few arguments that arose amongst this crew of women. It caused an interesting mix, and the result has been delicious food that we all enjoy. Ma saved dry bread and salvaged some dried mushrooms. Added to her own onions and spices, it wasn't long and the smell of roasting bird stuffed with Ma's dressing filled the house. Hannah and Maudie made sweet potatoes with raw sugar and maple syrup. Ethel undertook the pies made from pumpkins brought from the root cellar and mince meat canned early in the summer.

There are times when I think on it hard the way we've all come together out here. It is near a wonder to me that people under this roof have blended into an extended family that works well together. We owe most of this to Ma, who not only set a good example, but demanded the best from all of us.

Thanksgiving morning brought with it light snow. We were warm inside the sod house Pa and Johnny had built. They hauled clay from the bank of Sweet Creek and made bricks with a mixture of straw and sand. Set to dry in brick forms, these were as sturdy and durable as stone. They built the main house and Johnny slept in the living room, but with the expected arrival of all of us folks, Pa found it necessary to build a bigger house. Four bedrooms and a huge kitchen were added on. It made it possible to have more than one root cellar. John Miller witched a well and that was dug and chinked with the sod bricks as well.

The men all went to the barn and sheep sheds to feed and care for the animals there. Pearl and Del Cole were deep in conversation about the weather.

"Pearl, I don't believe I've ever seen as bad weather warnings as I seen this mornin'. That's a mighty overcast sky and the wind don't quit." Del Cole's voice was troubled as we watched the wind churn clouds across the sun.

"The stand of young trees Pa and Johnny set out are too young to offer much protection, so the wind sweeps hard across the plains at times," I replied.

We stayed very busy until the Thanksgiving meal was ready and everyone assembled back in the kitchen. Ephraim Hobbs, Del Cole and Hank Simons took in the table laden with food, the appreciation washing over their faces in waves of contentment and approval. The storm outside was forgotten as we bowed our heads

Wildfire

while Pa said the blessing and then carved the huge wild turkey.

As I sat there, Mattie's image came bursting into my thoughts. I remembered the previous Thanksgiving at the boarding house. I need to deal with this before the yearning overcomes my good sense and I begin losing ground to my rampant desire and itchy feet. I could see Mattie with her apron tied around her middle, dolin' out food and orderin' the girls around. Mattie was a bundle of never ending energy. A real joy to behold in the kitchen. My heart recoils from the absence of Mattie in my life.

The day after Thanksgiving, we woke to a howling wind. Clouds gathered on the horizon, black and flat, rippling with wind. Grey and purple thunderheads streaked the overcast sky. The weather grew colder and blowing snow mounted through the day. The darkening sky was full of birds swept by the wind. Trees were full of their calls as they perched there. Pa sat at the kitchen table drinking coffee, worry all over his face.

"We got extra work for us because the cattle have to be brought in and all the horses tethered in the old barn, until this storm is over, so they'll not wander and perish in the cold. Last year, a dozen cows wandered out and got lost," his voice troubled and tense. "You men be careful out there. The clouds set low so there's hardly any daylight."

I saddled up Wildfire, my Gold Coin Arabian. He was ready to bust and run, always had this full burst of energy that had to be reined in and controlled. We rode out several times before we rounded up all the stragglers. Pearl rode the Little Blue out of the barn and was off without a word. It was a time when we could use all the hands on the farm. Snow piled drifts swirled high around the buildings and sheds. We shored up the buildings with shocks of alfalfa that served both as feed and protection for the cattle. Del Cole, Ephraim Hobbs, and Lone Bear rode steadily with us throughout the early morning light.

"The fence on the edge of the property should keep everyone in shouting distance of the farm house. If we get separated, find the fence and follow it to shelter," I cautioned everyone.

The spring calves were big enough to range with the heifers, but occasionally some cow would get head strong and head out by herself. Pearl brought the Little Blue around, and it wasn't long before the cows got the idea. The Little Blue herded them into a corner of fencing, rode close and bit them. The calves who were new to all this would run off, tails straight up in the air, and bellowing their heads off. I observed a cow with a bum leg and drove her into the shelter of the barn. I pulled ointment and swabs out of my saddle bag and dallied the lasso around her hind legs. I tied her down and hobbled her back legs then when I got to touching places that hurt, I wouldn't get kicked. There was a sharp rock about the size of a pea embedded in her hoof. I wedged it out with a pair of pliers and pus and blood shot out. I swabbed it out, but she hobbled off. Critters don't seem to have sense enough to lie down.

"She'll be OK. It'll just take a few days to heal though. Keep her in the barn for now," Pearl instructed.

Several times during the morning, I had Del Cole and Ephraim Hobbs come face to face with me. Their

Wildfire

eyes reflected alarm, aware that people get separated and lost in this weather. Their eyes held the fear we all felt. We all tried to be calm but eye contact spoke to the toll it was taking on all of us. Cole pulled on his heavy jacket and hat. He shut his eyes and drew in a ragged breath. The fear in his eyes sat dormant ready to grab at him from nowhere. He always wore a red bandana around his neck. Ephraim Hobbs refused to get more than ten feet away from the rest of the searchers. Visibility was bad, but Pearl and Joe Lone Bear had no problem striking off on their own. We spent hours bringing in cattle and horses.

All hands collected by the windmill as it pumped. We broke the ice in the tanks with an axe so all the cattle could drink. We were all nearly in the house before Ephraim mentioned Del Cole was missing. "I haven't seen Del for a long time, come to think on it."

"It always gives me a heavy feeling in my gut when this happens. We'll need torches for the four of us while we ride along the fence lines. People who don't live in this country have no idea how confused a person gets when a blizzard whites out everything so be careful." I hurried to gather torches for the four of us.

I rode back along the way I'd come and had pretty much given up finding anything. I came up a hill, as I rode along the fence line I could see tracks under the trees and traces of blood streaked the frozen new snow. In a copse of fir trees I observed broken branches. Snow covered the still form that lay beneath the trees. The wind blew snow in circular patterns that erased the path before me so there were no tracks of Del's horse. I dismounted Wildfire and lit the torch that burst a fierce hot red as I plunged it in the snow. Del Cole lay still beneath the snow and made no sound as I pulled him up and over the drift that covered him. An angry cut spattered blood that flowered across the new fallen snow. I bound the cut with Cole's bandana and grasped another from around my own neck. A chill crawled up my spine as I looked at his lifeless figure. I reached beneath his shoulders and dragged him across my horse's rump and over the saddle. A path of blood left the print of Del's boots clear up the back of Wildfire. The horse whinnied and thrashed around, fear showing in his eyes. I tied a tether rope around Del's waist under the horse's belly and drew it up the other side around his shoulders. Finally, I lashed it around the saddle horn. We started off at a slow pace as I held the torch aloft, hopeful someone would see it. I pulled my Colt and fired several shots to attract attention. Wildfire, my Gold Coin Arabian, reared his head and his nostrils flared at the sound. He pranced around in a circle, anxious to be off. The snow fell cold and wet on us as I made my way along the split rail fence. It seemed like hours before we were within a mile of the farmhouse. Ma saw the torch and sent Maudie and Ethel out with lantern light to bring us to the back porch. Pa heard the shot and met me some distance from the farmhouse. Together we bore Del into the house.

Maudie and Ma tended the cut on Del's face and rubbed his arms and face as they warmed him at the fireplace. Ma told us, "I'll clean that cut on his forehead and put stitches in it. Ease him onto the bed minus his boots and socks. Later I'll undress him, I'll need help from the rest of you."

Wildfire

The shock from the loss of blood, and the blow to his head, plus the whiskey Ma had given him sent him into a trance. He looked wide eyed and vacant. All of us stood silently watching as Del slipped into a deep sleep. The snow piled higher outside but we still needed to attend to that livestock so they would not wander off and die somewhere during the days to come.

As I strode out into the snow and wind again, my mind began to relive the time it had taken to find Del. Until now I hadn't given much thought to the place I'd found him. It was strange the horse wasn't around. Usually the rider can depend on even the most spirited horse to stay nearby. But Cole's horse was no where to be found. My mind kept going over what I had seen at the time I found him. Why was he under a tree? And where was the horse? I rode out to the place I'd found him and beyond and in a draw below the trees I found my answer.

The horse had been overpowered and lay in a mass of blood where something had torn him apart, strung his entrails all over, and then fled, probably when I arrived. I became uneasy sensing golden eyes were watching me in the darkness of the night. I drew my Colt revolver and spun the chamber just to be sure it was loaded as I inched forward. The horse lifted his head as I approached, wild eyed and in agony. He lifted his head to move but fell back exhausted I raised the gun and fired point blank at the horse's head. I felt surrounded with an eerie consuming whirlwind of energy of unseen predators. I stood and peered out, fired several more shots and held the Colt steady expecting the worst. Suddenly a swiftly moving force of bodies whirled past me and sped away. As I turned Wildfire again toward the farmhouse, I was deep inside my own head about what I had just witnessed. Fear coursed through my brain like shards of glass. Shock set in and I began to shake. It spurred all mighty fire into my action and I cut the horse's flanks with my heels. As aggressive as Wildfire is, it was impossible to make him move any faster. It seemed we were suspended in space. It took an eternity before I saw the lights of the farmhouse again.

As I burst into the house, Pa was removing Del's clothes and we all saw at once the bite marks on his feet and legs. Ma brought alcohol and swabs and began to clean the wounds. We all looked at each other, fear bouncing back and forth between us as we worked. The impact of what had happened would stay with us forever to the edge of our lives. The gashes on his thigh were deep and these had to be cleaned but we needed a doctor to look at these wounds. He'd lost so much blood, one pant leg was completely soaked. He looked off into space, his face empty and bloodless. His voice was incoherent as if someone else spoke.

"Pa these were huge animals that attacked Del. They got his horse and it was still alive when I came across it. Whatever it was, we need to find the critters and get rid of them. Best set some traps and run them regularly till we trap and kill these varmints."

Pa's eyes were stretched thin across his face with concern. His brows furrowed with worry as he worked on Cole.

"I seen lots of wild animal attacks in my time, but this is a vicious bunch of bites, like the work of more than one. Whatever it was, attacked the animal first and then knocked Cole off his horse."

"Looked like a frenzy of a pack of animals. All these wounds look bad. Emory, get the whiskey and pour him a stiff drink. Get as much down as you can," Ma ordered. "We need to keep some stimulant down him until we can clean out all these bite wounds. You say they downed the horse?"

"Yes, it was still alive when I got there. I must've spooked them."

"Likely you were their next victim if you hadn't had a gun, son. You took an awful chance going back." Ma's voice shook with emotion.

Thinking on it left me shaken. I decided to warn all the men and bring them in the farmhouse as soon as possible. We finished up with Del and then Ma stayed with him while the rest of us gathered in the kitchen. Breakfast waited in the warmth of the farmhouse. Maudie, Ethel and Hannah served a special sausage casserole baked slow in the iron stove.

"The kitchen smells good. I'm dyin' for a cup of coffee." Ethel poured coffee into my tincup.

All of us shucked off our heavy outdoor clothes and settled into straight back chairs around the table.

"This is extra for all the hard work this morning," Hannah announced to us as she served slabs of fresh bread. At the center of the table was a huge slab of churned butter, jam, and jelly. Silence fell as Pa intoned the blessing over our food.

"Bless this food and its strength to our bodies this day. We thank thee for the nourishment and blessing of the extended family gathered here. Our lives have truly been blessed because without their help we'd have been at our work hours longer than it already took. Be mindful of our friend Del Cole. Heal him and make him whole. We thank thee Lord."

By morning, Cole had not improved and began to run a fever. Ma brought snow from the yard and packed it in doeskins for compresses, but he continued to pitch and turn with delirium. He would shout and plunge out of bed till it was necessary to restrain him. Ma ripped pieces of sheeting, and Pa and I bound Del's wrists and ankles as loosely as possible, but firm enough to hold him.

Mama lamented to Pa one afternoon, "It's been three days now and Del still is out of his head most of the time. Sure wish this storm would let up so someone could ride out for the Doc. It'd be a load off my mind to have him take a look at Cole."

"He's probably in the best hands there are right here with you, Sara Ann. Don't fret so about it," Pa soothed her.

It was a week before the weather turned calmer. Ephraim and Hank plowed out the yard and hauled in more shocks of hay to shore up the barn. Pa built the cattle sheds with a slanted roof so the excess snow would slide off.

Maudie and Ethel washed out Del's clothes and bedding in hot water and cranked them through the wringer. They put the clothes out flat against the fence in the yard, where underwear and shirts and sheets froze solid. After a few hours, they put them in the wash shed on lines where they would dry and smell fresh as any clothes line dried washing ever would. The women worked steadily going in and out in the unforgiving

Wildfire

weather. Their faces so intent on their task, they never noticed everyone's sympathetic expressions.

The wind churned storm clouds across the sun. It sat like a broken egg yolk inside the clouds. In the distance the storm rode like a great beast denying any respite from its terrible wrath.

Chapter 3

<u>Pioneer Women:</u> The West remained largely a male dominated society throughout the 19th century. In Texas, for example, the ratio of men to women in 1890 was 110 to 1. Women continued to face traditional legal barriers and social prejudices. A wife could not sell property without her husband's approval. In Texas women could not sue except for divorce, nor could they serve on juries, act as lawyers, or witness a will. But the fight for survival in the trans-Missouri West often made husbands and wives more equal partners than their eastern counterparts. Prairie life also allowed women more independence than could be had by those living domestic lives back East. <u>America</u>: "The New West, The New Frontier," (Chap.18), pp.669-670

<u>Omaha World Herald</u>, May 12, 1890, Nellie Ward of the East Bottoms, who hit Mrs. John McElhatton with a bucket will be tried Saturday. She claims to have acted in self defense.

The Sleigh Ride To Town

It was a week before the weather turned calmer. The wind blew snow across the bright kitchen windows where it sat like expensive lace. The sun pierced

Wildfire

through the tiny openings like needles of light. We plowed out the yard and hauled in more shocks of baled hay to shore up the barn.

At the end of that week, Pa came to me. "Why don't you and Pearl get out the old sleigh and hitch up the work horses to it? The girls can go along with you to town. There's Christmas presents to buy and you'll need to stop at Dr. Dickinson's office. See if he will come back with you to look at Del. It'd ease up Sara Ann's mind lots just to have him look Del over."

Pearl was enthused at the idea of going into town. The idea put speed in his step as he hurried out to the shed and began preparations. Over an hour later he bustled into the house smelling of saddle soap with a string of sleigh bells in his hands.

"I'm going to clean these up and the sleigh will be all set. I told Hannah to round up some buffalo robes and furs for the trip. Maudie isn't interested in going out in the sleigh, but Ethel is excited about it. We'll leave first thing in the morning."

Mama sat at the kitchen table with a pen and pad making out a list of stuff she needed and everyone had suggestions to add to the list. Finally, she handed me the pad, satisfied it was complete. I collected the total sum of $20 for all the things on their wish list.

At dusk there was light snow from gray skies, and the wind shifted massive cloud banks. Morning came crisp and clear as the sun rose like a golden disk. Winter had been on our tails for awhile and it had finally caught us. Icicles formed on the moustaches of Ephraim Hobbs and Hank Simon where their hot breath met the cold brisk morning air.

The horses caught the excitement as we hitched them to the sleigh two deep. They were Roan colored with heads huge as hams and feet hard as iron skillets. Their broad backs could pull the weight of several contraptions like this sleigh. Pearl shod them right after our arrival here. Big Red pranced around nervous cause he wasn't going, and huffing and snorting, sallying up to Wildfire. My Gold Coin Arabian pranced around the corral showing big teeth and pawing the ground, twisting his head as he watched us.

Pearl eyeballed the two horses. "It looks like they're not pleased at being left behind. We could tether them behind the sleigh in case we'd need them in town."

We left at daylight. Slick with frost, the land stretched flat and frozen, gleaming like new china plates mile after mile, as far as you could see. Sounds soaked into the silence of the brittle cold. The yip of a coyote shattered the winter calm of silence with a high pitched wail like fingernails scratching on a blackboard. Snow sparkled like sandpaper that dusted the hillsides, dented with blue shadow. Snow blew like smoke before us, blinding us against the sun. Sun dogs appeared on the horizon. We reined in the excited horses as we came near the town.

The sleigh cut the snow fine. Except for ears that might escape the wool hats we wore, the rest of our bodies stayed warm. The buffalo robes turned out to be the best idea of all. Once the saddle horses got the idea of what we were doing, Big Red and Wildfire pranced along behind the sleigh. Ears alert, eyeing us and listening for the tinkle of the bells as we moved along. It would've been impossible to use a wagon or buggy on these roads. Drifts in places were higher than a man's head and packed down so hard from the wind we were able to go right over them. As far as you could see were hills all white and glistening under the bright sun. We finally reached the outskirts of Cairo and eased up on the horses some. The town was covered with a blanket of white from the recent snow. Only footpaths broke the open streets where people had walked.

Pearl looked around at the silent street. "Likely we're their first customers since the snow fell."

Ethel was concerned. "Looks like it to me. What if the stores aren't open? Maybe we just wasted our time."

"I wouldn't worry about Cairo being closed down. No matter what time of day, it seems you can find someone who'll not only let you shop but be glad to see you," I comforted her.

Hannah looked like a snow princess in her heavy coat and bonnet. Pearl hadn't seen her "dressed up" since we'd had our last gathering at the house and was showing his appreciation at being in the company of the young woman. Hannah peered at Pearl, aware of his interest. They snuggled close together under the robes in the sleigh. It was apparent he was enjoying the whole event. We all were.

Pearl gazed into her lovely face as he inquired. "Hannah, what's the first thing you're gonna' buy at the Mercantile Store?"

"Glory, I believe I'd like some hot tea to warm me up before I start shopping," she replied. "After that I'll need some time to pick out all the things on this list Sara Ann gave me."

"It's so much fun spending other people's money. We'll have a time finding everything they wanted," Ethel patted her handbag contentedly.

We entered Cairo and came to the Platte Hotel, where we stopped to let the women off. We found a stable, tied up the team, and tethered our saddle horses. Pearl gave the blacksmith a gold piece and told him we'd be gone about an hour. Ephraim and Joe had been so quiet I asked "What's on your mind fellas? Cat got your tongue."

"Well, we ain't much for tea and fancy cookies, so if ya'all don't mind we'll go the Whistle Stop Café we heard about over by the grain mill," Ephraim said. "It ain't nothin' personal, I just don't feel right about all that fancy stuff I hear they'll have at the Platte Hotel."

"Suit yourselves men. Try to show up in about an hour to help us pack up the sleigh. And for Christ sakes watch yourselves. There's some lowlifes hang out there sometimes," I warned.

The two men struggled down the boardwalk and the rest of us went to the dining room at the hotel. We were greeted by the host and owner.

"Good to see you folks. I'm Adolph and I'll send a waitress out to take your order. You can be seated right here. Just make yourselves comfortable." Adolph poured water in the goblets on the table.

Pearl helped Hannah into a seat and sat beside her. His eyes reflected excitement with secrets he held there. No matter what he did there was always this aura about him. A waitress came from the kitchen and greeted us. She asked, "What'll you people have today? Maybe a sandwich or some nice soup." She recited the menu for us about their daily specials.

"I'll be orderin' coffee. Coffee always has a special zing to it on a crisp morning like this. The last of the cup tastes ever bit as good as the first," I handed her the menu as she turned to the others.

Ethel thought she'd like a bite to eat, and Hannah was partial to a crumpet or a homemade roll. Pearl decided on soup and the waitress made notes. I ordered a corned beef on rye. Hannah and Ethel had tea, and Pearl and I had coffee. As we sat there in the cozy room, a cloud passed over the sun. I had this sudden uneasy feeling I couldn't put my finger on. I looked around the room as if something might be hidden there. I hoped I was mistaken. I had this vague feeling that something was wrong.

"You seen Dr. Dickinson around lately?" I inquired of the waitress.

"Not today, but believe I seen him over at the Mercantile Store yesterday-day before. Don't just recall exactly when."

"We need to have him come out and treat a man at my Dad's place that got injured," I said.

"Oh, that so, what happened?" she inquired.

The hackles on my neck went up about then as I surmised the lady was more interested in news than helping us out. I just provided gossip for the locals as soon as we were out of sight.

Before I could stop her Ethel spoke. "He got attacked by something out on the range. Hurt just terrible bad by some animals."

"Well, if I see Dr. Dick I'll sure tell him you need help. What'd you say your name is?"

"I'm Ethel Peers. My daddy is Emory Peers out on Wood River homestead. We been there for nearly five years now."

"That so? Well, I don't get to know everyone who comes by here. If Doc comes around, I'll certainly tell him you need help though."

I felt a little more at ease when we finished our food and were ready to leave. I'd rather Ethel hadn't been so candid, but that was my sister. Always outspoken, always sorry for saying too much. Couldn't do anything about that in all the years I've known her. My warnings go through her brain like rainwater.

We braced for the North wind that blew strong on us as we wandered out. The women had decided to walk the two blocks to the Mercantile Store while Pearl and I brought the sleigh around.

As we rounded the corner onto Main Street, we pulled up at the Whistle Stop to pick up Joe and Ephraim. Nobody was in sight, which made me damned uneasy. Suddenly the door to the Whistle Stop flew open and Joe was the first one ejected. He dove headfirst into the snow. Ephraim came behind him. Some sodbuster had him by the scruff of his neck and the seat of his pants. Joe seemed to be unconscious and Ephraim sat dazed and incoherent. Pearl and I drew our guns and the ruffian who had tossed Ephraim out eyeballed the two of us.

"Don't nobody get no ideas with them guns, if you know what's good for you," he sneered. His eyes had a venomous look stretched tight across his face.

Wildfire

"No problem if you'll just clear up why you've manhandled my men just now," I demanded.

"This here man claims he's been cheated."

Immediately behind him another man appeared, seedier looking than the first. His gun drawn, he flipped off the safety, and spun the chamber, letting us know we were challenged. Pearl took all this in, and with a single motion retrieved his gun and fired. The bullet stung the man's wrist and he flung his gun to the floor. A look of amazement crept across the varmint's face. His eyes raked Pearl up and down.

A voice raised from behind Pearl and me. "You boys just lower them weapons and step back a few paces," It was Pete Sikes, the County Sheriff. He'd heard the gunshot and came out of the feed mill to investigate.

"Just so's this here sodbuster'd understand your orders sheriff," I wasn't about to let my guard down.

"Slats Mahoney don't have no choice. He goes for that gun he just dropped, and he'll be lyin' on the ground same as these fella's he's throwed out of his establishment. Only he won't be so lively. Now Eddy, you know better than to start a rumpus like this. How come you two are feeling so pestery this fine day?" he inquired.

"I just drove around to pick up my men and found them all tore up here," I said.

Slats countered, "That one there," pointing at Joe Lone Bear, "Claimed I cheated him."

"Well, you're not above it and everybody knows that," the sheriff shouted at him. "Now you keep your tongue flappin' with this nonsense and I'll put my sweet disposition on hold and stomp the hell out'n you my ownself," he threatened.

"Do you mind if I look after our men sheriff? They've been worked over pretty bad," I was about to put my own disposition on hold if I didn't get some action here.

"Better do that son. Just who the hell are you two anyway," Pete Sikes inquired.

"I'm Jesse Peers and this here is Pearl Lux. We come to town to get supplies for my dad, Emory Peers," I told him.

"Well, ain't this a pretty kettle of fish! If I hadn't took this in with my own eyes, I'd thought a robbery was in progress. Either that Lux fella is a damn good shot or an awful bad one. If the latter be the case, this factor here was lucky. Either way I'd say he's lucky he's alive. Now if you two side hill gougers don't mind, let us look at these men you've nearly beat to death. Just stay where you are till we get the story on you two."

We looked at Ephraim and Joe, Pearl helped Joe to his feet. Both men had been battered with something and were incoherent. Ephraim was the worse off. They'd knocked him cold before they threw him into the street. His eyeballs fluttered as the pupils rolled up into his eyes. We helped the men to their feet.

Sheriff Sikes spun the cylinder of his Colt, "We'll all move over to my office and I'll send someone for the doctor."

We loaded Ephraim and Joe into the sleigh while Sikes walked his prisoners along the boardwalk. He fingered his Colt lightly as he walked along. I could see he couldn't decide whether to draw or just follow the two sidewinders empty handed. Finally, he had some kind of revelation and drew his gun. The snow didn't encourage the prisoners to run as the streets were blown waist high in places. Sheriff Sikes sent his deputy to fetch the Doctor.

Before long, Dr. Dickinson burst into the sheriff's office. A short stocky man his energy infectious. One look at the injured men sent him into a frenzy. Pulling out bandages and instruments, needles and suture thread, cleansing some cuts. It was over an hour before he finished.

"You gonna run them two in for a long stay somewhere? They only owned that café six weeks and it's been nothin' but one brawl after another. You can't imagine what riffraff they sprung from. Truth is you fought somethin' loathsome." Dr. Dickinson's words fell like spittle from his mouth. Everyone nodded in agreement.

"They have a bad reputation all over the Nebraska territory, and they may be wanted in some others as well." The sheriff seemed to be informed about these two miscreants we'd tangled with.

Joe and Ephraim were beginning to come around and take in their surroundings, and it was my guess they thought they were going to jail too. Ephraim looked up at me, his face split like a ripe melon, a bloody smile for a mouth. "I give that guy five dollar gold piece and he short changed me. Said it was only worth a dollar. When I called him on it, Eddy, the bartender, stepped from behind the bar. We didn't have a prayer. Slats had a two by four he's fashioned a handle on. Like gettin' hit with a ball bat only worse because them ridges cut. You start bleedin' before you know what hit you."

"I figured as much but you're all bruised up as well. Best get some whiskey to take the edge off the pain." The doctor glanced back and forth between Ephraim and Joe like he couldn't believe what he was looking at.

"Doc, one of my men is laid up at our homestead. He was attacked by something when we were out wranglin' cows just as the storm hit," I said. "Ma has kept him alive, but we're not sure what's wrong. It's been about five days ago since it happened. Once we took care of the damage from the storm, Pa asked us to come in for supplies and to look you up."

"You say he was attacked by wild animals or something?" Shock registered on the doctor's face.

"You bet. Ma has been with him near day and night. She'd be a lot easier in her mind though, if you'd do us the service of coming home with us. After you'd tend to Del, we'd see to it personally you got back to town."

Doc finished up with Joe and Ephraim taping some bandages on, taking a pulse, tying a support on one of Joe's arms.

"I guess I can do that. I need to go home and get a few things before I can leave town though."

"We have to pick up two women, Ethel and Hannah are with us, and we left them at the Mercantile Store. With Christmas near they wanted to buy some things and get supplies for Ma."

"Your ma's about the finest woman I've known around these parts. She should've been in the medical profession, cause she can deal with everything from measles to broken bones," he said. "You say Ethel and Hannah. Now just who in tarnation is this Hannah?"

Pearl spoke up, "We brought Hannah from Indiana with us when we trailed a herd of cows out here. She's got no family and we needed help on the trip. She's doing fine on the Peer's farm."

"Well, she has no family yet but I believe Pearl is gonna change that Doc. Just a little secret between you and me," I winked at him.

Pearl's face took on a startled look like maybe he thought what I'd said was a secret.

Sheriff Sikes bid us all farewell and assured us he'd deal with the two ruffians who had jumped Joe and Ephraim. He didn't exactly apologize for what happened--but it was close.

After giving us directions to his house, Dr. Dickinson went back to his buggy. Pearl and I drove the sleigh around to the Mercantile Store. You could hear church bells in the distance, faint as the tinkle of a piano key above the noise of the town.

Ethel spotted the men out the window and gave a screech. "You fella's are all just like a bunch of little boys. Lord almighty, if you ain't a sight to behold. What happened to you?" Hannah peered out from a huge blue hat she'd tried on. Ethel stood with her mouth agape.

I had trouble keeping my face straight. I turned away to get composed. This was no time to break out laughing, but it was hard. Suppressed chuckles bounced around in my chest and I snorted. Pearl wanted to know whether I was alright?

"Yeah, just got somethin' caught in my throat is all. A man never knows what they'll get into when it's least expected."

"It's all your fault Jesse. If you'd make those men stay put, never woulda' happened and you know it," Ethel stormed.

"Oh, you're right no doubt about that. Hannah probably thinks we're a real bunch by now," The look on my sister's face was worth a thousand words.

Hannah gave the fancy hat back to Abby, the store clerk, and pulled on her velvet hood. The shopping event was officially over and it was time to return home. They paid for their purchases, and Pearl and I helped carry all the packages to the sleigh. We stored them away under the seats of the sleigh.

Hannah found the fabric and patterns, that she wanted and thread, yarn, knitting needles and such Ma put on the list. Ethel had selected shirts, gloves, socks, and all the groceries that were on the list. She'd added cotton batting and alcohol after our recent experience at the homestead. She said they'd spent all this time trying on hats and looking at lace and satins that Abby had dug out for them. They both seemed a little reluctant at leaving it all behind.

Finally, all the people stowed away inside the sleigh while I rode Wildfire, leaving Pearl to cuddle with Hannah. We left Cairo about 4 o'clock, the sleigh bells ringing gaily as the horses trotted along. Ethel was buried under a buffalo robe, her eyes dancing with excitement created by the day's events. Joe and Ephraim were tucked to their chins in buffalo robes. They had found some comfort in the sleigh and slept quietly, waking in a start now and then at some sudden noise.

We moved along the streets to Dr. Dick's house and then out onto the country roads. The late afternoon sun cast a glistening glare of solid white that hurt your eyes. Dr. Dickinson surveyed our transport with an eye of appreciation. "I haven't seen one of these things since I've lived out here. My daddy had one in Missouri where we lived when I was a boy," he reminisced.

While we traveled along, he discussed the Mahoney's, the two men our fellas tangled with today. They homesteaded on Wood River and harvested ice from the river. They sold it in the spring and summer months. There were four boys and a girl in the family. The father fell into the river when they'd begun cutting ice one cold winter day and froze to death. The old man didn't come up till spring and froze solid as a rock when he popped up during the spring thaw. The family went to hell after that. Mother Mahoney was known to take a buggy whip to the whole bunch from time to time. That fall the daughter high tailed it away from home, and the boys turned on their Mother. They beat her beyond recognition and wouldn't permit the Sheriff near the place. "It's against the law to move a dead body, but to this day neither of the Mahoneys has had a Christian burial far as anyone knows. They're a bunch of riff raff and the best advice I could give anyone here is put some distance between yourself and the place they're in and never return."

Ephraim and Joe were still protesting they didn't do anything. To which the doctor replied, "You don't have to. They're just hoodlums that should be avoided.

I hope Sheriff Sikes has got enough goods on them to send them up for a long time."

We settled everyone into the sleigh. Hannah and Pearl snuggled beneath a buffalo robe where all you could see was Pearl's hat and the peak of Hannah's velvet hood. His arms were around her in a comforting embrace. Both looked so contented The blue dress she had chosen that day made a lie out of every other color in the world and stole the words right out of Pearl's mouth. I believe these were the happiest days these two young people had experienced ever. Hannah was still finding her way amongst us. Pearl, secure in his manly role had become her confidant. We all held the belief that there was promise for them of a future solid and perfect if they chose it. We were so hopeful they would remain with us on the plains.

The wind caught the top of the conifers along the way and shook them hard. They threw shadows that made the landscape seem alive. Wildfire became agitated prancing sideways along the path of the sleigh. Big Red sidled up to him, and the two trotted along side by side. They say if you listen, a horse will talk to you. I think if you listen closely, they whisper. Wildfire chewed his bit and voiced his discontent. Both horses became agitated as hell, and it made it hard to hold Wildfire down. He was ready for a hard gallop. They knew we were near the homestead. The full blown moon shown down on us as we traveled along. The lantern on the sleigh threw moving shadows inside the darkness. Our sleigh cast an eerie shadow on the snow drifts of the horses galloping along, looming over the drifts as we moved.

At last we came to the archway of the homestead and the cattle guard. The sign read Double Star Ranch with the two stars circled like the print of our branding iron. We pulled the sleigh up back of the adobe farm house, then everyone got out and stretched. Pearl bounded out to help with the two injured men, while Doc Dickinson unrolled and rose up from his buffalo robe.

"Yessir, that was a mighty nice ride there, Jesse. Couldn't find anything finer. Well, let's see to all these patients I have to tend to."

B. J. and Cynci came out to greet us and help us in the house. I introduced them to Dr. Dick while they unloaded all the purchases we'd made in town. Pa shook hands with the doctor and led him into Del's room and closed the door. After awhile, Mama's finger opened that door like the scar of a wound, as she peered out at the injured men and closed it again. Apparently she satisfied some personal need before going on to help the doctor.

The rest of us put Joe and Ephraim to bed, each one groaning and crying out from any unnecessary movement. There are times when my brain becomes so inflamed with anger and frustration, I can't keep it out of my gut. I wanted to smack a wall since the culprits who had visited these injuries upon them weren't around. I thought about it long and hard what the outcome of their injuries might mean. I was hopeful the good doctor would be able to mend these men and make them whole again.

Sweet Water had already begun compresses to ease the swelling on both men. Her eyes were heavy with sadness as she worked with Joe. I hoped that her ability might spell an easier night for both men.

At length Doctor Dickinson came out of Del Cole's room. His face reflected the concern and alarm we all felt. We all agreed that regular planned events had taken an irregular turn in ways that we dared not even guess about the consequences.

He was quiet for a time before speaking. "I think these were wolves that attacked this fella'. You need to clean this litter of wolves out, watch your livestock, be vigilant of everything. The snow makes it hard for the wolves to find the animals they ordinarily feed on. The wolf population has been a problem out here a good many years. Del has something else going on besides his injuries. Either he has some kind of infection or he has rabies, or he has both. His body has not been strong enough to overcome all this."

"I done all I could, Doc. All that I knew to do for him." Mama began to cry softly.

"Good Lord, I'm not blaming you and don't you blame yourself, Sara Ann. He'd been dead awhile if you hadn't been so good at caring for him," Doc consoled. "Don't you even consider it your fault. That's nonsense. What's more, I know every person in this house will do all they can to make Del as comfortable as possible till he either gets well or he doesn't make it. If he gets well, he's going to have problems the rest of his life. You need to expect that. He may not have a normal life. "

"Can we offer you some food or some hot coffee, Doc?" Maudie held a hot cup of coffee out to him.

"Well, that'd be nice. Then I gotta show your Mama how to care for these other two."

"How about a sandwich? We got some good vegetable soup too. Made it yesterday so it's really tasty by now," Maudie led Doc to the table all set up for our guest.

"Now that'd be mighty nice of you, Maudie," Doc eyed the soup and the ham sliced ready for sandwiches.

Hannah, Ethel and Cynci gathered in the kitchen to collect dishes and silverware, napkins and glasses. They set the big table in the dining room, and Papa told everyone to sit while he said the blessin'. The women served food all around, and then Sweet Water carried bowls of soup to the men in the bedroom.

"I don't believe Joe and Ephraim will have any long term affects from their bout with Slats. But that gismo he uses is known to do a bunch of bruises and splits in the skin. I sewed some of the cuts, but others I left, cause they'll heal better that way," Doc voiced this aloud convincing himself as well that he'd done the right thing.

Ma and those who stayed home were full of questions and I had to recount what had happened.

"All I know is, I never want to be on the other side of Pearl's gun when he decides to shoot for real," I had a revelation right then about what a sharp shooter Pearl was.

Mama wanted to know what I meant and I had to explain how he shot the gun right out of the varmint's hand. They all looked at Pearl with interest, wanting more explanation.

Pearl chuckled. "The way you put it makes it sound special., Jesse. All I did was try to protect our hides from harm. That factor was aimin' to do us in you know. If he thought he could get away with it, he'd have done it too."

We sat at the kitchen table over our supper. It was much too late to be takin' a trip through the brittle cold of December. "Doc, you better spend the night and Pearl can take you back tomorrow," I insisted.

The talk turned to Del Cole and what was to be done for him. Dr. Dickinson recommended continued bed rest, but said he'd need to be moving around some to get strength back if he's ever to get well. Mama agreed with that and said they'd do as good as they could.

Doc Dickinson asked, "How you going to deal with the critters that attacked him? Once you start trackin' these animals you'll need to watch your own backside out there, so it's not a repeat of Del's attack."

"Likely we'll set traps and run 'em daily to see that they are caught and destroyed," I realized I didn't know what was to be done.

"Well, if you set traps, the Indians will steal them. If you put out poison, their dogs will get into it and there'll be more trouble over that. No, you'll have to track these critters and destroy them. To my knowledge, stalking critters can be all over you before you know it."

"I know they stalk you and sometimes you never know they've been there till you find tracks the next day," Pa's hands flew up in a motion of alarm.

Pearl and I exchanged looks, knowing full well it would be our task to follow up on this activity. The hair stood up on my neck at the prospect of what was to come.

I could hear Cynci going on to Morning Star that the three men had "bad spirits" that hovered over them. She thought they needed to purge themselves with a good sweat and a plunge into the snow. Pearl started to say something about a pack of nonsense, and I raised my hand. I hoped he wouldn't feel the need to tell her that. He read the look in my eyes and didn't say more.

The doctor and Mama spent the evening with the three patients. I was aware they were called during the night, but nothing happened to disturb the rest of us. By morning the bedroom where they slept was quiet. As the sun rose bright and clear, it crept over the edge of the earth. Clouds sat like a deck of cards dealt by a chalk white hand, the sounds all around amplified by the cold. With a cup of coffee in hand, I drew back the drapes and felt the sun wash the room in golden light. It was good to be alive and greet the day for the gift it was.

Chapter 4

But the fight for survival in the Trans-Missouri/West often made husbands and wives more equal partners than their eastern conservative counterparts. Prairie life also allowed women more independence than could be had by those living domestic lives back East. One woman declared that she insisted on leaving out of their marriage vows the phrasing about "obeying" her husband. "I had served my time in tutelage to my parents as all children are supposed to. I was a woman now and capable of being the other half of the head of the family." Similar examples of strong willed femininity abound. Explained one Kansas woman, "The outstanding fact is that environment was such to bring out and develop the dominant qualities of individual character.–Women of that day learned at an early age to depend on themselves–to do whatever work there was to be done, and to face danger when it must be faced, as calmly as they were able." America, "New Frontiers: South and West," (Ch. 18) P.670

The Omaha Herald, May 18, 1890: Quick Divorce at Chadron. Judge W. L. Greene of Kearney and Reporter Scott opened district court here today. There is a docket of nearly 200 cases, but Judge Greene struck a gait in dispatching business that astonished the attorneys here and bids fair to clear up the docket in a week. Five divorces were granted this afternoon in fifteen minutes and most of the work cleared up. Attorneys Ager and Griggs are here for the Burlington, which has several heavy damage suits set for trial. Besides these the White River irrigation case, a big suit growing out of the failure of G. B. Smith & son, a year ago, promises a hard fought legal battle.

Mattie Kelly's Dilemma

Early July in Indiana was always a pleasant time of year. The first hint of summer was in the air. The sun burned down like a golden disk from a clear sky. Not a cloud up there, the kind of day the breeze blew the sheets dry quickly. Mattie and Sadie were busy with laundry stripping all the beds and cleaning the sleeping rooms of Mattie's boarders. It was a huge job that took weeks to complete. Sadie put another load of sheets out to dry, wiped sweat from her face and started back for the house. She saw a young woman dressed in dark calico and a straw bonnet riding a sorrel pony. She came up the main road out front. She dismounted and tied the pony to their hitching post.

The sign out front said, "Rooms for Rent." A small clip board allowed Mattie to change numbers on the sign. "$2.00 a day including meals. Two vacancies. Inquire within."

Mariah Calish had come to Valparaiso to visit her Uncle Gideon and Aunt Isabelle. Isabelle had talked to Mattie at their Mercantile Store recently. Ms. Crowder told Isabelle, Mattie was in need of help over at the boarding house. Elated at the prospect of having a regular job, Mariah rode over to Mattie's to see about working for her.

Mariah rapped the door knocker, and entered the front porch. The small entryway sheltered her from the July sun. Sadie answered the door.

Mariah asked, "Are you Mattie? I'm Mariah Calish and my Uncle owns the horse stables outside of town. My Aunt Isabelle said you need help here to cook and clean. I ain't never had a regular job but I helped my Ma and we had twelve kids in our family. That has to count for experience keepin' up with all those kids."

"I'm Sadie and I'd say you're experienced if you helped your Ma keep up with all them kids. We need somebody mostly to keep up the sleeping rooms. Come on out in the kitchen and meet Mattie. She's under the weather this mornin' so she asked me to get the door."

Mariah and Sadie entered the kitchen and stood before Mattie, who was peeling potatoes over the sink. Mattie was pale as a ghost and smoothed stray hair off her face. She adjusted her apron and shifted from one foot to the other where she stood. It was obvious she was very uncomfortable.

"I'm lookin' for work and like I told Sadie, I don't have no experience 'cept I helped my Ma out at home. There's twelve kids in my family so I know all there is about cookin and cleanin for a big bunch of people. I'm here with my Uncle and Aunt, the Calishes out at the horse stables." Sadie's eyes cut back and forth between the three of them as Mariah spoke.

Mattie turned to Mariah. "How old are you Mariah?"

Wildfire

"I'm eighteen Mattie. My folks own a farm outside of Bennet where I was born and raised. I got sisters old enough to help Ma so I thought I'd come to the city and see if I could get a job."

"We got so much to do here and then we been out to Ambrose Lux's place for several years now. We keep his house up too. We sure could use some help around here. Especially since Mattie ain't doin' well and all," Sadie said.

Mattie looked sallow and worry lines cut deep across her pretty face. "Don't be getting ahead of yourself, Ms. Sadie busybody. We got twenty rooms here that I rent out mostly to men, who work here in Valparaiso. We cook three meals a day besides. You livin' with your Aunt and Uncle too? You could stay here with me if you wanted. Save you a trip every day, and it'd be nice having you right here in the house."

"What could we work out so I could stay here and help?" Mariah inquired. "I don't know nothin' about pay or hours or stayin' or livin' here or at your boarding house."

Mattie felt her offer wasn't generous when she said, "Well, I could offer you $.75 cents a day and board and room. We could see if it works out and how you fit in. Are you interested?"

Mariah was elated. "Am I interested? Lord, that's lots for somebody like me. I'd jump at the chance to help you and Sadie out."

"Then it's settled. Can you start tomorrow? Bring your stuff and move into the little room off the kitchen. It's quiet and wouldn't be anywheres near the boarders' rooms."

Mattie leaned heavily against the sink. Sadie brought round a chair and Mattie sank immediately onto it. Finally, Mattie spoke , "You'll find out soon enough if I don't tell you. I'm six months gone with a baby and I've had a rough time. I'm twenty-eight years old and getting a bit old for this kind of thing."

Sadie spoke, "Coulda' done somethin' but you wouldn't listen to me. Havin' this kid when it's father chased off and left you." Sadie's anger boiled like thick soup.

"He doesn't know nothin' about this and you're not to tell. You hear me," Mattie demanded.

"Only because I promised not to tell, or I'd have wrote that guy in a heartbeat and told him what I really thought,." Sadie came back at her.

"Don't matter what you think. We'll just let things take their course and see just what comes of it. Besides, I'm here and he's in Nebraska, and I ain't about to follow. Don't make sense to even entertain the thoughts. Now Sadie, promise you won't get carried away. You too Mariah. I'd like to extract a promise from you not to let this get rumored around. So far I've been able to hide the whole thing, but that will soon end. Hope you won't change your mind cause we need the help, and you should know what you're getting into."

'That's fine with me. After eleven kids followed me, I sure know what birthin' is all about. My Ma had some problems herself, so I'm able to cope with about everything."

"Well, I don't believe we need no snotty nosed brat round here, but Mattie won't listen. It just disgusts me, Mattie goin' through this by herself," Sadie wasn't noted for pacing her opinions.

"I'm not alone, as you put it. Any number of fella's would've jumped at the task. The trouble is most of them are lookin' at this business and not at me and my dilemma."

"What about Ambrose then? He's around like a pet coon on a chain. Just wants to be part of your life so bad, I can hardly stand his pain. Mattie, you gotta' deal with him."

"I'd do that but not right at the moment, Sadie," Mattie came back at her.

"Well, kindly think on it anyway," Sadie said.

Mariah's eyes nearly bugged out of her head. She was speechless, taking in all she'd just learned. She moved to the sink and picked up the paring knife. "Looks to me like you got a real hard problem here, Mattie. People don't go for this kind of stuff. It's bad for you and worse for the little one that comes of all this. You don't appear to me you're able to handle anything more today, so why not take it easy and let Sadie and I finish up here?" Mariah asked.

Sadie helped Mattie to her feet and walked her to the back porch. Mattie laid down on the couch and closed her eyes.

"If we need to know anything, we'll come out and ask. You rest till you feel better," Sadie said. Her voice was full of pity.

So the deception began with a triangle of women with a single goal and more work than they knew what to do with. Mattie with her head for business, Sadie with her warring disposition and inner fire that drove her day by day. Now this third woman, who would solve their problems.

The two women in the kitchen pulled together a mid-day meal and had it ready to serve by the noon hour. Stragglers began to come in and be seated. Conversation was muted, but the general gist of it was curiosity about who the new woman was, and where in tarnation was Mattie.

Sadie settled the latter question by telling them, "It was none of your damn business. Can't a hard workin' woman like Mattie have some time to herself? Next thing we know you'll be prying into all our private lives and nosin' someplace where you shouldn't be. Wasn't it enough we had a new person to slave for you? Or did you want more even than that? Honestly, you're a bunch of pests if I ever seen some. Now give us a break while we get this meal served, if you please." She pranced out of the dining room like the Queen Bee herself. She was enjoying this part of it. That was obvious. Mariah was so shocked that anyone Sadie's age would dare stand up to a bunch of men that numbered at least fifteen. By two o'clock the two women had cleared the dining room, and the dishes finally were done. They sat with coffee cups in hand at the kitchen table.

"I don't know about you, but I need a break of some kind. There's just way too much going on here for me. What do you think now? Do you think you can stand it here?" Sadie asked Mariah.

"Oh, I'm going to stay here. I wouldn't miss a day of it. After that speech you give those men, I wouldn't miss a thing that goes on around here. How long you worked here, Sadie?" Mariah was anxious to learn all she could about the two women she'd be working with.

"I can't remember exactly, but I'm twenty-two and I guess I've been here since I was twelve or thirteen. It's a long time anyway. My old man was so hard to live around and he wasn't above usin' his fists to convince a person of what he wanted, so I lit out and come over here to Mattie. At first I stayed at home. But when I turned eighteen, I moved over here with Mattie. That way the old boy don't have a thing to say about nothin. I guess he missed my pay when I left, but that's tough."

"Who is this Ambrose you were talking about?" Mariah's inquiry didn't seem to bother Sadie in the least.

"Oh, he's a local businessman who lives outside of town on a acreage. He works for a man named Southworth that buys and sells horses and cattle to the local farmers. Southworth is rich, and I think Ambrose might not be far behind him. His nephew, Pearl, lived with him until last year when Pearl went West with Jesse Peers and trailed a bunch of cows out to Nebraska. Jesse lives out there with his folks, but he's spent time here. Too much time I guess cause Mattie's lost her good sense completely over him. I bet if he knew how things were he'd be here in the first train and take her back to Nebraska with him."

"Gosh, Sadie, that's pretty exciting. Do you suppose I'll ever meet anybody that I could feel that way about? Most girls have their lives all cut out for them by the time they're 18." The wistfulness in Mariah's voice made Sadie chuckle.

"Don't never talk to me about men and marriage and all the clap trap that goes along with it. I say leave me alone, let me live my life out without the likes of any of them. If you knew my dad, you'd know exactly what I'm talking about. I haven't seen one yet worth the powder to blow him to hell. That includes Jesse Peers with Pearl Lux thrown in. They're all a bunch of bums. Look at Mattie if you don't believe what I'm sayin'."

"Oh, that's hard to believe that they are all bad. Didn't you say Ambrose was like a pet coon?" Mariah pointed out.

"Well, I gotta admit, Ambrose might be just one teeny weeny exception but he's the only one," Sadie admitted.

By supper time, Mattie wasn't any better so the two women worked all afternoon getting food together. The two worked in the sleeping rooms making up beds and cleaning as well as they could.

"I think Mattie better go on to bed and around 4 o'clock you should go get your stuff and be back in time to serve supper around 6 o'clock."

Mariah thought about Sadie's comments. "Why don't I just stay till 7 or so and then ride out to my uncle's. Then I can come back in the morning and move in. It'll give my Aunt and Uncle a chance to discuss this whole thing and get used to the idea. How would that be?"

"Well, I know how you feel so you better go ahead with your plans. I'll be like a fish out of water till you get back. Most of the time it's alright, but occasionally there's a bust up cause someone got drunk, or played cards upstairs and didn't like the hand that was dealt.," Sadie whined.

"I just thought we'd get more done if I stayed late and went home," Mariah reasoned. "I feel sorry for Mattie, but I sure hope she gets along better now."

"What's the worst that can happen, girl? If she loses that baby or keeps it, it'll be a problem. In fact, it might be better if she did lose it, then go on with the way she feels."

"One time my Ma went eight and one-half months and the baby came stillborn. She had lots of problems, quite a bit like Mattie was feeling," Mariah remembered her own life at home.

The day moved along and the supper hour arrived. There were eighteen men at the table, and Sadie kept the kitchen going while both women served food. There was a huge pot of macaroni and cheese with mashed potatoes, green vegetables, relish trays and a platter of bread. Dessert was chocolate pudding with a dollup of whipped cream. Nobody complained and that was because Sadie chewed everyone out at lunch time.

Mariah decided Sadie had done right. She was relieved no one asked about Mattie. Looking at the line up of men, there was no one under forty and all seemed to be more interested in the food than the person who served it. No husband material around here, she decided. It was a big relief when the last dish was done and it was time to go home. She'd forgot all about the horse. She asked for a bucket of water before she took up the reins to go home.

"There's some corn out on the porch if you want to feed your pony. Won't hurt to give him something before you take off." Sadie showed her where the sack of ground corn was kept.

Mariah scrounged for a small amount of corn and patiently fed the critter then led him to the stock tank for water. With a sigh she mounted up and rode off. The sun still shown bright on the horizon and evening stars were beginning to mount into the sky. Mariah felt this glow inside she was so happy. She flicked her reins and brought the pony into a trot. A ball of warmth somehow rested in her tummy bright and cheerful.

The next day, Mariah moved her possessions to Mattie's boarding house, and settled them into the larger sitting room off the kitchen. Aunt Isabelle and Uncle Gideon brought the things in their buggy, along with a new bedspread and mirror. Aunt Isabelle said, "We got these things and I made the spread for you, Mariah. You may as well have these things to fix up your room. Looks like you have room for that rocker and the little settee we had in your room at our house. Gideon will bring those things over later today and bring them in for you."

Gideon looked pleased as a mother hen. Smoothing and adjusting things in Mariah's room suited him just fine. Mariah had told them Mattie was not well and needed help badly. Later Gideon had suggested to Isabelle perhaps he could look in on the woman and "help" some. He was more curious than anything at the prospect of the robust, ambitious Mattie Kelly being sick. Somehow his curiosity devoured all his caution, and he became quite zealous in his attention to matters at the boarding house.

Mattie stayed in her room, Sadie and Mariah had everything under control. This peeked Gideon's curiosity more than ever. During the next few days, he found things he needed to do for Mariah at the boarding house.

Chapter 5

Boarding houses were always a part of organized activity on the frontier as America became settled. The push Westward, development of industries, work crews and the railroad being built, created a need for the boarding house. Some had large rooms with cots set side by side. By 1889, the boarding houses supplied places for work crews and cowhands to find bed and board. A bed for the night and at least one meal a day.

<u>THE LOCAL MARKETS</u>: Fresh Eggs are selling at 7 at 7 1/2cents Live Poultry: Chickens, hens, 7 1/2C; roosters 5 cents. .Pigeons: Per doz., $1.20 , Veal: Fancy, 7 at 7 ½ cents, thins and large, 4 at 5 cents.. Butter: Creamery: fancy, 15 oz. 16 cents; choice country; 10 at 12cents; good country: 7 at 9 cents.

<u>FRUIT</u>: Apples: Per bbl. $4.50. Bananas: Per bunch, $1.75, Lemons: CA. $3.00 per basket. Oranges: per box $2.50. Strawberries: Per 24 qt. Case, $2.50 Pineapple: Per doz. $3.00, Cherries: Per 10 lb. Box, $2.00. Omaha Bee, 1897

Mattie and Ambrose

The two men rode along behind the Mustangs they'd brought from Cyrus Soutworth's property. They'd been up early toiling away in the early morning sun. The horses were lean, their feet the color of clam shells and hard as stone as they clipped along the gravel road beside the meandering creek that bordered Gideon Calish's property. The creek made a sound like a snake gliding through grass Ambrose sat astride an Andulusian stallion, carrying him through another day of mindless activity, as he rode through the countryside. He watched the windswept trees along the valley floor beside the shallow creek. He could smell rainfall out there somewhere.

Ambrose and Zebediah Frame, his hired man, delivered the string of horses to Gideon Calish at his stable outside of town. They were delivered there to be shod and sold at auction next week. July was always a good time to auction livestock. Spring crops were in and farmers had time to spend before harvest time began.

Ambrose and Zebediah ran the horses into a corral and closed the gate. They both dismounted and tied their horses to the hitching rail outside Gideon's office. Gideon met them at the door.

"Here's a bill of sale. The horses are mustangs and they are sound. Zebediah's been working them some. Pearl had this job down pat. I miss him since he's gone West. Had a letter from Emory Peers that Pearl's working out fine out there. He's a real prize to have around."

"You need to bring him back here. Can't have enough people like Pearl around to train and work horses. I'll get you a check. You used to live at Mattie's as I recall," Gideon inquired.

"Yes, I still have meals over there now and then. Can't cook worth much and Mattie takes pity on me."

"My niece, Mariah, went over there to work. Too bad Mattie's not well. She must be real bad. It's sad to see a robust person like Mattie fail," Gideon said. His eyes cut across the two men as he spoke, taking in any reaction he might find there.

Ambrose looked startled. "You say Mattie's not well? Didn't know as much. I'll look in on them on my way home and check on her. I appreciate your mentionin' it Gideon." Ambrose was deep inside his own head trying to understand what he'd just heard. He'd seen Mattie about a week ago when she'd come out to clean, but hadn't said one word on being sick or nothin' like that. He decided it wasn't serious and dismissed it from his mind.

Gideon wrote a check and shook hands with Ambrose. The two men walked out to their horses and mounted up. Dust rose in clouds as they rode off. The sun shown down intensely on the two men. Indiana summer had set in. The sky was clear and brittle, the sun heavy on the skin. It hadn't rained for several weeks and dust settled on the saddle horses as they rode away.

Ambrose stopped at the Mercantile Store to buy rope and nails he needed. Ben Crowder put them up for him. He bought sugar and coffee they needed. Ben wrapped his packages tightly so they would fit in the saddle bags. Mrs. Crowder inquired about Pearl.

"Sure miss having Pearl stop by for supplies now and then. He growed up real fine didn't he Ambrose?" she asked.

This surprised Ambrose, "Wasn't aware you were so attached to the likes of Pearl," Ambrose stated. "Life is full of surprises, ain't it, Mrs. Crowder. We get attached to some of these youngsters even if it was stressful at times." He had a problem fathoming how Mrs. Crowder could have this revelation since at one time, she had drawn different conclusions.

Ambrose paid Ben for the goods and the two men started for home. He'd forgot Gideon's news about Mattie till he got clear out to the acreage. They put supplies away and Zebediah went to the barn to work.

Ambrose made some notes in a ledger and sat at his desk pondering Mattie. Dust motes spiraled in the hot sun through the windows where he worked. It was mid-morning and it struck him he needed to know more about this Mattie Kelly business.

He called Zebediah, "Let's ride over to Mattie's and see what she's servin' for lunch. How does that sound to you?"

Zebediah replied, "That sounds fine. If you stay around here the prospects of any food is pretty slim."

Ambrose chuckled, "I guess we're thinkin' along the same lines."

The two men saddled up horses and rode off down the country rode. They arrived as lunch preparation had begun. Sadie and Mariah were busy in the kitchen slicing roast beef and ham. A pot of bean soup simmered on the cook stove. The windows of the kitchen were open to let in any breeze they might catch. Sycamore trees grew all around the house for much needed shade and caught such breeze as might drift around the house.

Ambrose asked, "Where's Mattie? I haven't seen her for awhile. Gideon Calish says she's poorly. Mattie got the flu or somethin'?"

"Now Ambrose, you're as bad as these whiners we got round the boarding house. Mattie isn't well and she needs to be left alone."

"Well Sadie, you may get by with that stuff where your boarders are concerned, but I want to know just what the particulars are and I want to know now," Ambrose demanded.

"Well, let me see what she says. Seems to me you could spend your time better than botherin' the kitchen help when we're so damned busy we don't know half the time which end is up," Sadie retorted.

She went to the back porch where Mattie had heard most of the conversation. She sat in a rocker trying to be as composed as possible. Somehow, she knew the time had come for her to face the whole issue and deal with it.

"Tell Ambrose to get out here. I'll try to reason with him the best I can." She was upset and it was apparent.

"Tell him to mind his own business, Mattie. I'd tell them to leave if they don't like it. They're just in time for lunch and they'd showed up conveniently so they'll get fed."

"Well, you know that won't satisfy Ambrose. So send him out here."

Wildfire

Sadie fumed and walked back to the kitchen. "I see you showed up in time for lunch. If Zebediah wants to wash up he can. Mattie said she'll talk to you out on the porch, Ambrose. Don't go upsettin' Mattie, you hear me?" she threatened.

Ambrose looked relieved. "You got room for two more for lunch, Sadie? I'm not mindin' my manners here. Gideon said his niece was workin' here. This here's Zebediah Frame and I assume you're Mariah Calish."

The young people greeted each other. Mariah led Zebediah to the washing basin and poured hot water for him. Ambrose walked to the porch. Full of dread and worry he peered at Mattie hard as he entered the porch. She sat passively dreading what was to come.

"I understand you're not well. I don't mean to intrude, but you were fine awhile back when you came out to the house. What's going on that you're not even in the kitchen today. You get a man upset and wonderin' what's happened."

"Well, Ambrose, you know I wouldn't concern you unnecessarily. Hopefully, this will pass and I'll be just fine again." She evaded what was going on. She wasn't dealing with Ambrose squarely.

"You mean this is just an upset like flu or food poisoning, and you'll be alright soon?" Ambrose inquired.

"Well, something like that. It may take a little longer than a few days though. I'm hoping to be right as rain in a week or so," she replied.

Ambrose pondered on this. His experience with women was limited. "You're too young to be dealin' with a change. I know women go through such things but I've not learned much about such. Perhaps you could enlighten me."

"Lord God, Ambrose, you've been an owner and breeder of horses but you know nothing about humans. We're full of desires and some never act on them. Perhaps if you had you'd better understand my situation."

"You're sayin' it's more than flu or food poisoning then, right?" He was warming up to the subject but couldn't quite fathom Mattie's answer. A little kernel of suspicion began to grow and at last it took root, Mattie's problem was not a passing thing. "You don't have the cancer or some disease, do you?"

"No Ambrose, nothing that bad, although it will seem bad enough." With this statement Mattie began to explain what it was all about. A recognition crossed Ambrose's face as he listened. Mattie told how she'd not loved wisely, but she just couldn't help how she had come to feel about Jesse. Then there was this business she had. She had resolved to stay and not sell it, and let the chips fall if they must. She was about to have this baby and keep it besides.

Ambrose registered shock and dismay, but this soon turned to anger. He began to rant about Jesse Peers. He couldn't contain his disgust with her, his anger with Jesse. Didn't Mattie know she'd lost her mind and become a complete nitwit

At first Mattie was disturbed and deeply ashamed, but as she reasoned this she had a revelation about it all. "Everybody knew we were mad about each other. Times bein' what they are I'm bringing a life into the world that whether we accept it or not has the right to

Wildfire

be born. Besides, I love this baby and I will do for this child whatever I must and to hell with whatever people do or say. Now you think about what I've just said and whether you feel the same way or not makes no difference to me, Ambrose Lux."

Ambrose was chastened like a child. He'd been chewed out and informed the best way Mattie knew, and it humbled him. The shock of what he'd learned sobered him. The idea popped into his head (I told you so) but he didn't say this.

He rose and said, "Well, Mattie, you should rest as you'll need your strength. That's all I have to offer right now. But I will think on this and I will be back to discuss matters again. Believe that."

Mattie replied, "You needn't if it bothers you."

As Ambrose rose and left the porch, both of them knew this was not the end of their discussion. How they would resolve this relationship was doubtful and would take lots of caring attention to save it.

Chapter 6

Range Wars: The growth of the cattle industry placed a premium upon land. Conflicting claims over land and water right ignited violent disputes between ranchers and farmers. Ranchers often tried to drive off neighboring farmers, and farmers in turn tried to sabotage the cattle barons, cutting their fences and spooking their herds. The cattle ranchers also clashed with sheepherders over access to grasslands. – Conflict faded however, as the sheep for the most part found refuge in the high pastures of the mountains, leaving the grasslands of the Plains to the cattlemen. There also developed the perennial tension over grassland use between large and small cattle ranchers. The large ranchers fenced in huge tracts of public lands, leaving the smaller ranchers with too little pasture. To survive, the small ranchers cut fences— In Johnson County, Wyoming, in 1889, the cattle barons lynched James Averall, a small rancher, and Ella Watson, a prostitute embroiled in the dispute. The vigilantes were brought to trial but the case was dismissed when the four witnesses to the hanging refused to testify. <u>America</u> "New Frontiers: South and West," (Ch.18), pp.666-667

Loup River Mystery

It got colder during the night and the sounds amplified with the drop in temperature. I opened my eyes to a new day, aware that so much was missing from my life right now. My emptiness made a lie out of everything I do every day. Pearl and Doctor Dickinson were sound asleep, their deep breathing in perfect harmony with the muted noises from the kitchen and the crack of cold and stillness outside. It was almost too much to absorb all that had happened the past few days.

Someone had been about starting the fires in the cookstove and heating stove. The ring of stove grates and shift of wood bore witness to the new day, lighting a lamp, setting the hot water kettle to boil absorbed my conscious thought and brought me a kind of peace I thought I'd never again achieve once I'd left Indiana. The spinning of the windmill, the cattle lowing, the horses trotting about in their stalls attested to the beginning of another day. The first day of the rest of my life.

Pa came to the bedroom door. "Time to get up. Breakfast will be ready whenever you fella's are ready for it. Pearl, you gonna take our good doctor back to town?" Pearl roused in his bed.

"I didn't think I'd do that today as Jesse and I need to figure on how we'll track and kill these predators before we lose anymore men, cattle or horses."

" B. J., you and Hank want to take a ride in the sleigh today?" Pa asked.

Both men agreed they would go but B. J. added, "Cynci would like to go with me, senor, if she could be spared."

Pa's eyes lit up, allowing there was more than just a sleigh ride. It would relieve some of the tension in the house at the same time. Pearl's eyes cut across mine. There was some humor there as he spoke. "B. J. needs to council Cynci on some of the stuff she pulls now and then."

B. J. said, "What you mean, my fren? She seem jus' fine to me. Always my good and sweet Cynci."

"You been taken in and thrown out by her so many times, I'm surprised it's a mystery to you, B. J.," Pearl insisted.

The conversation going nowhere but in circles, I steered Pearl outside to the barn. "I d thought I wouldn't have to tell you not to say more about Cynci. He won't see your way no matter what. She's the best as far as he's concerned."

"She's got other talents too but no one seems to own up to what she does. She just goes on doing her deviltry, Jesse, and you know I'm right, " Pearl insisted.

"It won't do a bit of good to bring this up with either one of them. Besides, you and I got a whopping problem of our own."

We all moved to the barn and began cleaning stalls. Hank fed the horses and returned them leading Little Blue back into her stall. He had this strange look on his face as he turned to me.

I said, "What is it Hank? Little Blue do somethin' to you?"

"There's tracks over by the chicken run. Big ones. Too big for a wolf, but there's horse tracks too. Made in the last couple days since our last storm."

"Let's take a look," I said.'

Wildfire

The three of us walked quickly to the yard and behind the buildings. Corn cribs sheltered this portion of the yard. This was joined with chicken fencing that kept the chickens and geese away from the large animals around the barn. The horses hadn't been shod, front or back feet, and the hooves curled outward. Only a lazy wrangler allows his horses hooves to be like this. Most people who aren't inclined to do this work themselves, for a price, have a smithy do it. There's one in every settlement around.

We were looking at tracks and trampled earth where someone had stood. This was not something we'd invented with our imagination. Sometimes fact and fiction were so close, if you weren't careful you'd miss it. Nobody said a word, nobody had to.

"Let's don't mention this in the house. We'll see where this takes us. After we eat, we'll saddle up and have a look around," I told them.

A couple more months of weather that would dip below zero lay ahead. Clouds riffled across a clear sky without enough wind to turn the blades of the windmill. Sounds cracked the silence and bounced across the still air.

Laughter traversed across from the house. It broke the tension from the strained silence moments before. It was a relief to me, and surprise washed across the faces of Hank and Pearl.

When we got our outdoor clothes off and entered the house, everyone was seated at the huge table. Hannah and Ethel came in with hot cakes and sausage. Mama and Cynci followed with pots of cornmeal mush and scrambled eggs. Pa said our blessing.

Mama looked around at all of us. "It was great you could tend to us, Doctor. My mind had a great load lifted the minute you walked in the door."

"B. J. and Hank will take you back to town," Pa said. "We need to tend to this business of these predators fast as we can. I'm thinking it may be a tedious job finding these varmints and ridding ourselves of them."

"Ma if you'll fix us a jug of coffee and some sandwiches, Pearl and I will leave soon as we finish here," I said.

This statement was later known to cause anxiety in our Hannah which led to many conversations between Pearl and herself. You see the most casual remark would set off a firestorm of opinions. Even the most common of remarks can cause an uncommon affect that would ricochet over and over.

When breakfast was accomplished, Hannah came to Pearl, cleaning and oiling guns and checking equipment. She surveilled this quietly and Pearl became aware of her curious attention to details.

"I see you are cleaning and checking guns and ammunitions," said Hannah.

"I was hopin' I'd not have to tell you that," said Pearl with a wide grin on his face.

In all seriousness she went on. "I suppose we'll not see much of you till you've tracked and killed these critters, whatever they might be."

"You read my mind, Hannah. I'd not thought you a mind reader, but here you are telling what's in my inner most thoughts." His attempt at humor was wasted, as Hannah was not being toyed with.

"I suppose you and Jesse will be wound up in this thing till you've accomplished what you've set out to do and then some. And if it results in freezing in the cold or being attacked yourself, no matter," she continued.

"Now yer scarin' me on top of the rest. Do you believe we'd take unnecessary risk to accomplish this task?"

"Yes, I do, and more besides. At first, I wasn't concerned, but since our trip to town and what happened there, even you must see it's a wild and raw country. You'd throw caution to the wind." With this gut wrenching statement, tears fell and Pearl, willing and able, moved to comfort Hannah.

At first, he had a change of heart. He thought of canceling out the whole thing, but as he held her close, it did occur that the thing at hand needed to at least be looked into. So with his calmest most persuasive manner, he began to explain the dilemma that would continue to plague them if nothing was done. He needed to at least discover what had occurred and why the attack was so vicious. He did recall to her Jesse's brave attempt to search for Del Cole on the fatal night. What might have come out of it, if Jesse had not gone back to search?

As he said all these things, Hannah began to relax. Pearl brought out a large red bandana, wiped the tears as Hannah blew her nose and composed herself. With all this said, Pearl held her close once more and filled with elated passion, kissed her many time and held her there. Pearl stood over six feet tall by now. Muscular and long legged, he had dark brown hair, chameleon eyes like glass marbles, sometimes green sometimes blue, and at this moment, they were electric with the confidence of being Hannah's lover. Yes, sometimes the most common events can lead to uncommon events.

By the time they'd returned to the kitchen, food and coffee was packed for the side saddle bags. Pearl and I set out for the barn and in the time it took to saddle the horses, we were ready for what lay ahead. My Gold Coin Arabian was anxious to get underway. It was all I could do to rein him in and hold him to a steady pace. Once more we went to the back of the hen house and checked all the footprints we'd seen before. The horse's hoof prints led off into the sand hills toward the Loup River now frozen over with ice and nearly closed. The horses felt our anxiety, responding to the pressure of our signals to press ahead.

By mid-day we had tracked along the Loup River about 15 miles and we came to an old abandoned mill. Not expecting to find an inhabitant, I was surprised to see smoke coming from a chimney of one of the buildings. We dismounted and tied the horses to the branches of an old tree. We were on an outcrop of shale and sandstone that jutted some fifty feet in the air. Below, a corral butted up against this wall that formed the back closure. As we inched closer to the edge, the cold melted into our feet and legs as we crept along. In the yard stood various sheds in a sad state of decay. Horses were loose in the corral. They whinnied and trotted about, aware we were there. We watched closely for any sign of life. The door of the biggest shed opened and a man came out, looked around and walked to the corral. He was followed by a Mastiff about the size of a young colt. The man ordered the dog to heel, and the animal trotted obediently at his side.

The horses sensed the dog and trotted around nervously. The man carried a crate of some kind and it was too far to see what he had or fathom what he was up to. He opened a shed and there was a sudden uproar of barking and whining, the likes of which would put yer eardrums out. The Mastiff with the man became agitated and the man reached into a crate and grabbed two rabbits by the ears and threw them into the shed with the dogs. The melee that followed was unbelievable. The mastiffs attacked in a frenzy killing the rabbits. They yelped and tumbled over each other in their frenzy to catch the rabbits.

"I don't have my opera glasses but, Pearl, I believe that sodbuster just threw live rabbits into that dog kennel. What do you say?"

"I believe you've seein' right, Jesse. What do you suppose is goin' on down there?"

"I'm supposin' it's a man's own business what he does but, by damn, it seems a mighty cruel way to treat animals," I mused.

"What do you say we've found our attackers and they ain't wolves. Is this a matter for the sheriff or do we have to have some more attacks before he'll be convinced? Hell, it's only some rabbits, but it seems bad to bait dogs unless you're raisin' 'em to hunt and kill." Pearl added.

"The varmint has now got himself an empty cage he's hauling back to fill up again with fresh live bait. He's goin' back to the house, looks to me like," I said.

The man disappeared inside. We were about to ride off out of there, when a bunch of Sauk Indians rode up on their ponies. They milled around the yard and called out to the varmint inside. He came out again and it appeared the Indians were in heavy conversation with him. After a little more palaver he went to another shed.

This shed had an active chimney smoking that spiraled upward into the cold winter air. The day wore on and now the sun had descended to the western sky. There would still be several hours of daylight but we didn't want to leave right now.

The varmint came out with several jugs of hard liquor, and it appeared the Indians had some money to pay him. There was something amiss, and the factor must've demanded more money. Several of the young bucks jumped down and walked toward him.

"It seems there's a little argument about the price, I'd say, wouldn't you Jesse?"

"You guessed right. Are we gonna see a little fracas here?" I asked.

The man raised his revolver and shot in the air. The Indians stirred around and made like they were ready to mount up.

"Look. One of them just threw something on the ground. They've grabbed up their liquor and are makin' off with it," I said.

"That guy looks like he's ready to shoot 'em down," Pearl said with alarm.

The Indians rode off with four jugs of moonshine. The varmint bent and picked up something from the ground, examined it, raised his revolver and fired it into the air.

"You can see those Indians spurred their horses into a gallop. They're not takin' a chance on getting shot by stickin' around," I said.

We stayed a little longer, but things were now quiet around the buildings. We slipped back down the shale butte and found our horses milling under the apple trees.

I pondered on what we had seen and what it might mean. I knew we'd witnessed not only a dog handler, but the worst kind of bootlegger. He trafficked in the young bucks who were the renegades. I knew we were not safe on the homestead, and we'd been lax in not being more cautious. That sodbuster ne'r would've been out by the chicken run and that close to the house unless he felt safe nosin' around the property. That'd explain why whoever he was had probably been out the night of the storm. If he hadn't been out there, the dogs sure as hell were. Thinking back on it put almighty speed in my action, and I flipped my reins at Wildfire. He responded with his usual burst of energy into a full gallop. The two of us rode on in silence the rest of the way. Both of us looked this way and that, more cautious than we'd ever been this morning.

"Hannah was more aware of what this was all about than me. I was not nearly as upset as she was about our trip today. Like I told her, how were we to know if we didn't take a look. She was so upset, I had to comfort her and tell her things to relieve her mind," Pearl said seriously.

"I saw you comfort her and it did not seem you were in any way concerned. It almost looked to me like you were more than up to the job. What I could see anyway," I teased.

Pearl chuckled, "Didn't know you had your eyes peeled for such matters as Hannah and me this mornin'."

It would be months before we would have enough "proof" to take it to the authorities. Early spring brought about many changes for us however.

Chapter 7

During the twenty years after the Civil War, some 40,000 cowboys roamed the Great Plains. They were young—the average age was twenty-four—and from diverse backgrounds. Thirty percent were either Mexican or African American, and hundreds were Indians. Many others were Civil War veterans from North and South who now rode side by side, and a number had come from Europe. The life of a cowboy, for the most part, was rarely exciting as motion pictures and television shows have depicted. Being a ranch hand involved grueling, dirty, wage labor interspersed with drudgery and boredom. <u>America</u> The New West, New Frontiers: South and West, (Ch.18) p 664

Cynci, Sauk Slave Woman

Cynci (pronounced Sinsee) was always a source of curiosity where all of us were concerned. I had a hand in rescuing her from some Sauk warriors out in the Iowa territory near Fort Des Moines. Over time, we had all talked to her trying to glean some sense out of how she came to be a captive of the Sauk Nations. I'd learned she likely was the infant of an Iowa territory settler whose homestead was raided by Sioux Indians, who then traded her at a young age to the Sauk tribe. She eventually lived with them for well nigh two score years, and it was apparent she was not treated well. At that tender age she became the slave of a widowed squaw, whose husband and sons had been killed either in tribal warring or by the United States army.

She remembers being carried on horseback at an early age, I figure three or four to a pow wow somewhere in the Black Hills that Crazy Horse called home. Squaw whips were a common property of elder Indian squaws and they brandished them with gusto when some infraction occurred.

From Cynci's tale of a life of misery and abuse, to my thinking her life had not amounted to much. As she reached a marriageable age, it seemed to have gotten worse. The old lady would barter over her, being a greedy old fool, for personal gain. Cynci had worked hard all her life with the Sauk Nations. Cynci at times was as evil as a snake hiding it cleverly enough to take in some other wild squaw causing enough deviltry to eventually get her sold off to these Sauk warriors that brought her our way. She had numerous scars and burns that stood as proof of her miseries with the Sioux Nations and later with the Sauks.

We probably provided the best years of her life. Mama supervised Cynci's exposure to our white culture by being patient and kind in her dealings with the woman. The dusky wild squaw was still ingrained in there and would forever surface and strike whenever Cynci decided to pull some vicious mischief knowing full well she had outdone some of the Indians she lived among.

B. J. was a half breed Apache vaquero who migrated from Mexico to the United States. He and Cynci entertained us during that long winter. Pa had built a sod shanty 12 X 24 in back of the property, one story high, basically a flat plain room of sod with windows on three sides. It had the same slant roof as the out buildings that made it possible to clear heavy snow from the roof. We had a massive amount of hired hands that came and went through the year. One of the main reasons I wasn't in a big rush to get back here to Nebraska, figurin' Pa always had access to men lookin' for a few extra dollars and a roof over their head.

Mama supervised the building of bunk beds at one end of the room putting up 18 men if needed. A heavy table and stools occupied the other end of the huge room. A wash stand stood with a pump sunk there to allow daily washing. A stall out at the side of the building provided that occasional shower these men all needed after working in the fields ten to twelve hours during harvest. Mama complained about the body odor at meal time till Pa gave in, waffling under her nagging on the subject mainly to keep peace.

The table was big enough for the ongoing card games that B. J. was known to set up. It was large enough to seat 18 people as the need arose during the summer harvest time. It became necessary at times to serve meals there, with the kitchen help carting food back and forth.

Pa had an ongoing relationship with some Indians from the Omaha Nations that he cultivated. The Indian's would ride in carrying the carcass of a deer or some wild geese, sometimes pheasant and grouse. Since Pa and Ray had little time to light out and hunt and there was this constant need for meat, he bargained with the Indians and built up this business of trading with them. Their favorite trade was brown unrefined sugar and whiskey. Sometimes they wanted bullets and always guns which Pa was careful about. He also didn't want to rile them by refusing their offer. They bad mouthed him anyway calling him bad medicine and said he didn't trust them. They made lots of noise but in the end would settle for a reasonable trade with Pa.

After we arrived from Indiana, Lone Bear and Sweet Water had taken over this task famously and we had a variety of foul and venison for cooking. It also meant Pa didn't have to butcher his precious milk cows for beef.

On one occasion they had a Nez Perce Indian called Lone Buffalo with them. Cynci, being a meddling squaw, began conversations with Buffalo. With her endless flow of cash from the bunkhouse, she bartered a pair of fine beaded moccasins which she wore post haste. The design in bead work that the Nez Perce were noted for, consisted of roses with green stems set into white beads. The moccasins contained a small sleeve that held a filleting knife. She preferred moccasins to the stiff leather shoes Mama had given her.

B.J. took all this in and wanting to be the main buck in her life inquired where she had learned the Nez Perce dialect. The outcome was she taught him sentences

Wildfire

with exclamations and all the clap trap that went along with that. Not long after B. J. bragged to Joe Lone Bear that he could speak Indian and he did just that. Shock and disgust registered plain on Joe's face. He slapped his thigh and informed B.J. he might never want to try those sentences out on any Indians he knew, cause he was speaking low life trash Indian talk. We laughed about this, but B. J. was hard put to learn just to keep up with his dusky woman, and soon Joe had a pupil. B.J. learned to talk with traders as rapid as you please.

B.J. and Cynci were always playing and it got wearing at times, depending on who got caught up in it. Sometimes we all were and Mama would chuckle to herself over some mischief Cynci had pulled. She never felt the need to single one or the other out for a tongue lashing, which many of us had surrendered to from time to time. We still had the confounding occurrence of some item disappearing: broaches, rings, earrings, mostly things belonging to the women. It should've given a clue as to the culprit. The item would show up in some opportune place and Cynci was all innocence about it.

Maudie had gotten pearl earrings for her birthday in early November, and Ethel had made over them so at the time. Sure enough they turned up missing, and were found eventually in Ethel's possession. The shock was apparent on Ethel's face full of anticipation and fearing the worst--until she realized she'd been set up. Promptly, her eyes stretched wide across her face with anger flaming in torrents of rage. Cynci, nowhere to be found, turned up playing cards with B.J., Joe and three other cowhands in the bunk house.

Ethel was unable to conserve her words. She ranted and raged until she spent herself totally, collapsed in tears and threw herself head first upon her bed. She shrieked so loud it could be heard in the bunkhouse. About then applause and laughter erupted out there. It sounded as if money had exchanged hands among the lot of them. I hoped I was mistaken on that.

Pa's eyes lit up with this inner glow when I happened to look upon him. Slowly, it began to dawn on me. If things played out as I reasoned, it would not belong and we would see retaliation take form and shape. Cynci came back in the house that evening like some saint with a halo over her head. The Indian squaw in her left a warring soul more evil than good at times, and would be forever leading her in a path of destruction--just for the hell of it. B.J. watched with appreciation of her talents, if you would call them that. The squaw man was full blown and developed and Cynci drew him in and threw him out regular as rain on the prairie or wind from the sand hills. He was struck dumb with her shenanigans, approving and still distrustful.

That dusky lady had him wound around her little finger. Though she was lovely to look upon with that brown and black hair and eyes like buttery chocolate, her confidence did not lie in the kitchen. Though Mama tried her best to teach her some basic skills, we could always tell when Cynci was in charge in the Kitchen.

Mornings the eggs were always leathery and evenings the mashed spuds were lumpy. We were given to teasing her which got us chastised as a group by that squaw lady. She threatened everything from throwing it to the pigs to letting us go hungry. When

Wildfire

Pearl told her that's what it was, "slop for the pigs," he was anointed with hot coffee that left him scalded and gasping. He went to my Mama. "Mrs. Peers, we are only telling it like it is."

Mama was appropriately understanding while she put ointment on his back where the coffee had spun in rivulets. Sweet Water agreed we needed to do something about Cynci and her fit throwing, but what?

Mama said, "I'll speak to Emory on what we might do to resolve the situation, but there was no where for Cynci to go, and if she does B. J. would not be far behind."

So the solution going neither one way nor another, we were hard put to solve the dilemma for everyone involved.

Pearl attempted to coax her out of her disposition but the anger was ingrained so deep, no doubt by her former captors, the Sauks, we were doubtful the temper fits could be resolved without a confrontation. Some squaws were noted to carry filleting knives tucked in their moccasins. We were fearful of bloodshed or injury. After some negotiating with Pearl, we agreed to be vigilant and perhaps nip some of these events in the bud. Our best efforts were not rewarded as we spent the winter months not knowing what the next day would bring.

The final outcome happened in early March. The weather was noted to be changing and the farm house was in need of a thorough cleaning. This included beds and blankets as well as a scrub down of bed springs and a good airing of the whole lot. Ethel and Maudie with Hannah and Cynci in tow went to the bunk house where the bunk beds housed some twelve men at the present time.

Mama had left the women to themselves as the division of duty fell. Cynci didn't look at it that way. Ethel proceeded to tell her she was a shirker and a lazy bum. Cynci countered she was no different herself and not to be so foul mouthed and dishonest to accuse herself of anything of the kind. Maudie then dove headlong into their fracas and told them both they were about as useful as snow in July, and if they couldn't make themselves useful any other way to go back to the house. Both of them knew Mama would be in a state of mind herself if they returned to the house and did not help with the dirt and mess in the bunk house. The work began slowly. It was clear from the start Cynci was in a fine temper throwing things about and generally misbehaving. Maudie sent her and Hannah to get buckets of water for scrubbing the floor. They returned with the buckets, mops and rags. Maudie continued to harangue at them to get to work and Ethel told Maudie to shut her mouth. Cynci took a swipe with her wet floor mop and the battle was on. Hannah fled to the yard where she could see through a window not wanting to miss one blow of the event. The three women went at it tooth and nail and soon we heard shrieks and screams in the farmhouse telling us the battle was in full swing.

Pearl and I held our ground knowing full well we did not want to go in that bunk house any more than we wanted the gates of hell to open and swallow us. B. J. was more aggressive claiming Cynci would get the worst of it and we should stop the whole fracas at once.

Pa came in from the barn where he'd heard the worst of it even out there.

"I have to appeal to you fellows to do your best to stop this battle going on out there. It's senseless and has gotten way out of control. Being shut up we're all a little sick with cabin fever. We feel these days of March the worst before spring breaks and we can get to work outside again."

"Pa, we would have to wade in and stop all three of them and then what. We gotta' figure out a way to keep them apart for awhile, but how?" I asked.

We barged in and separated the three hellions in the bunk house, getting ourselves knocked silly with broom and mop handles and that clap trap. Maudie had a black eye and Ethel had a wop of hair torn from her scalp. B. J. finally stretched Cynci out spread eagle on the floor disabling her from doing anything but mouthing off. She was doing a good job of that too, as she spit in his face. He loosed one hand and cuffed her across the face. Her free hand scratched him full across the face and blood spilled there. Maudie and Ethel were a little more subdued by now and beginning to be ashamed of themselves. Looking around at the mess they'd made, we were all more than a little disgusted.

Pa walked out to the bunk house and chastised the whole lot of them. One look at B. J. and he made up his mind right there. "B. J., if you and Cynci cannot find a peaceful way to live here, then take her and head out someplace where you can. The Omaha's won't take you in, they know both of you too well. The best you might do is with the Oglalas and I don't know if they would be so good either. Just remember those folks are in the process of being relocated mostly to reservation land. Be mindful of what just happened at Fort Robinson recently.

When Crazy Horse surrendered along with his half brother and his other hostiles, the U. S. Army attempted to interrogate him. The officers there didn't understand a word he was saying. Some renegade burst in on the officers apparently aiming to kill Crazy Horse. General Mills thought it best to impound Crazy Horse for his safety. His half brother insisted he'd go with him; they'd had a pact to stay together to the end of their days. When they went to arrest Crazy Horse, he resisted and a young soldier ran him through with a bayonet. Crazy Horse had sworn he'd surrender and be peaceful ever after. He didn't live to tell about it. So you need to be wary not only of the Army, but hostile Indians as well. I don't want to hear that you ended your days in some senseless struggle. You need to think carefully about where your future lies."

B.J. agreed he'd take her off their hands, "Whatever we do you're still going to have these two in your camp. I'll only have the one to deal with where you'll still be stuck with the worst of the lot."

This tended to stir up Maudie and Ethel. Pa raised his hand in a threatened manner and they had second thoughts about saying anything. Pearl looked around for Hannah. She had escaped to the wash house and stood there with the sheets in a tub of hot water and soap stirring away.

She raised her face when Pearl entered there her eyes big as saucers and face streaming with tears. It may have been the biggest day of Pearl's life on the plains as he swept her up, cuddling her and caressing her, soothing away the alarm he saw in her face. It was sometime before he returned to us and I chuckled to myself as I saw this look on his face. The darndest incident can sometimes bring out some sweet rewards. If ever there was a man smitten it was Pearl Lux. For a moment there, I looked in his eyes and saw this deep yearning and yet something so profoundly happy. Here was our finest again doing the best he could and finding it a rewarding experience at that.

Earlier when we had gone to town, Cynci had plenty of money to purchase the things she wanted for Christmas. Deep inside my own head as I ponder on this dusky woman, I know she will never return to the white man's world. There's too much of the wild Indian in her.

Pa decided we should work out something with B.J. before he hightailed it out on his own. Mama thought it best to equip them somehow so they would be able to care for themselves.

Sweet Water collected the food essentials they would take along with a sorrowful glint in her midnight eyes. She knew full well Cynci would not prove out to be the best cook, but whatever came their way, such as fish or small foul could feed them.

The stallion and his herd of mares we'd captured down on the Dunes in Indiana, was growing. Three of the mares had dropped foals in addition to the one dropped by the dun mare coming across to the plains. B. J.'s mare, Impanada, was the stallion's first choice of all the mares, and she was noted to be more agreeable to his amorous overtures. I felt some of these horses belonged to B.J.

Pa instructed them about the Indian nations around Nebraska. He told B.J. the warring going on always seemed that no matter how peaceful the tribe seemed there was always the threat amongst the young bucks to be on the warpath.

The last day they remained was a sad one for Pearl and me. No matter what the problem with Cynci, B.J. was a first class wrangler who always carried his own weight. Pa threatened Maudie and Ethel if they didn't behave he'd whale the tar out of them personally. Their eyes flashed and they assumed a "show me" position. This was enough for him to grab both women and sheperd them into the back room where he closed the door. I guess we'll never know what he said to them. But from there on you could hear a pin drop. They came back to the kitchen shame faced and apologetic. I'd say his best weapon was the Catholic Convent in Indianapolis where they would have enough discipline for all of us.

Their departure was a sad one with all of us lingering over them. The mares were all packed with things they'd need along the way. The traps and extra guns and ammunition were packed on one of the mares and both Cynci and B.J. had bulging saddle bags as well. They weren't leaving empty handed, but we would worry about marauding Indians and dishonest whites as well. Pearl was curt for days afterward with Maudie and Ethel. He marveled at Hannah and occasionally I would find him gazing at her with this inquiring look. I knew he still held some concern over her earlier mental problems. To the rest of us though she seemed sound as a rock.

So early spring when buttercups grew and pussy willows showed knobs of new buds, B.J. and Cynci left us with their meager log and the small herd of horses the three of us had netted down in the Dunes by the great lake Superior. B.J. had his back pay from the trek out to the plains, some traps, two buffalo guns, a colt revolver besides his own holster guns and plenty of ammunition. They headed out on a balmy day where the breeze blew wisps of clouds through the azure sky. I hoped it was a good omen.

I saw B.J. again at a rendezvous in Fort Keogh outside of Miles City that next fall, where he'd come from Johnson County in Wyoming. He'd trapped beaver and traded buffalo hides from the Shosoni Indians. There'd been a craze for stove pipe hats come into style and the milliners back East had used beaver hides to make hats that could be folded up and poked out. The politicians of Washington were particularly wild about this style.

Cynci was considerably changed. No one suspected she was not a full blood Kiowa and she didn't object to people thinking so. I sensed they had some considerable trials coming through the Teton mountains and up the Yellowstone, through the Beartooth range and into Billings. They were going to Missoula where they would sell their furs and start out again.

At this time, I believe they were both in their late 20's. The fresh air and hard living had firmed them both up hard as nails. They had a couple of run ins with

Cree and Nez Perce Indians. They narrowly escaped being killed by Cree renegade Indians.

"B.J. got friendly with them Cree and paid for it too. He wouldn't listen to this woman tell him they were up to no good." B. J. nodded, apparently in agreement. "We waited till night and if this woman had not been wary we would be out there bleaching our bones in the sun. I say, come now and steal away from them before you are sorry."

They rode up the gulch to the right hand ridge, coming out above the gulch below. Well concealed there, they could see the Cree Indians as they rode past them. The whole bunch high tailed it together down the gulch and through the lodge pole pines of the Yellowstone. Cynci and B.J. stole out like silent shadows side stepping and dodging through brush and willows back the way they had come. They rode on for some time before they could relax knowing they'd given the thieving murdering Crees the slip. Cynci's buttery chocolate eyes flashed in the retelling of this tale to me. Deep inside my own head, I fathom this and other occurrences have helped to shape the woman she had become. The country was wild and full of venison and fowl. Shale hills were everywhere and caused a constant threat of rock slides. They had ridden a long day's ride high into the Beartooth range that day.

I met them again two years later at a rendezvous in Donnelly, Idaho, where the land and opportunities had abounded. B. J. talked about settling there in the Wallowa Mountains where he could trap and hunt. He had a dream of owning a small piece of land where timber grew and he could harvest pine and cedar for the mills around that area. I hoped the dreams would out distance reality and he would realize all he aspired to want.

Cynci was still his main woman and she was growing supple and beautiful. B. J. regarded her with that glow in his eyes that young men are prone to. They were nearly nature's opposites as far as disposition, and she was still noted to fly off the handle with some knit wit tantrum about nothing. Not as often as I'd ever noted before, however, which was a relief and of note to us all.

The family still reminisced about the day the women flung mop water and mops at each other. Hannah's eyes would dance at the mention of this occurrence and Maudie and Ethel hung their heads in shame.

Mama missed Cynci and often mentioned some trick she so often pulled from thin air. I guess Mama had some appreciation for things besides cooking and cleaning. She summed it up pretty well. "Cynci was a babe when the Kyowa's took her and raised her. She never touched a pot or pan till she came to us. She'd had a long history with the Sauk Nations, where she learned to tan hides, weave wool, and make bead work. She had a place with us and Maudie and Ethel need to think carefully to themselves why she left us."

Chapter 8

INDIAN POLICY. --The Dawes Severalty Act of 1887 proposed to introduce the Indians to individual land ownership and agriculture. The Dawes Act permitted the president to divide the lands of any tribe and grant 160 acres to each head of family and lesser amounts to others. To protect an Indian's property, the government held it in trust for twenty-five years, after which the owner won full title and became a citizen. In 1901 citizenship was extended to Five Civilized Tribes of Oklahoma and in 1924 to all Indians. But the more it changed, the more Indian policy remained the same. Although well-intended, the Dawes Act created new chances for more plundering of Indian Lands, and it disrupted what remained of the traditional cultures. The Dawes Act broke up reservations and often led to the loss of Indian lands to whites. Those lands not distributed to Indian families were sold, while others were lost to land sharks because of the Indians' inexperience with private ownership, or simply because of their powerlessness in the face of fraud. Between 1887 and 1934, Indians lost an estimated 86 million of their 130 million acres. Most of what remained was unsuited for agriculture. <u>America,</u> "New Frontiers. South and West," (Chap. 18), Pp.662-663

Medicine Bow Country

Deep shadows swallowed the landscape with occasional flashes of low light cutting through. Before the sun lit the shapes inside the darkness, Joe Lone Bear, his son, Ishtapa, and I rode out the gate of the property and made for the North Loup River. I rode Big Red today, the strong Morgan horse, we'd need to haul a heavy travois home.

Joe and his son rode buckskin roan horses. Joe sat astride the mare and Ishtapa rode the mare's two year old colt. They sat on leather Indian saddles radiant with red roses with green and blue leaves set in white. These were beaded with Sweet Water's intricate beadwork by her long slender hands, learned from her Red Cliff Nation of Wisconsin. My saddle was black leather with handmade silver buckles and leather strips pulled through them. My bridle and saddle came from Ambrose's trove in the horse barn back in Indiana.

Our tanned leather chaps and shirts had fur turned in for warmth against the cold in the Teton mountains. Our clothes and equipment blended with the horses we rode. It felt good trotting across the prairie. Big Red heaved with his loping pace, anxious to go faster if I'd urged him to do so. The squeak of good leather and the energy we felt riding along the flat terrain infected all of us.

The snow melted away and the brown earth of the plains could once more be seen. The green of spring and the return of the summer birds accompanied us as we came across the North Loup River. The cascading ripple of the rapids sparkled like moving glass along where I saw the markings of the other settlers' property.

Today we cut through the grassland and away from the river. We planned to meet Lone Buffalo and his brother Red Feather at the Cheyenne Nations reservation and head out hunting in Medicine Bow Country. Since our arrival last fall, I'd planned to take myself to the mountains of the Wyoming territory.

Soon it will be time to plant crops and get beef cattle to market in Omaha. I'd discussed this with Jesse and his Pa several times. At first, I wondered if my imaginings would fall short of what could happen. After my discussion with Emory Peers, I felt satisfied I could be away for even a month and not cause too much of a problem.

He wired his son, Ray, from Council Bluffs. Ray and his wife Virgie, and their daughter, arrived at the homestead a few weeks later. Their buckboard with all their belongings stashed aboard, tailed by their milk cow and a pair of goats came slowly down the road and settled in to help while I was gone.

Lone Bear had nearly recovered from his brawl with Slats Mahoney in Cairo. He would bring his boy and travel with us without being missed. Another month would be another story. When planting began, everyone including Hannah and Mrs. Peers worked outside from dawn till dusk. They made their plans for the garden. Hannah and Mrs. Peers were busy with seed catalogs discussing what flowers and vegetables they would plant.

Joe and I anticipated trouble in the wild unsettled country and watched every butte and forest for signs

Wildfire

of unfriendly strangers. The elevation changed as we climbed higher into the pine and firs. The oxygen in the air cleared one's head like a sweeping draft, leaving me dizzy at times.

By evening the sun caught fire over the rose buttes in the distance. Eagles peeled and shrieked from their lofty pinnacles, spying their evening meal from a lofty perch. We built a large campfire, rolled out our blankets and bedded down at dark under the stars. Each morning we rolled up our bedrolls and got ready for another day. We passed through the flatlands into the foothills where there was abundant wild game. They say a cowboy's blankets are his only home under the stars. Wherever he happens to be, the blankets unroll at the end of the day and he's at home.

We were up at sunrise feeding and watering horses as we began our search for the Snake River. Even though we were going through near wilderness, we heard the haunting whistle of the express train as it sped toward Laramie and Cheyenne. The distinct shrillness echoed through the mountains even though it was miles away. The iron horse that brought distant travelers brought mail, express packages, and freight as well to this uncivilized country. Times were changing.

My thoughts turned to Hannah, I wondered what she would think of a trip like this. Perhaps the train better suited her civil manner, her delicate fragile body. I missed her and already wished for a conversation whispered and personal, our daily exchange of fondness, the fervor of words from those warm lips, and her tender embrace.

Joe and I had planned a long time to ride into these mountains where we hoped to hunt some. Lone Buffalo told us of the fine feral horses he'd seen throughout the foothills. On the third day, we arrived at Lone Buffalo's hogan. He is Sioux, married to a Cheyenne named Early Dawn. Their dwelling sat deep in a ravine in the Cheyenne reservation. Early Dawn's family lived among the fir and aspens in rolling hills. Diminished light traced loose patterns across the ground where we made our camp. We hardly settled in after our long ride, when Lone Buffalo and two brothers-in-law came, making their greeting. They squatted around our little campfire. I boiled an extra large pot of coffee, and shared plenty of raw sugar. We poured coffee into their cups sweetened generously.

Lone Buffalo, from one of the most feared nations, had joined with Early Dawn into the Cheyenne's matriarchal society. The women owned all the property. The children belong to the mother. There are no illegitimate children in the Cheyenne Nation. Their sod hogan consisted of one large room with a cooking hearth at the end. Herbs, mushrooms, pemmican, medicinal plants and seeds, hung in bags and baskets on hooks from the ceiling. Modest shelves held a few pots and cooking utensils.

Lone Buffalo came to me. "Early Dawn carries her first child. She wanted to come along, but we convinced her riding hours on horseback would be unwise. Just because this is unwise doesn't mean she's accepting, so I promised to bring back a pinto pony for her. I told them about your way with feral horses. "

Wildfire

"I didn't know you were of a mind to look for horses as well as wild game." Thinking about this excited me. I could be dreaming on this, but my expectations suddenly grew with the possibility of bringing some choice wild horses back with us.

The next day we set out with four more men: Lone Buffalo, Deer Hunter, Red Feather and Little Coyote. Little Coyote was quite agitated and it was apparent Early Dawn was the cause. He pulled his horse up short and trotted off briskly ahead of us.

Lone Buffalo called out to his nephew, "No need to worry now, Early Dawn is home with her Mother."

Little Coyote trotted up and gave his brother a relieved pleading look like a lost and worried dog. It showed in his obsidian eyes. Buffalo said later that his wife had complained Little Coyote was not much bigger than the baby she carried and not much more able to take care of himself. The men laughed, but the boy heard the insult, hung his head. and hurried away he was so ashamed.

Ishtapa took all this in and rode up beside Little Coyote. Soon the two boys were in deep conversation. They were making plans of their own about what great hunters they would be.

By noon the sun hung high in the sky and morning mist burned off. Steam rolled from the Powder, and the air was clear and clean. My head spun from the high altitude. The open spaces flooded with sagebrush and pine trees. We vigilantly watched for signs of elk and deer. "The open places are full of prairie dogs. The little buggers aren't even afraid to have us approach," I said. "Their heads stick up out of holes like they are greeting us."

"I've seen horses maimed and riders hurt bad galloping fast over these prairie dog villages. They are in the darndest places and they sit and chatter while you ride by," Buffalo said.

"I saw a young woman break her neck riding through one of these places one day. Went right over the horse's head onto the bare ground. Broke the horse's leg. It was bad. She was the daughter of Chief Washakie," Deer Hunter said.

We stopped briefly for coffee and hardtack. Coffee was still hot in our canteens from breakfast. We walked around some. The boys drank black coffee like adults and acted important, while they threw stones at the prairie dogs.

We mounted up and rode on to the foothills and the Medicine Bow country. Red Feather spoke, "This country has huge cattle ranches set up by the federal government to get settlers to live out here. There's a reservation above here, maybe three to four days ride. Chief Washakie lives up that way. The sacred place of the Nations is there because of the mineral hot springs. Chief Washakie has declared it sacred and the Nations gather there for a Sun Dance during the Fall before snows come. Afterward they climb into the Teton mountains until winter is over. The Nations trap fox, beaver, even ermine, and bring them to the post in Spring. Now that the treaties are settled, these Indians were given land rights and allotments of food if they would occupy the land and take up ranching. Some of them have done that."

Red Feather's wife was a white woman whose family had befriended the Cheyenne during the fatal

Indian massacres that occurred throughout the western territories. She had come to live with them after her family died from Cholera. Red Feather asked her to join him. Unlike our Cynci with the buttery chocolate eyes and dark hair who lived among the Sauk Nations, his wife Esther was blonde with blue eyes and had been a preacher's daughter.

We rode into the foothills that day until the shadows cast from the mountains no longer allowed us to see. We rode among the pine trees, the smell sharp in the soft evening air. The coo of the evening birds settling in for the night told us it was time to carve out a spot. We needed to make a fire for the coffee and beans eaten with a little hardtack. Except for the mournful breeze that blew through the pines, nothing else stirred. I curried Big Red down and settled in my bedroll under the stars.

Dawn crept in over the crags and left a chill on the ground for sometime in the mountain country. The men were already up for hours gathering branches and deadwood for the fire. The coffee began to boil and the men gathered around, offering pemmican and flat bread.

Deer Hunter informed us, "There are wild horses up that ravine. They aren't too lively because they're winter starved so they'll be easy to catch. We can wait till we are ready to go home. Then we can scout them out and box them in somewhere. Pick out the best and take them with us. We saw a couple stillborn foals. The snow was deep this year so they're scrawny," Deer Hunter said.

Little Coyote asked, "Was a pinto in the bunch?"

The men said, " No, maybe we'll have to hunt some other herd before we'd find pintos."

"This was different than the Mustangs in Indiana. Winters were shorter there, and Mustangs were generally healthier by Spring. It takes a good lot of work to bring them in," I added.

The first day we shot an antelope and prepared it for our cooking fire. We filleted lean meat from the haunches very thin and hung from tree branches. We'd pack it in salt later to keep it. We brought lots of salt along to lure the wild horses in.

The second morning we found mountain lion tracks, no doubt attracted by the drying meat. We decided to keep a fire going all night now. We gathered stones and built a small mound that would hold heat. I resolved to be more vigilant at night after this. The Cheyennes slept lightly anyway. They seemed to have an endless source of energy.

The fourth day we woke to find our fire cold and the meat stripped from some of the branches of the trees. We'd fed some critter well with our effort. We packed up what little was left and sealed it in pouches. It shakes one to the core realizing we might have been first choice rather than what was hanging in the trees.

Each evening Ishtapa brought out a flute and played for us. The young men found willow trees along the river bed and carved a flute for Little Coyote. Soon we were hearing teacher and student playing harmony.

"We'll need to get ready to start back in about a day or so. Let's ride up that ridge today and see what horses might be up there," I said.

Wildfire

Joe Lone Bear brought out his pipe and tobacco and passed it while we saluted the directions on our journey. I stumbled through the ceremony once and I nearly choked, coughing, spitting and sneezing till they never asked me to smoke again. They didn't know what to make of me, as even their young men were anxious to join in. At first, they were surprised and concerned I choked so bad, but afterward Joe told me, "They thought you were putting on, but then decided you might collapse." He chuckled as he said this.

I guess my embarrassment was plain for them to see. "You mean to say they thought I was faking?" I asked. "After all that wheezing and choking, I felt like a damn fool. I've never liked tobacco even as a kid. I never tried smoking. Ambrose's cigars were enough to turn me off."

After that they made reference to my fit of coughing as "man not knowing his own limits" and left it at that. Ishtapa listened to this with delight, and I became the butt of his teasing more than once. These young men had a fine sense of humor which surprised me.

The last day we rode about ten miles into a deep canyon and found a herd of some twenty-five mustangs. One bunch of young bachelors hung around the herd. A buckskin stallion whinnied his alarm at our presence, eyeballed us and urged his mares into a gallop. He put distance between himself and the pack of bachelors as well. There were some foals in this group. The number of bachelors were significant though. A white stallion eyeballed us but didn't seem too concerned. We put down a salt lick by the water flowing among the rocks, clear as a glass, clean enough for drinking. We filled our canteens and then moved back of some boulders to watch. We were about to give it up when several young bachelors came down to drink, smelled the salt, drank heavily and then returned to the salt lick.

"We may have to give it another day to get anything going here. Give a little take a little, I always say," I quipped.

"Maybe they smart, too smart for us. We not be able to catch good if they too wary," Red Feather acknowledged.

The young horses turned suddenly and ran away. "Well, that might be it," I said.

"No--wait and see. They spread word, bring others. Put out ground corn, see what happen they hungry lookin'," Little Coyote insisted.

I brought out coffee and hardtack, while we eyeballed up the direction the horses had run. "They didn't stay long. Maybe we've seen the last of that bunch," I said.

We rode up another ravine and discovered a box canyon where dead fall and brush had been made into a fence. It opened at one side but was not apparent till you were right upon it. We rode farther out into the flatland near the shale buttes, where we scouted along the edges of the soft earth. A waterhole about 50 feet wide fed from an underground spring. We decided to give it a few more hours before returning to our campsite. We placed salt by the spring. When light began to fade, we gave it up and returned to our campsite. We could see the waterhole where all the critters came for water. Ishtapa and Little Coyote stayed behind. We started our campfire and dug into our supplies to make supper. I hung a tripod to boil water for coffee. I dropped in scraps of dried meat and wild onions and added rice and wild turnips. This could simmer slowly, while we had some coffee and a little pemmican to tide us over till the rice was done. The two young men rode up and dismounted.

"Looks like you quit too soon. There was a mare and some yearling horses. Looked like bachelors came to water hole above. Lick salt, wander around. They scented us, took off fast, ran a short distance, then began meandering around. Must've thought it safe, came back again. We decided to come back. Couldn't do much by ourselves anyway," Ishtapa looked disappointed as he said this.

"We'll go back again before we leave tomorrow and see what's going on up there," Lone Bear replied.

"Might as well pull up your sleeping blankets and take a load off your feet. We'll have something to eat here pretty soon," I lamented. I was disappointed we hadn't had a better day.

Darkness fell when a herd of mustangs came to the lake, sniffed the salt, drank, ate some of the corn, and reared their heads up. Must've been able to scent us and nervously wandered around. The stallion reared on his hind legs and challenged us. He let us know we were put on notice. There wasn't much we could do in the dark. In the moonlight we could see he was a pinto and several mares were with him. Some colts stood among the mares but they didn't seem to be interested in leaving, they just stayed around and fed. I could hear them nickering to each other as I drifted off to sleep. We would wait until daylight crept in. I'd bet anything they'd be gone by morning.

We all roused at dawn's first light and lamented the horses were gone. I built up our fire and I put some sourdough to rise, hoping we'd get quail or pheasant for our noon meal today. We decided to ride back up to the box canyon, only this time we came up on the shale bluffs where we could see the water hole below. To my surprise, the herd was there eating our corn and using the salt lick. We exchanged glances, pleased with what we saw. We sent Ishtapa and Little Coyote to the other side of the herd and around in back where they could scare them back our way.

We rode as slowly and as quietly as possible down the shale, into the flat land below. Shale can be a nasty challenge at times because it's slick from the morning dew. We sidestepped all the way down and came to a copse of conifers near the little herd. They were busy throwing dirt and rolling themselves to get rid of the black deer flies that are around this time of year. They looked a little shabby and seem to be paying attention to something that was bothering them. To the right I saw a mountain lion advance slowly on the herd.

"If we scare off the mountain lion, we'll lose them anyway. Should we take a chance?" I whispered.

"If we do it right, we can scare off the lion and turn the horses into the box canyon all at the same time. Wait till the mountain lion moves, we'll shoot and then head them off. If they come this way, we probably will lose them," Joe Lone Bear said.

The mountain lion climbed a tree and crept out on the limb of a huge old pine tree. Joe told Ishtapa to shoot, and we rode slowly forward as he took aim and fired. The horses reared their heads up in alarm, turned

Wildfire

and ran straight for us. When Ishtapa's gun fired, the lion dropped in a heap. We made for the stallion while the younger men rode hard toward the side of the herd. When the stallion saw us, he turned sharply and headed into the box. We looked with relief as he turned the mares into the opening of the canyon and all ran into it. He began running and trying to hurdle the boulders along the edges. At first I thought he was going to injure himself. As he galloped about, the rest of us closed the gap of the box canyon with more dead fall and brush. Lone Buffalo and Red Feather stood guard, ready to turn the horses if they ran at them. Ishtapa and Little Coyote galloped up just as they closed the opening and ran through it.

We let the herd settle down for a couple hours before I tried anything. The stallion reared up and challenged my first attempt to talk with him. I motioned to him as he watched me warily. Finally he stood quietly and eyeballed me as I walked around. His attention was on Big Red. "I guess he thinks you've come to do battle with him, old fellow." Big Red whinnied his discontent, not sure what was about to happen here.

I dismounted and took up my tether. I cast it out at him and he reared up again. I walked about as he watched carefully. I signaled I was open and he nickered and looked back at me. I spun my rope but it fell short as he jerked back and ran off. I pulled in the tether and Big Red walked up beside me. I mounted and rode up the box canyon a little way. The pinto stallion whinnied his anger and let me know he didn't like what was going on. I signaled to him I was open. Big Red and I trotted slowly up near him separating him from his mares. He burst past me and regained the herd. I rode close this time, dallied the lasso and snapped my wrist. As he stepped inside the loop, I roped his back leg. He bucked furiously and ran past me again, trying to get free. Big Red held fast and didn't budge. I threw the tether rope and this time it dropped around his neck. He bucked furiously, against the feel of the taut ropes. I loosened the back leg and let him run in a circle. He continued to do this till he settled down some. I signaled for him to join me and he eyeballed me again. This took several hours and we still weren't comfortable. For a winter starved horse, he was very strong. I figured now was as good a time as any to see what he would do. I pulled the lasso taut and he had to kneel. I brought up the tether line and dismounted. I shortened it little by little until we were about ten feet apart.

Buffalo and the others watched closely while all this was going on. They weren't sure what to do. I told them to lay low, it would take awhile before this one was going to settle down. I loosened the lasso and let him walk around me. I signaled for him to join in. I raised my hand and looked at his neck. He moved into a trot. I moved my eyes to his middle. He looked back, not sure what to do not accepting, but not scared anymore. I brought the lasso up taut and he knelt. I moved forward but he fought it. I came back out and signaled for him to join in. He watched warily while I continued to tighten the lasso. I was close enough to touch him. As I put the Hackamore bridle on his nose, he flicked it away. It was just a matter of time and patience now, but it would happen. He was tiring but something else was happening. He began to deal, open his mouth, show me lots of teeth. I slipped the Hackamore over his head and it was right this time. I grabbed his ears, rolled him on his side and lay across his great body. He heaved as if to be rid of me. Big Red backed up and the ropes held fast, while I told him sweet nothings and asked him to join in with me.

Lone Buffalo, Red Feather, and the younger men were watching now. Fear showed all over their faces, not really believing what they saw. We rested there for a short time and I uttered words of comfort to this beautiful stallion. What a prize he would be. We remained like this for a long time till he had calmed down enough to let him go. I signaled Big Red to come closer and the taut ropes loosened. The stallion stood, not sure what was happening. I thumbed a molasses ball into his mouth. He shook his head up and down and showed me lots of teeth. He chewed and eyeballed me, enjoying the treat, deciding it wasn't so bad after all. I removed the dally rope but left the halter on. He'd stay on a loose tether this time till we decided to leave. I wanted to be sure we controlled him while we brought in his mares.

"I've never seen anyone do that before, Pearl. You'll be a mighty favored fellow among my family if you'd show us how it's done," Lone Buffalo said.

"I just asked him to join me. Showed him I'm a pretty honest guy and I'd treat him right," I said.

"Pearl, you got a gift there. I think that stallion not go for it but you change his mind. How you do that?" Red Feather asked.

"People have a bad habit of beatin' the hell out of horses. They want them broke. You break a horse and you break his heart. He never gets over it. I seen people do all kinds of nonsense when all the horse wants is the confidence that you'll treat him good. But some nitwit will maim and mistreat even the smartest horse and then reward him with more of the same. Once you prove you can be trusted, these critters will do nearly everything for you. I don't mean they roll over and never give you any problems, but your meanness takes all the strength of the horse's spirit. There's nothing like sitting astride a good horse that trusts you. It's a bond that never breaks," I said.

I had converts in the bunch that stood around watching this. They weren't ready to believe that it worked, but I was ready to show them it does. Red Feather wanted to know how I planned to bring in a bunch this big and move them across so much land without any trouble. I felt it could be done with eight men to wrangle and watch for the stragglers. Besides, these horses weren't real energetic, they'd had a hard winter. I wished for some oats or grain to feed them. All that was around was a little green Buffalo grass that had begun to sprout in places where there was moisture.

Before nightfall, I again approached the stallion and fed him sugar and rubbed his ears and neck. I got close where he could smell my human smell, get used to the smell of leather and my scent. I wished a couple of the mares could have been gentled enough to take a couple of deer carcasses, but I had been daydreaming on that.

Wildfire

Ishtapa and Little Coyote were having heavy conversations. Ishtapa finally came to Joe and said, "Little Coyote thinks this might be bad medicine with these horses. We wonder how we can get ourselves and all this horse flesh over hundreds of miles to the plains."

"It won't be easy, but we will try our best. Some of these horses won't be able to travel at a fast pace. Some may not want to and will fall away. We have to decide which ones are road worthy, and then be prepared to leave some behind. They're used to wild country, and those bachelors will be more than glad to have this stallion share his herd with them," I told them.

"We'd better get ready to move tomorrow morning then. If we wait another day we may not have anything left if another mountain lion visits camp again. What he don't kill, he'll run off," Red Feather warned. He signed to his friends to shore up, and get ready to move.

The morning arrived sharp and clear. Lone Buffalo acknowledge the rising sun in the Eastern sky that crested the horizon and cast soft lights through the fir trees. Moisture sat in icy sheets that draped the mossy softness of the trees. Our breath rose in a cloud as we stirred, getting a lean breakfast of the last of the venison with leftover sour dough fried bread.

"Can't get no better than this, Lone Buffalo." As I looked around I could see that all these men were enjoying the scenery as much as I was.

"We'll take those short tether ropes Lone Buffalo brought and rope the mares. Pick out the Pintos first. Take all of them. Then the roans and buckskins. I feel right bad we lost that black stallion, but we did good with what we did find. I'll show you how long to cinch the tethers, so the mares can run at a good pace. I'll take the pinto stallion and keep him roped to Big Red where I can reel him in if he gets too wild to handle. We'll make better time than we did coming out here cause we'll be riding as fast as this bunch will go. The only thing we'll stop for is soft grass and water." I handed the boys the canteens, "Ishtapa, you and Coyote go pick up that salt lick. Take our canteens and fill them from the spring." I hoped we could take all the feral horses back with us.

Lone Buffalo filled a big canteen with the leftover coffee and tucked fried bread into sealed packs in the saddle bags on his roan horse.

"Ishtapa, you and Coyote follow up the herd. If you notice stragglers, come and tell me, as we may have some mares or colts that can't keep up," I said as we started out. I felt regret leaving this spot. In my mind, I would always carry a picture of this spot at the foot of the Teton Mountains. As we rode along, I could see the occasional ranch house that existed out here in this open country.

A brilliant sun was high above when we stopped at mid-day for a brief rest near grass and water, where the horses could meander around and feed. One mare showed signs of distress. I figured if she was that way by tomorrow, we should cut her loose and let her decide if she could keep up or not. The colt seemed to be as lively as any. The colts frolicked among the other animals without much urging to keep up.

The second day thunder heads formed in the west, and we searched for a shale ridge or outcrop for some shelter. The wind picked up and black clouds moved in overhead. Lightning flashed and struck the ground. Rain fell in torrents of icy cold water that ran down our backs and splattered off the rear ends of the horses. They pranced around with terror showing in their eyes. Sudden darkness enveloped us as the rain continued in a fierce downpour. I signaled to everyone, "Dismount near an outcrop where shelter can be found. " The rain ceased as quickly as it began. We made a fire in a shelter of rocks where people had stopped before us. We collected fallen rough timber and small brush and soon had a roaring fire that would dry us out as we cooked our brief meal. Ishtapa and Little Coyote shouted, "Look, we found goose nests with a few eggs in each." I watched with apprehension as they cracked them into a pan. I breathed a sigh of relief that there were no goslings in the huge eggs. The eggs were a fine addition to our fried bread. I threw in some dried venison and wild mushrooms.

As we sat around enjoying our breakfast and lots of coffee, four men from the Cheyenne Nations rode up. They had seen the smoke, and we shared a bit of the food and some of the dried venison as they gathered around our fire.

Red Feather signed to them asking what brought them this way. "They say they see fire and soon smell food. Came to see who was so busy they didn't notice strangers around. They interested in horses, Pearl. They ask where you get them."

Red Feather explained we'd been hunting and came across many horses up the ravine far above the mountain crest in the west. Our guests seemed very intent on the stallion, but when the food was gone, signed they must be on their way and left us. My gut feeling was alarm and relief as they rode away. There's always a sinister wave of apprehension in this country, and we had completely forgotten our own vulnerable presence. We had not been watchful and we had to be more careful.

We rode steadily the rest of the day in spite of one mare and foal that were constantly falling back. We came within markers where Red Feather knew we were near his homestead. "Sun disappear and cast shadow over Mother Earth. We come to upper Loup River - we have only a short ride."

"Sounds fine to me," I replied. "I'd not thought we'd do so well coming such a long way in two days."

Eventually we came to the sod houses of the Cheyenne people and ran the horses into a corral. Red Feather and Deer Hunter watered horses while Joe and I ladled out oats. I examined the mare, and her foal nickered nearby.

"Ishtapa, you got a job. Remember how you took over with that colt that the mare dropped on the way to the plains? Well, this little guy needs some extra attention."

"I'll do it, too," he replied. "I'd like to take him back to our place and see what I can do."

Early Dawn came out to greet us. Her obsidian eyes picked up the glow of the lantern light as she gazed at her new pinto stallion.

"I'll work with him a bit tomorrow until he gets the idea of what he should do," I said. "He's a fine horse

Wildfire

and sound as an oak. Just promise you'll never use a quirt on him and he's yours." All Early Dawn saw was a gentle horse with no fear.

We had our first good shower in ten days other than the natural one during the rainstorm. We chucked off clothes and showered in the makeshift stall Lone Buffalo had built. Esther took our dirty clothes to be washed, a wry look on her face. It was obvious she was a seasoned survivor of many of these trips.

When morning arrived, crisp and bright, spring birds whistled their brilliant song for the new day. The family moved through their ceremony of thanks to the directions for a new clear day.

Ishtapa's face registered an alarmed expression. Before I could ask what it was, he motioned me to the corral. One of Lone Buffalo's cousins was in the corral with the feral mare and her colt. Both ran around full of alarm. The mare whinnied as she collapsed heavily on the corral ground. She lay prostate on the ground, her eyes wild with terror.

Yellow Calf, Buffalo's cousin, had a whip he was using with force to get the mare up. He had welded it several times, and the shock was too much for me to absorb. At once, I vaulted the corral fence and grabbed his upraised arm to strip him of the whip. I threw it forcefully smashing it against him as I knocked him to the ground. He lay there surprised before anger took hold. As he attempted to get to his feet, he muttered guttural sounds aiming to reclaim his whip.

Ishtapa yelled, "Stop, Yellow Calf! Pearl don't do this way with horses. You can't do anything with the mare anyway. She's skinny and starved. She will die with what you did to her."

Lone Buffalo walked up behind us. Yellow Calf stood up brushing himself off. Anger bursting in indignation from his mouth. I didn't want to know what he was saying.

"You can't do this. I won't allow it," I repeated.

Lone Buffalo said, "Watch Pearl work for awhile. Learn something from a real horse trainer. You won't believe it yourself."

I bent down to the mare lying prostrate on the ground. She shivered as I touched her. I felt across her rump and back where the whip had braised the hide. She looked up at me with those huge eyes; she quivered pitifully and waited for whatever I would do.

"Ishtapa, bring us some fresh water." I took swabs and ointment from my saddle bag, and some herbs I mixed with her feed. The Jimson Weed is a loco weed, but used in moderation, could calm an injured horse. I put some in the ball of molasses and oats I held. After many tries, the mare stood for me, and I thumbed the molasses ball into her mouth. Ishtapa came up with a hide bucket of cold water. She drank gingerly, just enough to do some good. I walked her around slowly at first and then a bit faster. As the Jimson took over she relaxed, her eyes glued on me and what I'd do next.

At that moment, she and I bonded. In days to come, that would be a problem because she'd follow like a dog and the foal would be there too. Until I could get her back to the homestead, this would be a problem. I chuckled to myself as I realized, in this action of trying to please everybody, I had also extended it to the horses.

Big Red had seen this and understood exactly what had happened. When I came out of the corral, the mare stood looking after me. Big Red shook that big head of his as if he's saying, "Well, now what've you done?"

We spent the rest of the day examining the mustangs. Some we sorted out to train. Others I'd keep to take home, and the rest parceled out as gifts to Buffalo's family. The stallion would go to Early Dawn, but only if she understood what to do. "If I ever have a hint that these horses are being whipped or abused, I'll come and get them and take it up with the person who did such a thing."

Lone Buffalo grinned, "I think you got it across how you want things done."

Joe Lone Bear, Ishtapa and I left the next morning. The air was cool for April but the sun soon warmed us as we rode along toward the homestead. The mare and colt kept up pretty good after their mishap with Yellow Calf. We let them determine our pace. At one point, Ishtapa picked up the leggy colt and carried him on horseback.

"That colt will be worse than a dog when we get home," Joe lamented.

"We've got a good strong pen out by the barn. We'll put them there till they get used to us," I added.

It had been a great pack trip but I thought about being back to the Peer's homestead. When good things end, something was always there to take its place. Hannah would be there and life would be good.

Donna R. McGrew

Chapter 9

END OF THE OPEN RANGE:. A combination of factors conspired to end the open range. Farmers kept crowding in and laying out homesteads. The boundless range was beginning to be overstocked by 1883, and expenses mounted as stock breeders formed associations to keep intruders out of overstocked ranges, to establish and protect land titles, to deal with railroads and buyers, to fight prairie fires, and to cope with rustlers and predatory beasts. <u>America</u>, "New Frontiers. South and West", (Ch. 18), P. 666

Omaha Bee: 5/12/96 "Heck" Hammer, Insane. Heck Hammer, a man about 40 years old, who was born and raised in Council Bluffs and is well known here, is under arrest. Charged on the books at the city jail with being cracked. He was found yesterday in an alley west of the city building, fishing with an Imaginary fishing pole and his line in an imaginary pool. He was much better last evening, and his mania attributed to drink, will probably leave him.

Donna R. McGrew

A Letter From Ambrose

Little snow remained to hide the loveliness of spring that struggled once again from the earth. It filled the patchwork brown of the prairie with promise of buds on young trees, and with warmth would spring forth a profusion of green leaves. The sparkle of spring rains stretched from the eaves of the house flowing like wet curtains. The blue of the river bordered by trees and brush not long ago bent under a load of whiteness. All covered with a brilliant sky that pressed down and filled every crevice and ravine.

Del Cole healed physically, but mentally he was unsound. Mama wiped worry from her face and looked forward to calmer times ahead. He owed much to this woman whose proficient care and treatment mended and helped him heal.

Yesterday, Del, Ephraim and Eban rode to town to the cobweb of streets of Cairo. They came from flat land into a broad valley of houses held like birds nests among trees and gardens. This was a test to see if they could keep the house supplied with the necessities of the kitchen and feed bins for the cows and horses. A shopping list from Mama for white flour and baking needs was foreign to them. They complained later they were not accustomed to buying such. Would she please carefully check their choices as they might not have interpreted her list correctly.

She replied, "If the need had been for hard liquor or shooting irons, I am sure you'd not had a problem with that. You bought baking soda rather than baking powder, and yeast as well.

Del stated defensively, "Effie Syrie, the store owner, was nasty to us but did her best to help. "

"Refined sugar rather than raw sugar," Mama stated. "And blackstrap rather than dark syrup that I put on the shopping list. Cows and horses will no doubt get most of the molasses, not the people in the house."

"Effy watched carefully and will surely report to you next time you visit the store. We made these purchases and got out of there," Ephraim insisted. The three stood with hat in hand, embarrassment written all over them while Mama's eyes walked from one to the other.

Pa laughed at her sharp retort chiding her, "No matter, Sara Ann. The road to hell was always paved with good intentions. Perhaps next time you'll care to do some such shopping yourself."

A smile of success washed across her face the moment the three rode into the yard after dark. The horses trotted along sharply amidst the coal oil lamps, the packages stowed in the deep wagon bed. Their faces reflected the pleasure they experienced being trusted to go into town on their own like three kids out on a spree.

Del announced at breakfast, "Jesse, I brung mail for you and Pearl. Pearl got a huge package from Indiana that I got from Ross Still, the depot agent. Ross has the United States Post Office as well as the depot agent job."

There are no secrets anywhere, even now, since we are new arrivals to the household. My letter was from Ambrose, written in his heavy stilted penmanship. It took me better than an hour to grasp just what he was saying. This letter was dated September 1879, about the time we arrived in Nebraska territory.

Ambrose and Mattie had come to an understanding and had married in early June. The ceremony was performed by Father O'Houlihan from St. Pious parish in Valparaiso. They had not decided whether to live on the homestead or at the boarding house, although both seemed not to want to live in town. Mattie hired Mariah Calish to help Sadie and planned directly to add a third person to help out. Mattie was of a mind to think Pearl and Hannah would prefer to return to them. If this was the case, they would be most welcome.

As reality set in, shock took over and my hands shook so bad I had to put the letter aside. I needed to be alone and decide what this might mean. The blatant disregard they have. Announcing their intentions not just in getting married, but attempting to take Pearl and Hannah away from here. The thought of what all this might mean to all of us, especially to me, was overwhelming. How could Mattie do such a thing after we had meant so much to each other? My mind grappled with the idea of heading out immediately to see Mattie, knowing only too well it would be of no use. The wedding happened some time ago.

Pearl read his letter and approached me with a downcast face. Apprehension moved with every step he took toward me and said, "Marrying Mattie does not surprise me. Ambrose had a subtle romance with Mattie ever since I've known her. He always had a high regard for her. I never thought of marriage between the two, and it seems strange to me. He puts it like one of their on-going business deals. Remember the Black

Angus cattle we brought from the rail yard? That was one time I discussed this relationship with Ambrose. He said it was a forty-sixty percent deal after the Angus were sold. At the time, I scolded him for cooking up a deal she'd be involved in. I never knew from one day to the next what was happening between the three of you."

"After Annie Dodd died in that riding accident, Ambrose moved into Mattie's boarding house and lived there until I came along. After that we lived there a long time. Mattie told me Ambrose loaned her money when the bank tried to foreclose on her boarding house. That was around 1866 when the whole country was in a slump. No money around much 'cause of the aftermath of the Civil War," Pearl added.

"Hannah is afraid you'll get down about this and go off to Indiana again. She doesn't want to leave here. It kind of depends on what you do as to how I respond to Ambrose," Pearl searched my face looking for any clue to my inner thoughts.

"I need to think on this before I can answer Ambrose's letter," I replied. I had to recover from the shock of this letter before I could make a sound decision. I hoped they would be patient.

The atmosphere was heavy and I needed to go out somewhere. Bundled up against the chill of early morning, I saddled Wildfire and headed out along the North Loup River. I let Wildfire have the lead and with no urging he moved out at a gallop. His head was high inhaling the clean and soft air. It felt good to urge him into a gallop as we moved easily across the land.

Rounding the bend of the North Loup, there were fresh tracks and animal spore announcing the recent presence of horses and smaller animals. In a copse by the river lay one of our cows. The body still warm, udder full, a beautiful animal; no doubt there'd been a calf with her from the hoof marks around the cow. Some animals had attacked and brought her down. Bite marks went along the juggler vein, blood covered the snowy ground. Breaks in the brush and bushes led off up the edge of the stream and then disappeared. It appeared the riders crossed over and made their way to the other side of the river. They must have picked up the calf as it was nowhere to be found, and carried it away.

Pearl was about thirty minutes behind me. I came up with a start, my gun drawn, as he appeared beside me. With relief I recognized Pearl advancing on me carefully.

"Your Ma urged me to follow you. After our trip over here last week, I'd thought you'd be more careful of your actions, knowing these scoundrels are about," Pearl scolded.

"I'd not realized I'd come all this way till I found the cow. Let's look a little further and see if this riff raff has done anything else," I said. I did not want to accept what I'd stumbled on. Sometimes unrelated events center in such a way that causes a reaction too difficult for one person to bear.

We decided to make a travois out of some willows and haul the carcass back to the farmhouse. At least we could harvest the meat. Pearl helped bleed the animal out. We sliced the stomach open and gutted her before we continued on to the farmhouse.

As we came near the homestead figures appeared on horseback in the distance. We were alarmed as we watched them come closer until the figures took shape in the morning sun. Lone Buffalo rode up with some of his family. He signed hello while his piercing obsidian eyes cut across every detail.

"You been out huntin' already today, Jesse?" Buffalo asked.

"No, this cow was rundown and killed out by the North Loup River. Her calf was gone and the cow dead on the spot."

"You want help to skin it down and cut it up? These women are good skinners and could have that animal cut up in no time. Let my woman keep the hide and she'll be pleased with you," Buffalo added.

"That'd be fine with me. Let's drag this to the bunkhouse and see what Mama says."

Maudie and Mama ran out, crowding so close to each other their shadows were one. "What happened there, Jesse? Looks like we've lost another heifer. Land, what are we going to do about these rustlers? We have to find the varmints that are doing all this."

Mama set to work and Buffalo motioned his women to join in. Mama turned her face and greeted the Indian women, a look of relief washed across her face. Hannah watched with surprise and interest at how quickly Buffalo's wife worked. Soon we were all involved as the Indian women showed us how to cut the beef thin and dry it on racks.

By the time we finished, it was late for the dinner hour. Ethel and Hannah took a platter of steaks to quick fry with onions and dried basil. They boiled potatoes and cut slabs of homemade bread. Hannah turned steaks on the black wrought iron stove. Mama called to Buffalo, "Best wash up and have a bite to eat. Then we'll divide some of this up to share with you."

This pleased Buffalo's family as they murmured among themselves. They wandered to the pump in the bunkhouse where Ethel offered hot water, soap and towels. The men held back timidly while their wives washed up. Their beautiful eyes flashed uneasily between alarm and curiosity, taking in the ways of our family.

We invited them to sit around the long table and Pa motioned for the Indians to join us. Slowly, they moved to empty chairs. Two groups of people joined quietly together, and whatever separated us was gone. Confidence melted and touched the empty spaces and made all of us one.

Supper was a quiet affair while everyone concentrated on platters of nose tingling food passed around by Maudie and Ethel. The Indians looked at the dishes and utensils, not knowing what to do till Mama took up her fork and knife. I chuckled as Buffalo attempted cutting and forking food. Finally, he thrust his knife, lifting a generous bit of steak to his mouth. Once the rest observed this, hunger overtook embarrassment and food moved swiftly down the long table and disappeared into waiting hands. Last came Hannah with black coffee, cream and sugar a familiar favorite of Buffalo's family. The dark liquid was poured into tin cups and passed to each one. Ethel dished up slices of apple pie, the amber liquid congealed on golden crust. She had made it from dried fruit, baked fresh yesterday in our giant black iron range.

Pleasure washed across Pearl's face. He was truly at home with this blended group of human beings. Hannah passed among Buffalo's family as they nodded their approval of her and the family gathered here. Pearl's eyes glowed with the pleasure he felt watching Hannah at home in the center of all this.

The buttes along the west were solid rose, a path of red gold sunlight bathed the flat land. The sun dipped neath the horizon, a fireball slipping slowly over the edge. We bid Buffalo and his family goodbye as they left single file out of the bunkhouse. The women were wrapped in brilliant colored blankets edged in colors of the sun and moon; their feet tread softly in winter doeskin moccasins. They loaded their cargo of beef and jerky packs onto the backs of their gentle Appaloosa ponies, mounted and trotted single file down the broken path of the North Loup, disappearing in one long moving shadow along the river's edge.

Finally, I recalled Mattie and the lingering heartache over her marrying Ambrose. These lengthening days of spring had brought a mix of good and bad emotions. I cannot fathom that Mattie had made a choice, but I would honor her decision. Perhaps there was a path I had not figured on that would enrich my own life and give me the strength to live here in the plains as my parents desired.

I caught the eyes of my mother upon me, piercing deep, inquiring and worried. It was not my plan to be such a concern to her. She came and gently patted my shoulder. "Do not worry so about matters that you have little control over. The Lord has devised a path for you which you are bound to follow. You would do well to honor it and not go against His will. It seems we fight the hardest when we should let go. Thy will be done. Try to find acceptance and peace will come to you, and you will be happier."

"You make it sound so direct and simple, Mama," I replied. "I wish it could be so." Her words turned to prophesy. It would not be long and I would look back on this day as she predicted.

The day suddenly ended, leaving me exhausted and ready for sleep. I wondered how to accept the Lord's will and reconcile my feelings, but I was much too tired to worry further. As I pulled off my boots and readied for bed, laid my head upon a pillow and rested in clean sheets, the sounds of the house had already diminished. I drifted off to the gentle noise of animals in the barnyard, the high pitched wail of two coyotes invaded the stillness as keen as a razor's edge. A far off tale of woe baying at the moon, reminded me of my own burden of pain. Peaceful silence lulled me off to sleep.

Chapter 10

--the fight for survival in the trans-Mississippi West often made husbands and wives more equal partners than their eastern counterparts. Prairie life also allowed women more independence than could be had by those living domestic lives back East. –Many examples of strong-willed femininity abound. Explained one prairie woman: She learned at an early age to depend on herself—to do whatever work there was to be done, and to face danger when it must be faced, as calmly as she was able. <u>America.</u> *"The New West, New Frontiers, South and West." (Ch.18) pp670-71*

Omaha Bee: 5/12/93 Solid as a Rock: "If there is one thing more than another that impresses travelers who go East on the Burlington's "Vestibuled Flyer", it is the excellence of the track over which you ride. Smooth, solidly built, free from sharp curves and heavy grades and laid with the heaviest and most expensive steel rails, it is as near perfection as it can be made. "The Flyer" leaves Omaha at 5 p.m. daily and reaches Chicago at 8:20 the next morning. Sleepers, chair car, diner, Tickets at 1502 Franklin St., Chicago.

Donna R. McGrew

Back Home in Indiana

Pearl sat with his back to the kitchen windows in Mattie's boarding house waiting for everyone to wake up. The late summer in Indiana always turned balmy and warm. The sky an iridescent blue, the sun gleamed like a fiery eye. It was a beautiful day with a few clouds trailing cotton above the horizon. The wind blew gently through the open windows and stirred the leaves of the giant sycamore trees by the house. The barn stood open where Pearl had learned to rope and tie horses. The salves and bottles sat unused, the owner long gone that had needed all the tinctures and ointments that were stored on the shelves. The grain bins were empty, the windmill spun water into the tank that visitors or boarders sometimes used for their horses.

Pearl was perplexed. He'd been here almost a week and needed to be about his own affairs, and not meddling in Ambrose's life. Thank Mattie for all this fracas going on.

Last week, Sadie had been roused in the middle of the night to get Doc Williams as fast as her legs could carry her. She and Mariah had stayed with Mattie the rest of the night, fetching things from Doc Williams office, trying to make Mattie comfortable. By daylight Mattie was still having hard labor pains and Doc Williams kept saying, "These babies take time. Didn't take a few hours to make, birthin' him isn't any faster. Baby's not ready Mattie. I'd give you some Laudanum, but it'll slow everything down. You and the little one will both go to sleep. I've got some ether to give you when the time comes, but you're just not ready yet."

Wildfire

"Lord, Doc, is there something wrong that this is taking so long?"

"No, but Mattie your what 30-31 years old now? Most women give up this nonsense notion along in their mid-twenties. You've had a long time for your muscles and bones to set. We'll just have to wait a little bit."

Sadie plumped Mattie's pillows, sponged her face with cool water, and rearranged the curtains to let in more fresh air. Doc Williams signaled Sadie to follow him.

Safely in the kitchen, out of hearing distance, he whispered, "Go get my Mrs. Tell her to bring my white kit, the one with the red cross on it. It's from my medical school days. Tell her to hurry and plan to stay for awhile." Sadie was about to protest, but Doc Williams cut her off. "And don't fool around. We got problems here, so hurry!"

"All I want is some facts. We've been up damn near the whole night. Seems a body would have something happen by now," Sadie whined.

Mariah listened to all this before she spoke. "I don't think this baby will make it. My Ma had hard labor with her last youngun, and it came still born."

"Oh my God," Sadie cried. "Don't say no more. I just can't stand it."

Doc Williams hurried her out the door and motioned Mariah to follow him.

"We're goin' to move you, Mattie. I want you to try sitting up. Okay? Now slowly, grasp the foot of the bed and pull yourself up. That's right. Now put your knees here and here while Mariah puts these packing clothes under your knees. Next pain, let me know."

"My God, Doc, don't tell me I have to stay here. What are you thinking?"

"I'm thinking the Choctaws and the Pottowatomi Nations deliver babies with the mother on her knees. I've only done this once or twice, but this young one is stubborn. If this doesn't work, I may have to use forceps and I don't want to."

From the anxiety in Doc William's voice Mattie knew he was stumped. It worried her but she was beyond caring.

"I better like what comes of this when this is over," Mattie cried.

"One thing at a time there, Mattie. One thing at a time," Doc Williams watched her carefully.

A pain lifted Mattie into an arc, and her back came up as the bed erupted in a burst of bloody water. Before Mattie could catch her breath, Mrs. Williams was there with the suitcase open, putting out instruments and knives. With watchful eyes she washed her hands in the soap and water Mariah brought.

Sadie's eyes grew about the size of saucers. "Lord, Doc, what are you doin' with her?"

"I used this position a couple times when the baby was slow. This one is a stubborn little cuss. He'll be a pistol when he gets here. You just wait and see."

Mattie shrieked as the labor pain gripped her and Doc said, "I can feel a nice little foot right here in my hand. Now Mattie, I'm gonna turn this baby a little so if you have another pain, try not to push till I get this done."

"God, Doc, do something quick!" Mattie's face was ashen but when another pain came she tried her best to hold back. Sadie and Mariah brought fresh towels.

Mrs. Williams looked at Mattie with alarm. "Do you think you can help her? I'd say it's too late to try this."

"Put Mattie back on the bed. Show the girls how to hold her arms, and then see if we can get some pressure on her stomach."

Dr. Williams began the ether drip, and Mrs. Williams took the cone from him. Mattie responded some to the sedative, and Doc began to talk to her. Finally, he placed the forceps on the infant's head. Mrs. Williams placed the cone aside as she told Mattie to push. The next pain brought a gush of fluids as Doc Williams brought out the baby's head and then the shoulders.

Everyone in the room began to relax as the baby emerged, brought air in his lungs and gave a healthy wail. Mattie, very groggy but aware, looked at the doctor.

"I told you it was a boy. Looks like he's got all his fingers and toes too. Soon as the afterbirth comes, you can look for yourself. Mariah, hand me that wrapper. As he placed the baby in Mariah's arms, Sadie and Mariah began to cry. Mrs. Williams smiled at both of them.

Doc cut the umbilical cord and tied it off; then took the baby and placed him in Mattie's arms. Mattie was beyond knowing much, the ether had done its work. The infant waved his arms and legs and looked around. Mattie smiled. "Meet A. J. everyone. Ambrose James Lux."

The excitement in the room was just too much. Mariah and Sadie walked into the kitchen.

"Lord, it's daylight and that gang will be down here soon enough wanting breakfast," Sadie lamented.

Mariah brought out a huge bowl, "I made pancake batter last night with yeast so that'll be about right for breakfast."

"I never thought of another thing since Mattie got sick. Can't imagine what life will be like for awhile, but we have to see what happens. I bet we have problems with these sodbusters because of this," Sadie said.

Sadie's words were prophecy. As the story got around, business began to fall off Men moved out, some with disgust, others just because they followed the crowd.

"Can't imagine these factors could leave without checking out where they would sleep and eat. No thoughts at all about what they would do. Mattie shouldn't take a one of 'em back when they discover there's nothing else," Sadie sneered.

Ambrose had not been called when Mattie went into labor. In fact, he had learned of the event about two days later when he stopped by for supper. Still living at the homestead, he cooked some for himself, but as always came to Mattie's for a good meal now and then.

Ambrose didn't comment, Mattie was so stubborn, she had only herself to blame. He had married Mattie after many conversations with her about this. Mattie decided to name the baby for him if it was a boy. Cassandra if it was a girl after Sadie, because that was her Christian name.

He arrived on Wednesday afternoon after the birth on Monday. He walked into the kitchen. Sadie motioned him into Mattie's bedroom off the back porch. He came hat in hand, eyes lowered, accepting whatever was to happen, concern written all over his serious face.

"Well, it seems you've went and done it, haven't you there. Are you doing alright? Anything you need, or want? Just say the word," he said apologetically. "Seems someone could've come for me, all the same." A note of disappointment registered in his voice. Sorrow was written all over his face, full of worry and concern.

"Ambrose, I didn't die. I had a baby, and a big strapping one at that. Doc Williams says he'll be a real pistol. Do you think you're up to raising the likes of Ambrose James?" Mattie asked.

"Let's have a peek here. God, he's homely Mattie. Better let him grow a little before I'll get involved."

"I thought that's about what you'd say. His head got a little squashed during his birth, but he has a good appetite. Didn't know how I'd feel until now," Mattie said. "I love him though, and I hope you will grow to love him. Is that too much to ask.?"

"You've got it. I'll do my best. Maybe if we're going to be a family, we'll need to alter where we live. You ever thought about moving to the country and getting rid of this place?" Ambrose asked.

"Not now, Ambrose. Not now. Wait awhile. Seems I may not have a choice. Men became scarce as hen's teeth around about. Once they learned of the birth they fell away. Don't know where they went and don't care," Mattie lamented.

"It's a bit of a trip to Bennett. I don't believe they'll find anything there. There's a flop house here, down by the train station; but it's a rough set up and not clean. You more or less have to fight for a spot. Men that have stayed here will soon find out what they've lost," Ambrose assured her.

"No matter to me. The women can help out till I get better. Then we'll decide what to do." Mattie sounded pretty confident.

Ambrose reached over and pulled the flannel blanket from the baby's face. He stood there a long time and then gently touched the baby's golden curls. "He's a fine boy, Mattie. You take care and I'll check again before I leave. The women offered supper and I'm pretty sick of eating my own grub. Can I bring you something?" Ambrose asked.

"No, but thanks Ambrose. I never realized what good friends we are. You mean a lot to me, Ambrose." Mattie sighed and closed her eyes.

Ambrose hurried from the room, a strange look on his face, a happy glow about the eyes. His feelings were hidden deep inside, but very sincere and accepting of Mattie and her little boy.

The next day, Ambrose wired Pearl and sent money. *"Come immediately. STOP Need to see you. STOP Bring Hannah. STOP We'll talk, when you arrive. STOP Signed Ambrose Lux.*

Alphonse Crown, the telegraph operator at the depot, was all agog at the message. He told Ambrose if any answer came, he'd find him no matter where he was.

Pearl and Hannah boarded the train in Grant Station that took them through Lincoln, Council Bluffs, Des Moines, Chicago and Valparaiso. It was a three night, four day journey. The two had berths and accommodations that made it a comfortable trip.

Wildfire

"Land, did you see the size of the roast I had for supper? Never in my life had such a helping of beef," Hannah commented.

"Well, it cost enough, so it had to be good," was Pearl's reply.

"A whole dollar and all that dessert to boot," was her answer.

"There you're reading my mind again. Just opened my head and picked it right out of there," Pearl smiled. He was enjoying the whole event. Especially, having Hannah all to himself and giving her all his attention.

"Those waiters certainly are helpful and I suppose that required a handsome tip." Hannah smiled as she said this.

"How would you get that idea. I swear. How would you know," Pearl teased.

"I know and more besides. With you, it's all playful, but deep down you wanted everything just so. Now admit it," Hannah laughed.

"Anything you want just say so. I'll do my best." Pearl enjoyed getting Hannah flustered and he succeeded famously.

"I'll probably never be the same again, Pearl Lux. All the service, I may get used to it. Then what will you do," she teased.

"Oh, that's what I'm worried about. I can take the girl out of the country, but I can't take the country out of the girl," he replied.

"It's true you know. I love being a country girl. I never thought much about it, but I do love it. Of course, you didn't have a thing to do with that," she teased.

"Oh, now I'm hurt. I'll have to extract a promise that you'll never be so mean again," Pearl faked alarm.

Thus they spent the days. Nights their berths were across the aisle from each other. They peered through curtains, made faces, threw kisses, and enjoyed the whole trip just being together. They sneaked kisses in the corridors on their way from the diner. The tangle of arms and legs steadied them against the buck and roll of the train. As the train stopped for coal and water they watched the crowds that spewed from the train while another group climbed aboard. The conductor called, "All Aboard."

They arrived in Valparaiso mid-morning after a hasty breakfast in the diner. They collected their baggage and gifts and dismounted the train steps. Ambrose waited patiently, feeling anxious about how Pearl would accept the news. He was shocked seeing Hannah in her blue velvet dress with a bonnet the color of her eyes. The sparkle of happiness sprinkled all over her. The healthy vibrant woman didn't look a thing like the waif that had left them. And Pearl— Pearl was in love and it was written all over him. His manner and his expression made this apparent in every action.

Ambrose shook hands and then grasped them both in an embrace. What a wonderful surprise to see them like this. "We'll go right to Mattie's from here. If you need anything, we can get it along the way." Ambrose shepherded the two young people to his buggy.

Pearl loaded their luggage and helped Hannah into a seat. "We enjoyed the trip, Ambrose. It was great you'd thought to ask Hannah. I'd not have thought you'd be so generous. Must be lots on your mind to ask me to come. If the news is bad, Hannah ain't big enough to catch a fella' once he's fainted, " Pearl smirked.

Ambrose looked at him. He didn't know where to begin. How much should he tell. All he could do was come out with it. "You got my letter that Mattie and I were married last spring. Mattie had a baby last week. A little boy she named Ambrose James. Looks like he'll be A.J." Ambrose gulped for air.

Hannah and Pearl sat with their faces blank as shock registered there. Finally they understood. "Congratulations Ambrose," they both declared. When was the baby born? Was Mattie and the baby okay? How had they decided on a name? They wanted to know everything at once.

Ambrose tried to fill them in. By the time they reached Mattie's , they were getting somewhat used to the idea. Sadie and Mariah spotted them and ran out to bring in their luggage. Sadie grabbed Pearl and Hannah in a big hug. "This is Mariah Calish. She's working here to help me out," Sadie said.

"Is she workin' at Ambrose's too, just like you and Mattie do?" Pearl inquired.

"Yes and more besides. She lives here too. You can have the pick of rooms. Some of the boarders have boycotted us so there's lots of room," Sadie lamented.

"'How come? Why did they boycott you, Sadie?" Hannah asked.

Sadie realized she'd opened a can of worms. "Come on in and we'll explain."

Mattie was awake and the baby fussed softly. Mariah put fresh diapers on the baby, then held him up for all to see. "A.J. weighed ten pounds at birth. Ain't he a pretty one though?" She added proudly.

Ambrose said, "That's the homeliest little baby. I'm not a good judge of newborns but he is no beauty contest winner."

"Well, that's all you know, Ambrose. He's a doll and don't you never say otherwise, you hear me?" Sadie retorted.

Mattie smiled to herself. It was like having your real family arrive. Hannah had turned into a tiny beauty, Pearl was just their pearl. He was gorgeous, Mattie thought to herself.

Little by little the story came out. Once the baby was born, gossip had it there was something wrong with him. One story was Mattie and Ambrose weren't really married. The boarders started acting funny and then moving out. Sadie told them Ms. Crowder talked about Mattie and Ambrose, and then acted like things were just dandy, when they purchased things at the Crowder's store. When Sadie and Mariah heard this they started going to the Mercantile store on the South side of Valparaiso.

On the seventh day, Doc Williams said Mattie could sit and dangle her feet a little. She sat passively on the edge of the bed. When Doc Williams left she motioned Mariah to come close. "Help me to that chair. If I don't start moving around I won't be able to move at all in another day," Mattie whined. "I can't stand this another day."

"I'm surprised they kept you in bed so long," Mariah said. "Ma always got up by the second or third day. She claimed she felt better that way. Apparently, she tried to stay in bed when I was born, but Pa like to burned down the house trying to cook. She figured it was better that way than having him wreck the house."

Mattie began to move about, diapered the baby, sat in the rocker to nurse him. By the time Pearl and Hannah arrived she'd begun to feel much better and taking meals in the dining room. They sat with Mattie at one end of the table and Ambrose at the other. As the days flew by, Ambrose became more at ease. This was all so new and different for him.

When Pearl and Hannah had been there two weeks, Pearl approached Ambrose. "You said you wanted to talk in your wire, but you haven't said much since I came here. Was there something special you wanted to discuss?"

"Let's take a ride to the acreage and we can talk. The women are so wrapped up in Mattie and that youngster, they won't even miss us," Ambrose said.

They saddled up a couple of Mattie's horses and headed out along the country road to Ambrose's place. Pearl had an attack of nostalgia riding along the road. The memories of his distant childhood, living at Mattie's, school days with Ada Hornby, the rescue of Hannah, Benny's murder. It all came back in a flood as he talked to Ambrose.

Ambrose reminded him of the time Jesse first came to Valparaiso, the cattle Cyrus bought for us to take West, and how Jesse had carried on with Mattie. Things began to swim in Pearl's brain like so many hornets buzzing around before they sting. All at once, Pearl understood what Ambrose was trying to tell him. "I remember how Sadie had such a time over Jesse going to St. Louis with Mattie. So you're saying they had more than just a fling? It went way further than that. So why did she send him off?" Pearl inquired.

"She wasn't sure when he left. Hell, nobody knew it until about a month ago. I had to pry it out of her. I thought she had the cancer or something. I nearly lost my mind when she admitted what she'd done. I asked why the hell she didn't tell Jesse. She said he was a Nebraska boy and he had promised his Pa to take over in the plains once the cows were there," Ambrose said.

"Jesse was a miserable man all during the trip out there. If it hadn't been such a treacherous trip with so much going on, he'd still be in a kind of funk," Pearl said.

"She said she was older than Jesse, and with this business she owns, it just didn't make sense to let him know. She wasn't even going to marry me till Sadie got wind of it. She held out and said she'd go it alone. Besides, Mattie is Catholic and wouldn't consider doing anything. I think Sadie thought she should've though." Ambrose's expression was somber.

"So she finally decided to marry you. Jesse and I both got letters about the same time from you. I thought Jesse was going off again. He's a sensitive man, more than anyone realizes. He never wants to let on how easy he gets hurt, but it's there. The poor guy deserved better than he got," Pearl peered out at the fields near the homestead.

"Well, I hope he marries somebody, someday, that'll make him a good wife. He's one sharp fella'. Cyrus thought both you and B. J. was about top of the line.

He's always going on about something especially about you." Ambrose's face had a strange sadness about it.

"Cyrus is a good man. What do you think of Hannah Ahrens this time? Ain't she somethin? The blue of that dress she has on makes a lie out of every other color under the sun. She looks so good. Jesse's mother likes Hannah lots. She's so good to her. Had a real purpose taking us in like she done," Pearl pulled the horse into the driveway of the homestead.

They arrived at the house where they watered the horses and then tied them out front at the hitching rail. The afternoon sun beat down on them. Dust motes spiraled up from the ground. The trees whispered in the breeze, a cardinal called his mate. The gentle whippoorwill called from a tree top. Ambrose thought they needed rain. He and Pearl wandered around the house. When they entered the silence was overpowering.

"You and Hannah discuss marriage at all? We thought maybe you'd want to bring her here, raise some kids, get back with Cyrus. He'd take you in a heartbeat you know," Ambrose said.

"Haven't really thought about coming back. It'd be up to Hannah though. She might not want to come back. She's made some friends already. Jesse's two sisters are fond of her. Some of our neighbors have daughters and sons about Hannah's age. I won't rush her but I'd seriously consider marriage if Hannah was ready," Pearl wandered about the house.

Ambrose listened without expression on his face, no smiles on that face, not even looking for one today. They strolled through the empty house. Pearl noticed some bridles and horse gear in his old bedroom. Memories of times gone by crowded his mind, saddened by so many thoughts it was unsettling.

"Ada Hornby still at the school, Ambrose?" he asked.

"Yes. She'll teach school till she dies. Most ever kid in town has had her at one time or another. I suspect she'll still be there when little A.J. is old enough for schoolin," Ambrose replied.

"I hope he has a better time of it than I did," Pearl lamented.

"Well, we better get back. By the time we get to town it will be supper time."

They rode through the countryside while the sun beat down on the dusty road. The clop of the horse's hooves echoed along the clay road. There was a buggy tied at the hitching rail in front of the boarding house.

"That's Gideon Calish, Mariah's uncle's rig. They do lots for Mattie since Mariah went to work here. Beats all the way they show up to do some wallpapering or some darn thing all the time. Regular as rain they're here doing repairs and stuff," Ambrose scoffed.

Pearl turned what he and Ambrose had discussed over in his mind. He decided he wouldn't say anything to Hannah. Not now anyway. The afternoon sun was intense on their backs as they opened the screen door and entered. All was quiet inside. Mattie and the baby were asleep. Mariah, Hannah and Sadie sat in the kitchen, a teapot and cookies on the table by the open windows. The odor of cooking was fragrant and delicious. A forerunner of the supper meal soon to be served hung heavily in the air.

Pearl and Ambrose had removed their hats and stood looking at the women deep in conversation. Something was being savored here besides the tea. Pearl was the first to notice as Sadie dropped her eyes to her hands, folded in her lap. Mariah's eyes were staring at Sadie. When Hannah saw Pearl she blushed prettily. "I'd not thought I was worthy of such rosy cheeks, such a lovely face to look upon," Pearl observed.

"Perhaps you've missed something, Pearl. Though it may be a pleasure to look upon, you've misread my expression. Perhaps I should explain my look of embarrassment," Hannah said.

"Please enlighten us as to what was so intense in your chatter? You hardly noticed we'd come in the house," Pearl inquired. He suspected what had happened. He would've bet anyone, even Sadie, that she would spill the beans.

Ambrose was already alert that something was going on, something he had hoped to postpone. He surrendered himself to the situation.

Sadie looked up as she spoke. "Hannah didn't know about A. J. Not just that he arrived but who his father was. She asked why everyone was so mad at Mattie, the boarders had left. Hannah remembers how soft Jesse was on Mattie, so it wasn't a big secret what had happened. Ambrose, we tried to be sensitive as possible, but the fact Mattie doesn't give a fig what anyone thinks makes it fairly obvious what the situation is."

"It's just as well you told Hannah. I think Pearl was about to tell her anyway," Ambrose lamented.

"I wasn't going to tell her quite this way. Now that the news is out, let's move on and make the best of things. I'm just concerned that you and Mariah will have a change of heart and desert Mattie," Pearl persisted.

"Ain't never entered my mind and never will," Sadie exploded.

"That's about how I feel too. What if Mattie sells her boarding house though? What then?" Mariah asked.

"I don't believe either one of you need worry. I always need housekeepers and I don't believe Mattie is going to give this business up. Not very soon anyway," Ambrose assured them.

"Well, I know I let the cat out of the bag, but you know it was for the best. Hannah was wondering about this blonde, blue eyed youngun, and it just slipped out," Sadie replied.

Pearl glowered at Sadie and she stared back at him.

"Now don't you two have difficulty about this. It's all my fault for asking so many questions. It's all my fault!" Hannah cried.

"Well, it just slipped out. I couldn't help myself," Sadie sighed.

"Let's just move on. We need to get this out in the open. Uncle Gideon keeps nailing me with questions about Mattie, and I never know what to say. If it was Sadie who he asked, she'd just say 'Mind your own business'. But I can't do that," Mariah said.

"Now that it's all been said and done and everyone is satisfied with what's been said, Hannah and I need to be getting back home. That's about what you expected to hear Ambrose?" Pearl inquired.

Wildfire

"Well, if you won't move back here, I guess we need to get you back to the Peers homestead soon. I hate to see you go. You know that. I thought maybe you'd be of a mind to move back," Ambrose said with regret.

Supper found them all seated with five boarders. In addition, the Calishs, Ambrose, Mattie, Hannah and Pearl were seated in the dining room. Mattie brought the baby while Sadie carried his basket. They sat him in the bay window where Mattie could watch him.

Sadie and Mariah served vegetable soup and ham sandwiches. The sun shone brightly through the windows. Suddenly Hannah stood, walked over and lowered the shade. She said, "He's so blond you can't even see his hair. You and Ambrose are both so dark. I suppose that'll change as he gets a bit older." Hannah studied the child who was wide awake gazing around.

"I don't think that will change much Hannah. I believe he'll be blonde with eyes as clear as colored glass. He'll be a real heartbreaker, I'm sure of it," Mattie's answer was firm.

Mrs. Calish asked to see baby pictures of Mattie and Ambrose, just to see who he favored. The conversation in the room had gone completely to hell. Then one of the boarders mentioned there was a hold up at the bank. The conversation quickly changed and the topic about the child was forgotten.

The following day, Hannah and Pearl rode horseback around Valparaiso and out into the country. They trotted along the streets toward the school they both formerly attended, then rode past the Crowder's store. The hot summer sun poured down on the dusty road. There was not a cloud in the clear sky. It was the first time Hannah had been to Ambrose's place. Pearl led her around the property pointing out his work pen where he'd trained the Mustangs from Cyrus Southworth's place.

At one point, he held her in his arms and kissed her tenderly. "If you say the word we'll stay right here. Ambrose wants us to move in. There's a little matter of marriage and making a move back out here though. You have my sincerest offer of marriage. I've cherished you always and would do that forever. If you need time to think on it, I'll be patient." Pearl's face was composed, his words reflected exactly how he felt.

"That was about the prettiest speech ever came out of that mouth of yours, Pearl Lux. What's more I'll hold you to that proposal. If this was a weak moment, it's too bad. You're right, you've about taken my breath away. I will need to think on it though if you'll allow me," Hannah's answer was calm and direct.

"It's my thoughts that you need to return to Nebraska and not try to live here. That's up to you though. You just say the word. Whatever you say goes," Pearl said. The pain in his eyes told the real story. Hannah could see he had made a promise to give her the chance to make her own decision. She took his face in her hands and kissed him tenderly. To see that awful pain disappear from his expressive face was assurance enough for both of them.

Chapter 11

The President of the United States and Congress appropriated funds for a public highway as homesteaders continued westward. It reached the state of Illinois by 1890 and soon regular stagecoach service beeame a reality. The Concord's Coach was ideal for wild country and visually they were beautiful. The coach was red, and the running board yellow. Each door had a handsome picture, The doors were handsomely decorated with landscapes each one different. This was the description of coaches destined for Wells, Fargo and Company. In 1852, Wells Fargo provided mail and banking services. By 1870, it had a monopoly on the Express service West of the Mississippi-The stagecoach-The most famous Concord was the fastest means of transportation in the far West. The incredible Deadwood stage created a legend. It traveled from Cheyenne, WY to Deadwood, SD. Its reputation grew from fighting off attaeking Sioux and marauding highwaymen all through that part of the United States.

Donna R. McGrew

The Runaway Coach

After B. J. and Cynci rode off from the homestead, I took myself a trip into Cairo to have a conversation with Sheriff Sikes. Pearl and I continued to watch the homestead and search the surrounding area of the Loup River. We assigned watches that rotated amongst our hired hands. Several times we came across cows with sudden death. They'd been brought down by someone or something and killed instantly. We suspected what probably happened but cows are known to wander, some worse than others. The property was large and, in spite of the fences, it was still possible for them to find a downed post that allowed them to get out. Mostly, these were cows with small calves ready to wean. Usually this meant the cow died and the calf disappeared. By spring there'd be enough new calves to gather and decide which ones to keep for beef steers and which heifers showed promise to be used for breeding stock.

It was a ponderous job and Pearl showed lots of patience with being a cowboy. I hoped he'd be happy with our current horse herd, but I could be dreamin' on that. He spent lots of time chasin' down lame cows and treating their ailments, but he preferred the horses.

Sheriff Sikes wasn't hard to find. I noticed him walking along as I rode down Main Street. He motioned for me to meet him at the Platte Hotel Dining Room. I put Wildfire up at the livery stable and walked to the Platte.

Sikes was seated at a table, and the waitress came as soon as I sat with him. "Bring us a couple of cups of coffee and some of them sweet rolls you got there, will ya?" he asked.

The girl hurried away and the Sheriff turned to me. "Hope you're here on a goodwill visit, son. I'd like a bit of good news this morning."

"Well, it depends upon how you view what I'm about to say. Del Cole is up and around. Joe and Ephraim are well and lots wiser about lots of things. It's amazin' that people turning 20-25 years old have so much to learn in a painful way. It seems that's about how it was though. I don't believe Del Cole will be right for the rest of his life between the trauma and the fever. "

"That's why I've come to town to see you, sir. I believe we have a clear cut case of cattle rustlin' goin' on, a sidewinder sellin' rot gut liquor to the Sioux injuns, and the same factor trainin' dogs to attack and kill whatever gets in front of them. We put sentries around the clock on our holdings and have found our cows met sudden death regular. There's no way to prevent cows getting out and about now and then, but this has got plumb ridiculous. We've lost two dozen heifers, all with calves about to wean. The cows have been fed off of some. The calves were small enough to be hauled off whether in a cart or on horseback."

Sheriff Sikes sipped his coffee. "That's a devilish lot of information you're givin' me this mornin', but I have been aware of the bootleg liquor getting into the Injun Nations. The agent reports it regular. Didn't seem to know where it comes from though. You got any idea about that too? I hope your sources are reliable on this, you understand."

"Saw it with our own eyes up on a tract on the North Loup River, about 15 miles from our place. Pearl and I went up there trackin' from our property. Somebody has made themselves right at home by our hen house and chicken run. Spyin' on us apparently. We were right down careless and changed our ways fast after we discovered what's goin' on up at that place. One day, we seen this varmint bait his dogs with a whole damn crate of live rabbits. The next thing you know, nine-ten young bucks rode in and bargained for liquor. The varmint blew enough bullets into the air to run 'em off. It was a day that put a good deal of fear in me and I ain't exactly a novice at this frontier life."

"Well, it sounds like you've had some problems that you found answers to. I believe Slats Mahoney and his two brothers may be the culprits. That's the property where they harvested ice off the river and put it up. They used to bring it around and sell it in town to folks. Their old man fell through the ice and drowned one year. There was a bunch of kids, but the three boys are the only ones stayed. I think they run the rest of 'em off. Always did think they murdered their old lady 'cause she trounced them good with a buggy whip a few times. Ain't seen hide nor hair of her for two or three years now. Never went out to investigate neither. People called me yella' but I notice nobody volunteered to join me when I put out an offer to pay a posse."

"Well, Sheriff, I don't know what's to be done, but I do believe you'll have three or four volunteers right from our place if you need them."

"I'll write up a report and decide what to do. Seems if the injuns are involved, the United States Army might be interested. As for the rustlin' that could be a job for a group of cattlemen interested in savin' their herd. I'll keep you informed, " the Sheriff continued.

I called for a second cup of coffee all around. After we finished the rolls, I headed over to the Mercantile Store for a list of stuff for Mama. I added a bag of stick candies, paid my bill, and got myself over to the livery stable. I mounted up and headed Wildfire, my gold coin Arabian, toward home. He busted lose with this surge of energy he's noted for. It was a good day for him to run off some of his pent up steam.

About five miles out of Cairo right by Sweet Creek, the stage coach passed me like the gates of hell had opened and spit them out. The driver had his whip leveled at the horses and was screamin' profanity at the top of his lungs. He was yellin', "Whoa Thar." No man was riding shotgun that I could see. The coach careened and a wheel stuck fast in the creek bed and tipped sideways as they crossed.

A young woman peered from the back window and screamed, "Get me outa' here, please!"

I opened the coach door and grasped her round the mid-section while she clung to my neck. She grabbed hold of me in a vice grip, the likes of which surprised me. I climbed aboard Wildfire and took her to the bank of the creek where I set her down. I told her I'd be back soon as I had the coach straight.

The coach sat lopsided and it was obvious the coachman was tipsy. I slapped him side the head and his head lolled as he came up with his whip. "Them sidewinders done run away their last time. Gonna' get me a shotgun and kill the both of them," he shouted.

"You'll do nothin' of the kind, you damn fool. Where's that bottle you been nursin' all day?"

"Got no bottle. Horses runned off on me," he slurred.

"The hell you say!" It didn't take much to locate a half empty jug under the seat. I flung that out over the edge of the bank.

"Now I'm gonna' sober you up and then I'll take you on to town, you hear me!" I yelled.

"Mind yer own damn business, you idiot," he said. He knew better than to move a muscle. I reached down and plunged him head first into the icy water. He came up mad and gasping, but he settled down after that. His shotgun man ran up on the bank of Sweet Creek and yelled, " Them horses run away, sure as shootin'. Couldn't do nothin with them," he whined. "I jumped off, wasn't takin' no more chances."

"Well, that's where you made your first mistake. Don't never want to jump from a runaway. Yer lucky you didn't break yer damn neck . Horses are somethin like folks. They go along for months or years and all a sudden they gotta let go. You can whale on 'em or whatever you feel the need to do, but you'll just make a strong remembrance in that animal's brain. The next time, you might not be even this lucky. You've near scared this young woman to death here, and you ought'a be ashamed of yerself. Get yourself over here and shove this coach, while I guide the horses out of here!" I ordered.

It took several tries, but eventually the wheel rolled free out of the rut. I put the luggage straight and refastened things. When I returned to the young lady, she was somewhat composed but still upset.

Wildfire

"I'm right sorry, Mam, you had this happen. Were you about at the end of your trip?" I asked.

I watched her moist lips form the words that rolled off her tongue, her mouth soft and wide. I realized then who she was. Her sister, Maggie, had come with John Miller to our place before Thanksgiving. I hadn't known there was another single daughter in the Sikes household.

"Well, if you'll allow me, I'll carry you across to the coach so you can continue on home. It's only about five miles now," I informed her.

I lifted her onto the saddle and we crossed the creek. Rose's hair was black as midnight. Her eyes sparkling emeralds surrounded by the blackest lashes and brows I'd ever seen. She wore a fancy hat of lace and veiling that set off her pretty face. She smelled faintly of lavender. The reaction I had when I touched her startled me. I remembered how it felt when she clung to me, the feel of her soft skin, the strong grip of her gloved hands as they clasped my neck.

As I put her aboard the coach once more, a black curl caught on the buttons of my coat. I located her purse and handed it to her. "These men have assured me they will see you safely to your destination or I will personally look them up and make them accountable."

"Thank you for getting rid of that dreadful whiskey the driver was drinking. My daddy will surely thank you too for helping me."

Rose peered out the window of the coach as we moved away. Those eyes and that lavender scent would be something I could not get out of my mind. I had fragments of a black curl wound round the button of my coat. I pulled Wildfire's reins in to keep abreast of the coach as we sped along. When we came to the out skirts of Cairo, I signaled to the drive, "I'll leave you here. See to it Ms. Sikes gets safely to the station and her parents." I pulled Wildfire up and turned quickly back along the way we had come. I felt lonely as I started off for home.

As I galloped along, I gazed at the countryside with pride. I felt like I'd discovered a crown jewel with the events of the day. This immense land of the plains, the pristine silence and all its beauty, moved to the marrow of my bones. A sharp north wind blew across the countryside. It blew in the bare limbs of the trees. Spring was on the coattails of winter. It seemed to be in my heart as well.

Chapter 12

The early housewives' responsibility was extraordinary in the array of skills required. It demanded such things as brewing syrup for a cold, feeding livestock, stitching quilts, embroidering fine under things, and tending and teaching children. The art of homemaking was acquired at a very early age. In one day a frontier female included in her activities: dressmaking, carding wool, cheesemaking, ironing, milking, cooking, knitting, dying thread and winding it on spools, dress making, tending and weeding a vegetable garden.

Rose and Jesse

I turned seventeen in April this year. Papa got a card from Jesse Peers asking Pa's permission to visit me. There's a summer frolic coming up soon, and I'm thinking it may be just about right for Jesse to take me there. What Pa don't know won't hurt none.

Mama Greta, and sister Maggie, washed my hair this mornin'. I swear they like to wore out my scalp with their scrubbin' and carryin' on. They used vinegar rinse and I hate the smell; but I hate the snarls worse.

Mama dried and brushed and combed till I near rebelled on her, but there's no quittin' with Greta Sikes when a prospective husband pops up.

Out came the curling iron set to heat in the fireplace. My curls have to be straightened, and even then they don't stay put. My hair sweeps like a midnight sky, fine and black that reaches my waist. It's a big job to get it arranged just right.

Then out of the blue Mama said, "Jesse Peers is coming to dinner tonight." I nearly fainted. "Get out that paisley print I made you for May Day dance. Air it out and press it," she ordered. Lord she's a slave driver. Do this – do that. Then she told me, "Jesse sent over a card with your brother John. Don't know just how John knew him."

Maggie and I both exchanged looks. She cut into my eyes with those sparkling blue irises of hers. I could hardly keep from laughing. You see, Maggie and I go to my brother, Doctor Johnny Sikes, clinic in town when Mama sends us for groceries. In the waiting room was this tall blonde stranger in leather clothes. He even wore a holster. His handle bar moustache really made him outstanding. He had the bluest eyes I've ever seen and they twinkle with merriment. Mercy me, I hope he doesn't show up with that gun when he comes over here. Or Pa will just run him right off the property. His eyes looked into mine. In my youthful delight, I'm impressed with his worldly experience. All I saw was this wonderful man whose entire attention was focused on me. Bubbles of delight course through me and consume my very being.

Wildfire

Anyways, Jesse went on about John did this and John did that. I thought he surely knew my brother well. So I ask, "What are you here at the clinic for?"

And he replied, "I'm here with my brother John."

Well, I laughed right out loud because all this time I thought he was talking about my brother. It turned out we both have a brother John. We exchanged information about our families. His family homesteaded a place outside of Cairo. Recently, he came here from Indiana on a cattle drive for his Pa. He reminded me how he had stopped the coach the day the horses ran away. I blushed—remembering the way he swept me out of the coach that day and set me on the shore while he straightened out the coach and driver. That was when I came home from Grant Station.

Then Jesse formally introduced himself to Maggie and me. We felt really daring talking to this stranger. Silence fell over us like an iron quilt when my brother walked out with his brother Johnny. Johnny Peers had his hand bandaged and Doctor John had stitched him up. He'd been sharpening tools and slipped and cut himself.

Then Jesse said he wanted to see me. My brother told him he'd have to send a card over with his name and some particulars on it so's Pa and Mama will know who he was. Doctor John said he'd get in touch with Jesse about what my parents decide. Lordy me, I couldn't believe my ears.

"You let me know how you do with that hand, Johnny. Come see me next Tuesday and I'll check on it for you. In the meantime, try to rest that hand and don't use it if you don't have to."

All of us went our separate ways. I was walking on air and completely enamored with my current experience. I couldn't wait to see what would happen next.

That was last week. This dinner tonight was news to me. Mama's such a matchmaker, it sure didn't take long to fix things up once she found a willing possibility. Her words poured through my thoughts like rainwater. Her plans flowed over me in a torrent. Good thing I'm agreeable with all these plans. I don't believe it would make a whit of difference if I hadn't, though. I shook my head in alarm.

Then Pa came in the house. Perspiring and sweaty from his farm work, he took a bandana and wiped off his face before he spoke. The bones of his face looked taut underneath the skin. His eyes flinched with a flat look. He hides a cruel side of his nature when he can control it before he speaks. "John says Jesse Peers wants to meet us and take you out. Do you know anything about that Rosa?"

He always used Rosa when he was the sternest. I could feel myself tense up under Pa's scrutiny. Then I remembered Jesse Peers and I said, "I know the family. You've seen them in church. They own a pew on the right hand side up by the altar." Might as well make it look as good as possible I thought.

Mama Greta nodded her head in agreement. I could tell she'd found a winner in her game of lovers and friends. I had scored big with her.

Pa replied, "We'll see just what kind of man this Jesse Peers is. He doesn't need to think he can buy his way with us like they did the pew at the church. He'll prove himself or we'll be shed of him."

Mama Greta was cheerful, fluttering around just like the social butterfly. Behind Papa's back, Maggie winked at me.

Jesse arrived around five o'clock, and I waited in my room till I heard Mama greet him. Pa come early from the yard and scrubbed up before supper. I heard Maggie answer the door and Ma greeted Jesse as I hurried downstairs. "Come in Mr. Peers. Have a seat. My husband will be right in. These are our daughters Rose and Maggie."

Jesse gave Mama his hat and sat on the settee before Pa came in; Jesse looked uncomfortable. He had been forewarned by his family and all his friends about Pa's temper. "I didn't realize our farms were so close. I always thought they were across the township from Platte Valley to Sodtownship," Jesse said.

"It can't be more than eight miles I'd guess. I never thought about it before." My skills being what they are, I feel wanting in matters of such concerns.

Pa walked into the room, towering over everyone. He extended his hand as Jesse rose and shook it. Pa wanted everyone to know he was in charge here. He gazed down at Jesse as he shook his hand. This was a tactic of his that made us all pay attention.

Ma called us to supper. We sat in the dining room today rather than the kitchen. The clean and polished furniture, the smell of roast pork and apple sauce, suddenly, things I've never been aware of brought about a knowing. Greta Sikes had a very intricate plan. The impact of awareness followed me as Maggie and I placed food on the table. The atmosphere of the room strained, the swinging door to the kitchen where Hessie Riddle was busy filling soup bowls readied for our reaching impatient hands.

Papa was inspecting the linen, silverware and flowers on the table. He gave a contemptuous snort as he seated himself. He's an expert at intimidation; this was not lost on Jesse. Jesse stood nearly as tall as Pa but lost all impact compared to Pa in size. Mama came to the rescue. She asked Papa to say the blessing and we all bowed our heads in prayer.

"I understand you came recently from Indiana to help with your Pa's farm. There's been lots going on over there from what I saw at Thanksgiving. We saw your family at St. Aloysius church every Sunday in Cairo," Mama said.

"No matter all that if people are not known to us," Pa spoke up directing his conversation at Mama. "Our family has been here since the turn of the century throughout this area settling and making our homes here. We're not taken much with all the newcomers and such. I gather you brought a bunch of Indians with you all the way from Indiana. I'm not much in favor of mixing with the red skins. Found them untrustworthy, not of much worth as far as work and such."

"I think you'll find our cowhands, particularly B. J. Rivera, are as trustworthy a lot as you'll find anywhere. We'd have been in a sad state if we hadn't had the support of Joe Lone Bear and his family. His wife, Sweet Water, is a fine cook and their children are a continual amazement with their conduct," Jesse replied.

Pa couldn't let it go and his anger continued to boil and spill over. "Is it true you've brought two women with you that have some kind of mental problems as well? Doesn't seem advisable to associate with the likes of these women of doubtful character."

Maggie and I brought food to the table and that interrupted the conversation for now. Thick slices of roast pork congealed in rich peppery gravy. The subject was dropped but it would resume at Papa's first opportunity. His expression told me he's carefully watching Jesse's reaction to what he said. I felt sick at heart. Lordy, I'll never leave this house the way things are going.

Mama's expression told me she was way ahead of all of us with a plan of her own. She took in the situation while her eyes walked all over Papa. Once the food was passed and served, Mama said, "Your parents migrated from Holland if I remember right. Your Grandfather played with the Gdansk Symphony before coming to America. Isn't that so?"

"Yes, that's true. He spent some time in New York until my Grandmother joined him, and they moved to Indiana. He played with the Indianapolis Symphony where my Dad was born. My Mother taught harpsichord lessons; that's how they met. She played with the symphony as a girl."

Pa looked angry as his eyes snapped back at Mama. No one dared show the indifference she does with Pa. My friends and our cousins frowned on Mama's stand. It wasn't considered wifely because she wasn't obedient to Papa. Somehow I worry that the things I invented outnumbered what was really true. Once I learned to avoid people who tried to pry, life became easier. As I grew up I learned that the things I invented and the truth lay side by side like panes of glass. The truth was very clear, but there would always be two stories that were similar but not exactly the same. I may be daydreaming on this, but I believe Mama may have already won the debate. I found it paid to be vigilant on matters where Mama was concerned.

Papa continued to shove food into his mouth and chew loudly. She constantly reminds him of his manners with company. His dignity had been seriously impacted, and I sensed a storm brewing.

Hessie Riddle was busy in the kitchen with egg beater and cream. She made an angel cake today with thirteen egg whites. It's her specialty and was iced with whipped cream frosting. She shaved bits of chocolate around the top, and served it on Mama's best dessert dinner plates. Maggie and I carried the pieces of cake into the dining room. Mama served coffee all around.

"I see you girls had time to bake a fancy cake and clean the house from stem to stern. I'll have to see if I can't find something that interesting to do out in the barn. Maybe the chicken house could use a fresh covering for our layers," he exclaimed.

I nearly choked tryin' not to laugh. Mama and Maggie and I just did the henhouse. That's how we discovered there were plenty of eggs to spare for this dessert sitting before him right this minute. Mama spoke up, "Rosa is the best milker in the family, Hans. Or have you forgotten. Both of the girls are better milkers than any of their brothers." Her words sizzle off her tongue. Pa has made a poor choice to belittle us girls. "You brought dairy cows out to the prairie didn't you, Jesse?"

"Yes, we brought two hundred cows and Beauregarde, the famous breeding bull. Papa bought him from Pearl's Uncle Ambrose. There will be cows ready to calve for sale this spring once the weather breaks."

"We should discuss this matter someplace besides our dinner table when my daughters are present," Papa declared.

We struggle to keep our faces straight; chuckles were ready to burst from my mouth. Maggie and I both know more about the milk cows than anyone in this room. The milk cows with their big brown eyes are like pets, and we've watched the herd grow with delight since we were four or five years old. Some would say this should have been a "verbotin" matter for children so young, but we both loved milk cows. Besides, it's our cash crop that brings extra money for all kinds of things we do. Last year, when I was sixteen, I bought enough brocade and velvet to make Mama a "Crazy Quilt." It hangs on a quilt frame right in the bedroom Papa sleeps in. Papa called Maggie and me empty-headed silly girls at the time. Didn't take long for those pieces of fabric to turn into a bunch of beautiful quilt blocks my friends and cousins made for Mama. The center says: "To Mama from Rose, April 18, 1880."

Each time the thread unravels on such things, I worry about Papa's attitude toward Annie, Maggie, Ella and me. When Ella and Annie finally married, Pa made everyone think it was all his doings. Annie married Willie Runge, a conductor for the Northwestern Railway System. Ella married John

Schuetts, who owned a dray service in Grant Station. Pa told stories on both the prospective husbands like they were trash as far as he knew. He discredited both men and caused a rift until Pa discovered his daughters were going to marry with or without his permission. There were months when both daughters fled to relatives homes with all their possessions, vowing never to return.

Mama called out, "Hessie bring in the coffee pot, please. Does anyone want another cup?"

Hessie walked slow through the kitchen door. Hessie was different. Her Ma died birthing her. Had it not been for a midwife's careful care, Hessie would've died too. Obediah Riddle, her Pa, was so sad over his wife Delia's death, he never really got over it. Hessie lived at Corrie Braeghton's home till she was about two years old. Obediah hired a widow woman from Kearney to care for his home and Hessie, along with her own children.

Hessie birthed backwards and her face was a little lopsided till she was almost three, then she grew and became good as new. Pa called her butt ugly and Mama liked to never forgave him until he allowed Hessie to move into our house about a year ago. Hessie has these obsidian eyes, her body is lean as a willow, Mama thinks she sees and hears things we don't, another reason Mama was so taken with her. Pa always said Obediah was cursed by some redskin when he was young. Claimed that's why Pa hated redskins, 'cause they were evil. Hessie was right handed, maybe because her left side was damaged at birth. The right side works fine though and she walks

Wildfire

with a slight limp. Her wispy brown hair is always caught in a snood that crowns her face. Her eyes are as clear as black onyx as they glitter with merriment and sparkle with fire depending on her mood. She keeps the house clean and Maggie and I liked that just fine. If I marry a farmer, I'd want someone just as sweet as Hessie to help me out just like she does Mama.

Hessie had visions. The first time she warned us that something was going to happen, it like to scared us to death. We didn't believe her when she foretold how the trees along the property would twist like rags in the wind. That spring all the trees on the south end of our property were in the path of a tornado. Afterward, she peered at us with those black eyes of hers and said, "Didn't I tell you so?"

It looked like Papa enjoyed dessert even if he was so nasty to us. Finally he spoke, "Jesse, is it right that you are here to meet Rosa?"

"That's true, and I'd be pleased if she'd come with me to the Wood River Summer fest. We'd be in town before noon till near sundown, when I'd be pleased to bring her home."

"Safe and sound I assume, since you seem to have thought this through," Papa added.

Mama interrupted, "I believe Maggie will go with Johnny Miller. Isn't that right?"

Maggie was caught unaware and couldn't find her tongue. All she could say was, "Uh huh."

Jesse rose, "I'll pick Rose up mid-morning, and we'll spend the day in town."

"I'd really like that," I added. "I'll be lookin' for you Saturday, then Jesse."

Mama nodded in approval while Papa sat there with a scowl on his face. Maggie and I hurried to the kitchen and hugged each other, anticipating the coming Saturday.

We came into the dining room carrying the coffee pot, cream and sugar. Jesse said, "No more coffee for me; I need to be on my way. Pearl Lux and I have a rustler problem. No doubt we'll spend the next few days searching along the North Loup River."

This interested Papa, "You say you got rustlers?"

"I believe we do and more besides. Your son, Pete, was interested in the activities up around the Mahoney homestead on the North Loup River. I believe you're familiar with the Mahoneys. They own the Whistle Stop in Cairo."

"Yes, I believe I know who you're talking about." Papa seemed to have this revelation after Jesse's statement. His eyes became alert, a strange expression crossed his face. He sized Jesse up, extended his hand and shook it. "Pleased to have you Jesse. See you next weekend."

I was so surprised with this turn of events, my mouth fell open. Wonders never cease where Papa is concerned. Maybe he was seeing something here he hadn't really looked at before. Papa followed Jesse to the front door.

"If you need some help with that rustler problem, just let us know," he insisted.

Wildfire

In one quick motion Jesse unhitched Wildfire, put one foot in the stirrup, mounted up and rode away, lifting his hand in farewell.

Chapter 13

As life became easier the role of the homemaker became an ideal. Magazines such as American Woman's Home, Ladies Home Journal and Good housekeeping featured articles on the American housewife. She did more than prepare food and wash and iron clothing. She was charged with the responsibility of making the home not only a nurturing place but a place of beauty and love. Educators proclaimed to owe much to the American housewife. The love that strengthens and inspired the family provided a refuge for husbands and nurtured children. America had arrive at a new threshold for women.

Rose's Music Lessons

The ice of the North Loup River and its rivulets of streams along the homestead cracked recently like a pistol shot. Morning winds ate at the snow piles which turned to rushing streams that gathered and sat on the frozen ground to be sucked into the hungry earth. The air was warm to the face so I drank in the goodness and listened to the faint wind song spinning the windmill.

Wildfire

I savored the last of my morning coffee and walked out to saddle up Wildfire. Grass had started to grow in the slight hills and gullies, the first promise of warmer weather. Neighbors stirred about anticipating the work and toil of days ahead. I eyed the landscape looking for evidence of dead cattle or strayed livestock. The last painful months of winter were over, and I rode eastward toward the face of the butte where the Oglala Sioux had been outwitted by the United States army.

Wildfire stepped gingerly over the rutted wagon trails. His eyes glanced back and forth, his head was held high. He strained at the bit in his mouth and whinnied. He was ready to break and run hard. I gazed at the brilliant web of prairie tinged by the orange red glow of the morning sun, casts of green spread over the buffalo grass. Deer bounded away ahead of me. Another week and geese would be plentiful along the North Loup. An ecstasy of trilling migrating birds summoned their presence as well. I turned Wildfire back toward the sod houses in the distance, my eyes alert as I took in every detail of the prairie, especially the mounds and hillocks that might hide downed cattle or horses. I dismounted in the yard and turned Wildfire into the stock pen.

Stopping briefly, I picked up dried cord wood and entered the farmhouse, my arms piled high. Del Cole sat in the kitchen. Hannah poured his coffee cup full, her face held a strange grimace. He sat smoking his pipe. His skin was thin and white, gray creeping at his temples. His angry eyes were potent and scolding. Smoke curled up around him and wafted away, joining odors left from breakfast.

Ephraim Hobbs sat across the table from Del at the kitchen table. "Soon you'll have no excuse to sit in the mornings; we'll all be busy with planting time." The talk turned to crops and politics, railroads and such. Time to plow, time for selling off beef cattle.

Mama noticed Cole was afire. Maudie and Hannah moved swiftly to pound the smoldering coat. Still he grabbed his burning pipe and slipped it into his pocket. Maudie's eyes raked him while she scolded. Del rose quickly and rushed outside.

"We try not to make much of his actions, but we still watch and act as quickly as we can. Open the windows and let some air in," Mama insisted.

"He smells so bad I can't stand him," Maudie complained.

I watched while things calmed some. "You don't usually get upset about some smoke in the kitchen, Mama. What is it?" The women rushed around cleaning up the mess Del had made.

"Rose Sikes comes today and starts harpsichord lessons. I don't want her to think we've set here all winter without cleaning," Hannah said.

"Rose? You don't usually give music lessons do you, Mama?" I couldn't fathom how this could be. In the back of my mind was the evening I spent at the Sikes' home. I'm not sure I wanted to repeat the experience.

"Rose finished eighth grade two years ago, and Hans refuses to let her go on. I'm not surprised she's upset about this. Greta always boasted how smart Rose was. Maggie wouldn't have bothered. Hans says the girls will just get married anyway. They don't need education," Mama added.

"I'd not thought Rose was bent on education. She seems a little scatter brained. She and Maggie are a pair."

"How do you know that, Jesse Peers?" Mama insisted.

It wasn't my motive to trap myself with my own tongue, but there it was. Inquiring interest crossed the face of all the women in the kitchen, even Pearl was alert .

"Yes, tell us how you know that?" Pearl chuckled.

I recalled Rose's lips a heartbeat away as I carried her back to the coach from the river the day of the runaway. I smiled to myself, a little conspiracy I had not shared that I held and cherished within myself. I half found my voice, a whisper at best, while I recounted my evening at the Sikes' household. It had been a few days since then and now there was a time between their knowing and not knowing. I smiled to myself, savoring the intrigue and how I had teased them. I rose and headed to the barn to ponder what Mama had said. She was going to give Rose Sikes music lessons. I could just imagine Greta Sikes maneuvering this whole thing.

Del Cole stood by the stock tank, a look so desolate on his face, I was concerned. "Not to worry about what happened in the kitchen, Del. Be more careful of smoking, especially in the house. Are you burned or injured because of what just happened?"

"No, I'm ashamed I can't be more careful. If you want I should leave, I will," he lamented.

"Don't even consider that, Del. We want you here. Besides, we're trying to bring down the folks who are doing these things that happened to you. Sheriff Sikes and all of us are trying to figure out a way to end their rustling and arrest the people who caused this to happen to you. We want you to stay right here just as long as you want."

Del looked suddenly very relieved, as if he had expected the worst from me. "Maudie got pretty upset at what I done. Your Ma was upset too."

Del and I worked with the pump and brought fresh water into the stock tank. His body had healed well, but these upsets brought him to a place where he couldn't cope.

In the distance a speck appeared on the horizon. We peered closely at who might be approaching on the main road. Quickly, the dark shape lit by the bright morning sun revealed a horse and buggy moving swiftly toward the farm. It turned into the yard and came to a stop at the front of the house. Del and I hurried to see who had arrived.

Rose Sikes stepped quickly from her horse drawn buggy. "What a great day for a drive. Where can I tie

Wildfire

my horse, Jesse?" Rose asked. She was quite tall for a woman and did not wait to be helped.

"Del will take your buggy round to the bunkhouse. There's a hitching rail out there."

"Old Sukie could use some water, if you don't mind." As she handed over the reins, she smiled at Del, her teeth white pearls in her full mouth.

"I'll see to it," Del replied. The pleased look that relaxed across his face was a comfort to observe. Rose's friendly manner was not wasted on Del. He'd been more concerned than necessary. I need to take it up with Mama about all the turmoil in the kitchen. Rose and I entered the front door as I called, "Rose is here, Mama."

Mama took Rose's coat and purse. "It's good to see you, Rose. Are you ready for your first music lesson?" She wore a short velvet jacket that revealed her tiny waist and rounded hips as she walked toward me.

"Ready and anxious to learn as much as you can teach me," Rose insisted. Her eyes flashed briefly on my face; at that moment it seemed she was about to say something to me. It was a small intimate glance. Then the look was gone and Mama was in charge.

If love had an ambassador, Greta Sikes was the person. This was a setup if ever I saw one. I didn't mind a bit. In fact, I'm willing to bet Greta will use every opportunity to see that Rose and I get to know each other well. Pearl sat in the kitchen cleaning his pistols, and Hannah was watching him work as she dried dishes and straightened the table. He had this look of amazement on his face. Hannah had a different expression that washed across her face, the time between knowing and not knowing. Neither said a word, but their eyes had an intimate knowledge of what they suspected.

By the time the music lesson was over, dinner was ready and Mama insisted Rose stay for a bite to eat. Pa came into the house and it was clear he was amazed. "Good day to you, Rose! What a pleasure to have you at our table. Sara Ann, you didn't tell me we were having a visitor today."

"Guess I forgot to tell you, I talked to Rose and her Mama so long ago. Rose'll be with us every Thursday from now until she decides she's had enough of my drumming at her to practice. Isn't that right Rose?"

"That's about right, Ms. Peers. I may be a slow learner, who knows?" Rose said. There seemed to be a private joke only she knew about.

Mama handed Rose a basket of biscuits. "How's your folks Rose? Everyone fine at your place?"

"Mostly, Maggie went to Omaha to stay with my sister Ella. I miss having her around. Good thing Hessie Riddle is with us to help out or I couldn't have taken lessons, I guess."

"Obediah, Hessie's Dad, has had problems with the sheep people," Pa commented. "Obediah has been raising dairy and beef cattle and the sheep graze off the open prairie grass. With the Homestead Act, $14 will get you a great plot of land here in the plains. The trick is to stay five years. These sheep people realize what they are doing will drive settlers off. They tend to graze prairie grass needed by the farmers for their cattle."

"I thought people fenced their land and kept lots of interlopers out. Seems they can't buy enough fence and fence posts to protect their property," I said.

"Obediah and some of the cattlemen have banded together to form a group. Honest as the day is long, you can count on the group making their word good, but the sheep people cut fences and then feed on land that isn't theirs," Pa continued.

"Obediah was alerted by one of his group, about a tough looking bunch headed toward his farm. His friends gathered as the marauders arrived and lighted torches making ready to burn him out. Obediah wounded one of them as he bent to set his haystack afire. An exchange of shots left another man injured, but Obediah's group held them off and drove the thugs from his property. He didn't think they were just sheep herders though. I guess they found out that was true. Some of them were mercenaries recruited to burn the settlers out. The group tried to throw torches on the roof of some of Obediah's buildings. Obediah's group drove them back and during the last month he dug a trench around his home and out buildings. He's afraid they'll set a fire that will get all his buildings. They're a bunch of gun totin' fools. If they come back, Obediah will have reprisals until they feel they've paid him back." Rose's eyes swept around the table at the folks there. Her dark lashes fluttered, a small frown flickered on her face. She looked too fragile to be so knowledgeable.

It's been awhile since I've seen a woman who commanded as much attention as Rose Sikes. I thought about Mattie, always telling everyone what to do, so bossy and capable. Rose had something else going on. She commanded attention for her tender years. She was at least fifteen years younger than Mattie.

Ethel rose and filled bowls with hot food, passing them along the table. Dinner was always a huge meal, and today, we had roast beef with gravy and a large bowl of mashed potatoes. We still had carrots and beets in the root cellar. Sweet Water had oven roasted them with pungent spices. Mama put some more hot biscuits into a covered basket and passed them along to us.

"I've seen some of the sheep herds over by the South Loup River, sometimes thousands at a time like a moving carpet of gray as they feed along. I was out trailing a bunch of feral horses. They gave me a good work out for five or six hours one day, before I got them cornered. I used a good lot of patience and all the tricks I knowed that eventually got them to the corral. They were led by a mare, and she finally let me get close enough to let me work with her. It took a long time though. When she finally came with me, she walked into the yard, stepping high, suspicious, eyeballing me," Pearl chuckled.

" I see you have a quarter horse, Rose. That mare is pretty spirited for a woman's buggy, or are you the only one that uses that horse?" Pearl asked.

"Sukie? Goodness, she's as gentle as a kid's pony. I' ve had her since I was five, and Pa helped break her to the buggy. It's my buggy too. Pa gave me the buggy for eighth grade graduation," Rose said.

"I notice you used the word 'break'. Pearl doesn't break horses. He has a knack at getting horses to do about anything without a crop and never a whip. You'll have to stay over sometime when he trains a feral horse," I added.

"I'm going to the Sioux reservation next week. They have a bunch of ponies they want to bring in. I said I'd look at them and see what I could do with them. If they're good stock, I'll bring a few back to work here at the homestead," Pearl said.

"I thought you'd not be doin' much of that kind of thing lately." Hannah spoke up.

I wasn't certain how she felt about this, but as I looked in her eyes, I was allowed to see the open happiness reflected there. It gave me a start as I tend to see her worried lots these days.

At last, Rose said she must head for home. Pearl hurried to the hitching post and brought up her horse and buggy. The women began to clear dishes and prepare to clean up the kitchen. I helped Rose into her coat. She gathered up her purse, and we walked slowly outside savoring these last few moments. The sun shone down full from above, Rose's hair was a cape of ebony reflecting the pure sunlight. What a pleasure to help Rose into her buggy. Her mouth so close I could feel her breath. Her lips only a whisper away. I sensed a message confirming the news. Some secret my heart had already received, letting it loose in my senses like a kite with a broke string. I helped Rose into her buggy. "I plan to send my card to your Pa with my name and some of my particulars on it. It'll introduce me and let him know I want to court you. Some things are coming up I'd like to attend with you, if that's alright with you." I could see that was fine before she answered, "Yes,

Jesse, that'll be real fine. I'll tell Mama what you intend to do. She'll be pleased, be assured of that."

I watched Rose's buggy until it was a tiny spot on the horizon. When I returned to the house, silence fell among the people there. At my age I won't squander my time, wallowing in the pleasure of a conspiracy. I almost asked Mama if she knew more than she was telling, but she looked so complacent, so nonchalant, I changed my mind. Time would tell, you can bet on that.

Chapter 14

As the frontier wilderness slowly and steadily disappeared, rugged attitudes gave way to a more mannerly gentle way of living. While the difficult work of 19th century women proved important to the survival of the family, tasks in settled communities gradually became easier due to the appearance of household appliances. Nineteenth century women's social identity ideals tended to elevate their status in society. The widely held image shaped by changing lifestyles and imported European manners portrayed women as modest, tender, demure, cheerful, pious, proper creatures given to attractive blushes and sometimes emotional outbursts. Victorian customs of restricted clothing, delicate diet, limited exercise and fresh air, reflected the age's popular attitudes. At that time, the weaker sex was called a female rather than a woman. "Woman" was considered common and was applied only to females of questionable character.

Obediah Riddle

June was always humid; the North Loup river overflowed its banks. Mud hens and ducks dove for worms and caught water bugs that skated about on the river. The weather turned so hot heat lightning crackled inside the cloud cover like lightning bugs caught up in a cheesecloth sack.

Rose drove her buggy each Thursday to the Peers homestead and Sara Ann and Rose moved through beginning piano lesson books and into sheet music. The sounds from the parlor harpsichord floated through the house. Sometimes Rose stayed for supper but as June came to an end, work on the farm found Jesse busy in the fields far away from the house. Rose would visit briefly over iced tea with Hannah, Maudie and Ethel, and then hitched up Sukie to ride off.

Hannah saw her off with a wave. "Pearl, Jesse and I will pick you up for the Summer Frolic in Wood River. We'll be there early morning."

"I'll be waiting." Rose replied. The soft glow of happiness on her face told the state of mind she was in. She flipped the reins and Sukie trotted off down the road.

That morning Hessie and Maggie pulled Rose's corset strings tight while she clasped the bedrail of her poster bed.

"Lord Rose, you're getting thin as a rail!" Hessie scolded. "You don't eat enough to keep a bird alive. I'm thinkin' I need to take it up wicher Ma you're gettin s'thin."

"Now Hessie, don't go concerning Mama about my weight. There'll be plenty of food at the Summer Frolic and lots of other things too. The Breightons and the Syries both have quilting bees soon, and there's lots and lots of food at those things," Rose replied.

Wildfire

"You're waist measures twenty inches, Rose." Maggie looked again at her tape measure just to be sure. She sighed as she looked at her own round figure in the mirror by the windows.

"Seems I just have to smell food and I gain weight," Maggie lamented.

"My Lord, you're both about to waste away. Now you listen to me, both of you. Either you get to eatin' better or I'll go straight to your Ma." Hessie's obsidian eyes snapped with fire. The girls knew she meant every word she said.

Rose changed the subject. She knew she wouldn't win with Hessie ever. "How's your Pa, Hessie? We ain't seen him in awhile. He isn't ailin' or nothin' is he?"

"No, as a matter of fact, he's not. Thanks for askin'. He's started the upper story over at his house on Sweet Creek on that property he bought. He's got the outbuildings done. You can always tell what's important to these men around these parts. He finished a silo and barn the first year he lived there, but it tuk him five to get started improvin' the house. Effie Syrie's boys been carpenterin' for Pa. They were stayin' on the farm with him and helpin' out. Effie goes over and cooks and keeps the house straight as she has time."

"Those boys must be eighteen or nineteen years old now. I seen them one Saturday night at Wood River shinin' the Woodrow sisters. John and I seen them there. Old man Woodrow and his wife were there and he got a tad too much to drink. Ms. Woodrow rousted them out and they took their Pa home. Woodrow's run the feed mill in Wood River and they live right by the mill on the river," Maggie confirmed.

"We're going to Wood River next Sunday. I'm fixin' to make potato salad and Hannah wants to bring deviled eggs. Jesse and Pearl will take us to the Summer Frolic. I guess Maudie and Ethel won't be goin' but I heard Celia Dibern was going with our brother Augie," Rose replied.

"I for one won't miss those Peers girls at all. How'd you find out that Augie was going with Celia?" Maggie asked.

"Hannah heard it. I guess Pearl talked to Augie. Pete was talking about taking Alma Dibern, that's Celia's sister," Rose added.

"Well, ain't you full of news. I bet if the Diberns thought about that good they'd put a stop to August and Pete both coming around," Hessie interjected.

All this was forgotten as Obediah Riddle rode into the yard on horseback. He'd lost his hat, his face red and sweaty, his hair rumpled and unkempt. Sweat pooled in the underarms of his shirt. He rode one of his work mules that was all lathered up. Dust rose in a cloud around him and settled on the mule's back. He clung to the mules as he glanced around the yard. He lunged from the mule and ran to the barn where Hans and his sons, August and Ernest, were busy in the horse stalls.

"What's got you in such a lather, Obediah? You look like you seen a ghost!" Hans Sikes demanded.

Hessie hurried to the yard when she saw him ride up. "What's wrong, Papa? Whatever happened to you?"

"I just brought a load of lumber back from Kearney. The Syries are gonna help me finish the upstairs of my house. So I had to have some two by fours and some shingles for roofing. Well, I come along the south road on the lower part of the Oglala reservation, when I heard riders comin' up fast. They rode around me and took that fork road toward Ravenna. Them sidewinders turned and emptied their guns above my mules' heads. Scared the mules and I had a run away on my hands sure nuf. I let 'em run it out till they calmed down some, but my load ne'r went over. Don't know who them varmints were but I will if I ever see them agin." Obediah shook his fist, his voice registered the fear he felt.

"Do you think it was them sheep people down by Wood River, Obediah?" Hans asked. "Maybe it was some of them young bucks from the reservation."

"Don't know. Never seen them codgers before," he said.

"Best come inside and sit a spell. Have a cool drink, calm down before you ride on," Hessie pleaded. Hessie led her father into the kitchen and pumped fresh well water into a tin cup for him. She wrung a cloth out in warm water and Obediah wiped the sweat from his face. Hessie was alarmed and rightfully so. Obediah was terribly upset. Hans Sikes and his sons came in the kitchen.

"Best get your guns oiled and ready for anything that might happen. We'll ride back with you and see if we can pick up anything these guys might've dropped-- empty shells, tracks they laid, that kind of stuff," Augie said.

"There weren't nothin' outstandin' bout this bunch. Other than they were ridin' hard. Nothin' , nothin' at all," Obediah said. "The sheep people have been up further on the Platte River," Obediah added. "These people looked different. Rough bunch. Had some Mastiff dogs with them. Biggest dogs I ever seen."

The men saddled horses and rode out down the road with Obediah in the lead. They searched along the roadside to see what they might find. When they returned to the Sikes homestead it was dusk and everyone ate supper in silence. A foreboding silence fell, leaving everyone inside their own heads wondering about what had happened. It shook most everyone to the core.

At the Peers' household preparation for the Sunday celebration in Wood River went on all day. Early that day, Jesse and Pearl rode off down the road to Cairo and entered the cobweb of streets. They rode along Main Street to the livery stable. At the stable they found Otto Grob busy shoeing horses.

"You got a buggy that we could use for special trips around the countryside? Something that would hold about six people and claptrap for picnics and luggage, that sort of thing?" Jesse asked.

Otto looked at Jesse and Pearl. "Now what would you two want such a contraption for? Seems to me what you need is something to haul lumber and goods with."

"That's not what we need this buggy for. All I see around here is somethin' for two people. We need somethin' bigger," Pearl said.

"Well, there's a surrey in the shed. Nobody wants that thing cause it's for sightseeing. Something a whole bunch of people would ride in. I could give you a good price if you're interested," Otto replied. He took them to a shed in back of the livery stable. "The surrey's in good shape. It would hold ten-twelve passengers or part could be used for luggage and storage. About right for what you need." Pearl looked it over while Jesse made an offer of $20 for the surrey, a three-seated buggy with a flat roof. Otto took their money and stood scratching his head as they rode off. Between the two, they hitched their horses to pull it back to the homestead. Big Red and Wildfire moved warily into the harness while Pearl pulled cinches tight and buckled them in place.

The rest of the day was spent getting together the harness and picking out horses to pull the contraption. "I think those sorrel mares Pa uses chucking corn might be about right for the surrey. They show lots of patience for stopping and starting out in the corn rows," Jesse said.

The sun began to sink as Pearl and Jesse mounted the coal oil lamps removed from the sleigh and fastened them to the back of the surrey. As Pearl worked on the surrey, Big Red watched curiously. Pearl bent to grease the axels, and Big Red trotted up behind him. He bunted Pearl in the crotch and Pearl sprawled beneath the surrey. "Alright you Red devil! That's about enough of that stuff." Red shook his head as he whinnied at Pearl, showing lots of teeth. Pearl got up, brushed himself off as he eyeballed the horse. Big Red trotted off pleased with himself.

The Peers' household was not aware of the drama that had taken place at the Sikes home. After a quick supper, Pearl was busy for many hours greasing the surrey's wheels and oiling the exterior leather. At last satisfied, he came into the house bringing the smells of leather and grooming oil as he entered. A huge smile played across his face. Hannah was suspicious of all the activity .

"I suppose you've worn yourself out polishing on the wagon you and Jesse bought," Hannah snipped.

"I'd not thought you'd even missed me today. It's so nice to know you were paying attention. Perhaps you'll find your carriage comfortable and fit for the likes of yourself tomorrow," Pearl chuckled.

With that pretty speech, Hannah melted and was embarrassed she'd been so nasty when there'd been no need. "You mean all that was for Sunday frolic in Wood River?" she inquired.

""Yes, and I hope you've been busy getting food and the likes ready while I was out there slavin' away for your comfort," Pearl simpered.

"I might've known you and Jesse would have something up your sleeve. So busy you'd not even had time to bid me the time of day," Hannah said. "And for your information, I have been busy and you'll see in due time I worked very hard so you'll not want for food tomorrow." She slapped lightly on Pearl's arm. He returned the swat and as usual they ended in each others arms. This fulfilled the need of both the young people as they playfully swung around the kitchen holding tightly to each other.

"You got your dancin' shoes ready, Hannah Ahrens?" Pearl asked.

"I'm all set, Pearl Lux. I hope you're ready," Hannah replied.

Sleep was elusive at the Sikes' household that night. Rose and Maggie followed by Hessie, climbed wearily to their bedroom. The windows, flung open, ushered in the breezes filtered through the Sycamore trees near the house. Rose and Maggie brushed Hessie's ebony crown of wiry unmanageable hair. One hundred strokes was Greta's instruction to the women. Then Hessie picked up the silver hair brush and unpinned Rose's profusion of hair that escaped down her back. Curls snapped quickly toward Rose's scalp where sweat gathered. Hessie loved this task and Rose sat passively enjoying this final toilet of her day. Quietly she relaxed.

The three women slipped into their white batiste summer nighties and climbed into bed. Maggie and Rose curled their legs crisscrossed beneath the billowing nightgowns. A brittle moon rose rim on rim and shimmered into their windows. An eerie whoo whoo came from the Sycamores as the wind disturbed the lace curtains as if it was confused.

"Spin us a story, Hessie, about your Hidatsa," Maggie pleaded. Rose's face tensed, her eyes apprehensive as Hessie began the story. Maggie's request was unusual. Rose felt uneasy sensing something that was beyond her reach.

"Mary, our housekeeper, taught me about Hidatsa that lived deep within the earth and gathered spirits on their soul quest. She taught them about their ancestors seen in the eagles and hawks that lived high in the trees," Hessie began. The story was old and well rehearsed about protecting the earth and being thankful for the Hidatsa sharing her ample and generous bounty with all her creatures so that the warriors and maidens would know how to live. Their safe passage back to their earthly being would forever teach them these values. The three women reclined into their beds and all seemed peaceful in the household.

Before midnight, Rose and Maggie woke suddenly to Hessie's pitiful wailing. The girls rushed to her bed and grasped Hessie's hands as she wrung them in her lap. They couldn't wake her. She was in a trans. She rocked back and forth then sprang from her bed and bolted from the house. The moon shown brightly from a curdle of clouds. Heat lightning crackled midst the cloud cover and flickered in the sky. Hessie's feet slapped heavily along the worn path toward the river.

Rose and Maggie roused Greta and Hans. "Mama, something's wrong with Hessie. She's had a nightmare."

"This is women's business, this craziness," Hans Sikes spat.

"Enough of that Hans. Hessie had a bad shock with Obediah today, so don't be so harsh!" Greta insisted.

The three women grabbed robes and slippers before they fled down the path Hessie had taken. They hurried along the riverside searching through brush and bushes. Rose was the first to find Hessie and she called to her Ma and Maggie. Between the wind and the rushing rapids of the river, she doubted they would hear her. Hessie's eyes were huge and she stared vacantly as she moaned, "There's blood on the moon. The raven calls his warning of danger. Beware, beware!" The full moon shown down on her clad only in her stark white gown. "Beware there is blood on the moon!" she screamed.

At last Maggie and Greta came upon them and slowly they drew her up and held her as they walked back to the house. Maggie wrung out a cloth in cold water and bathed Hessie's swollen eyes; they tried to soothe her. She crawled meekly into her bed, the episode had left her lethargic. As Rose tucked Hessie in her bed, a glistening black raven perched on the windowsill and peered with a single eye into the room. Rose shivered and hurried to her own bed, threw back the covers and scuttled beneath them and hid her head.

The next morning, Hessie remembered none of the drama of the night before. She gazed around as if the answer to her confusion lay hidden somewhere in the room. The only proof she had were her soiled nightgown and her muddy feet. She refused to believe their story until they proved it to her. It left a strange foreboding in the Sikes's household. They had no doubt Hessie was a seer, but this vision was so sinister.

Rose asked, "Mama, do you think Hessie has foretold something?"

"I think she had a bad scare when Obediah came here yesterday," Greta replied. "Let's hope that's all it was."

It left everyone upset, especially Hans who was completely overcome. His face stretched tight with anger; his eyes spun with alarm. "I knew you were courtin' trouble bringing Hessie Riddle to this home. Didn't I tell you several times not to mess with her? She's had this curse on her since she was born, but, Greta, you wouldn't listen. Now you're responsible for what happens! No telling what will come of this!" Hans' voice was stern.

"Now Hans, I'll deal with this. But we cannot desert Hessie now when she needs us most," Greta pleaded.

"You mark my word. No good has come of her, and never will. I say send her packing! Let Obediah deal with her!"

Worry nagged at Maggie and Rose. They knew Pa always resisted having Hessie Riddle here, and they feared there was nothing they could do to stop him from forcing her to leave.

Friday morning, the sun rose out of the Eastern sky in a huge red ball. The humid air sat in droplets on the corn stalks and garden plants. It shown over the prairie fields so strong you could hear the corn grow. Rose and Maggie were the first up, moving around quietly preparing food before Hans and Greta would start their day.

"I'll make sausage gravy this morning. That's Pa's favorite. You stir up some biscuits and get them done before it gets any later," Rose said.

"I know Pa was upset about Hessie, but I'll not be making biscuits just to please him. Let's make some eggs too and get up a jar of apple butter," Maggie insisted.

Hessie came slowly downstairs and poured hot water into a pan. After washing up she poured the soapy water into a bucket and washed her muddy feet. Rose and Maggie watched all this preparation. Hessie did not believe what had happened during the night till they showed her the mud on her nightgown and feet. She wandered around meekly, not knowing what to say.

"Don't you remember anything about last night?" Maggie demanded. "You nearly scared all of us to death. Now Papa is threatening to make you leave. What do you have to say for yourself this morning, Hessie?"

"Now Maggie, quit it. Hessie's been through enough. Don't you mind her Hessie. Mama and I are concerned about you. Are you sure you're alright? You sit here and have some coffee. Just take it easy," Rose said.

"I'll pour a cup but then I'm goin' out in the garden for awhile, at least till breakfast is over. Then I'll come in and do the dishes and clear up the kitchen."

"Fine," Maggie snorted. "That'd be the best idea, to my mind."

Hessie left through the kitchen door and walked out to the flower garden. Inside Greta and Hans came downstairs followed by their sons.

Hessie sat heavily on a stone bench looking at the morning glories that spilled over the arbor. Bees buzzed in and out, flying from one blossom to another. Dew sat in droplets on the brilliant leaves, the vine's tentacles curled that supported them.

August wanted to know what last night's racket was all about. This set Hans off again, and Maggie and Rose were both in tears before he'd finished ranting and raving.

"Hessie Riddle will not live here any longer. We have had the last of her mental raving. She disturbed everyone last night. It's enough to give a man the creeps. She's unstable and unpredictable. Rose coddles her and Maggie is influenced by what she does. This comes to an end right now!" he pounded the table.

"Lord, Pa, I didn't know I was going to upset you so bad or I never would've brought this up," August lamented.

If anyone noticed Hessie wasn't in the kitchen, nothing was said. Hessie stayed in the garden till the men had left the house. When she entered the kitchen again, the three women welcomed her.

"Was your Pa still upset with me?" Hessie persisted.

"Yes, but don't you worry about that. We'll be busy here all day, and we need you right here with us," Greta insisted.

Mid the left over aroma of cinnamon rolls and coffee, the kitchen door swung in and out as Hessie brought breakfast dishes from the dining room. Maggie and Rose peeled potatoes and prepared the mountain of food needed by the family and food for the next day. Hessie cleared the breakfast dishes from the dining room. Pete, August, Johnny and Ernest had all been there for breakfast. Between meals and housekeeping the day went swiftly. Rose knew her Pa had called the family meeting; and, as usual, the men and their opinions were all that mattered. It caused a sadness Rose couldn't shake.

Finally, she turned to preparations for a happier event--the Woodriver Frolic. Maggie and Rose went upstairs to prepare for bed. Hessie followed after them once the house was in order. She reflected on the events of the day and what that might mean for her future.

Chapter 15

End of the Open Range - The rise of sheep herding by 1880 caused still another conflict with the cattlemen. A final blow to the open range industry came with two unusually severe winters in 1886 and 1887, followed by ten long years of drought.. Those who survived the hazards of the range, established legal title and fenced in the lands, restricted the herds to a reasonable size, and provided shelter and hay, against the rigors of winter. America, *"New Frontiers South and West," Chap. 18, p.666*

The Ravenna Incident

At Shady Grazeland, Obediah Riddle's housekeeper, Mary, heard the rain play a sleep song on the roof. Rain ran from the gutters on the eaves as it pooled in the rain barrel at the corner of the house in the yard. It was tornado weather and some rumbles of thunder along with sudden flashes of lightning, had registered in Mary's brain before she slipped once more into deep sleep. The rain on the garden meant fewer trips to Sweet Creek with milk buckets tomorrow. It was a pleasant sound to all the inhabitants of the house.

Obediah got up early, had his breakfast in the dining room, and read farm reports in the Ravenna newspaper. Mary served a huge breakfast to Obediah and his hired man, Adam Reedy, and then went back to the kitchen. The kitchen door swung briskly, bringing with it the early morning smells of coffee and coffee cake, and biscuits baking slowly in the old iron range. Mary kept an immaculate house and worked daylight till dawn to keep Obediah's house clean and orderly. Today, she made a simple list of things he would shop for at the grocers in Ravenna.

Shortly afterward, Adam fed the double span of mules and harnessed them to Obediah's heavy wagon. Obediah checked his wallet where he placed Mary's grocery list before climbing into the wagon and grabbing up the reins. He clucked to the mules and flicked his reins briefly. The mules trotted off down the road, their hooves making a steady staccato.

An hour later Obediah was at the Ravenna lumber yard, where he pulled the wagon down the lane between the rows of lumber cribs and stopped. He strode into the office, his air of importance enhanced the urgency of his mission. "Got my wagon here and I need lumber. Two by fours, joists, T-bars, nails, shingles, the finishing lumber I need to do the lattice and the roof. Can you maybe have it loaded by say one or two this afternoon for me?" he asked.

"We got other orders, Obediah, but we'll try our best. See the bookkeeper, have her make out your order and she'll see to it I get it. Soon's that happens, we'll set to work for you. Best check back by noon just so you have what you want," Emile Skulla said. He didn't like Obediah. Obediah was full of orders and short on cash. He rubbed Emile the wrong way.

Obediah pulled out nearly $500 in cash. Emile's face registered surprise. Obediah proceeded to the bookkeeper's office, repeated his order, and then paid the amount totaled on his bill.

As he walked out and opened the door, Obediah turned and said, "I'll see you about noon." He hurried out to the street and the grocery store, where he studied Mary's list and handed it to the clerk. He told the clerk he'd pick the stuff up about two o'clock, so would they please have things ready for him by then.

He hurried down the boardwalk to the bank where he deposited a $500 check written to him by the Grant Station business that bought raw timber. He held some money back and after completing his banking, walked on to the Pastime Card Parlor on Main Street.

Hardly anyone was at the Pastime. Obediah sat at one of the poker tables and dealt out a hand of Solitaire waiting for someone to join him. His face was tight and expressionless, he was disappointed no one was around, but continued his lonely game. He rolled a cigarette from his tobacco pouch, pushed his glasses up on his nose and studied the room. A column of sunlight fell through the dirty windows, filtering through the dust motes that danced up and down through a thin layer of smoke.

The bartender polished and straightened bottles on the back bar. He charged the beer on tap and filled a glass half full to test the pump. Emile Skulla entered the Pastime a short time later. Slats Mahoney came in with Alan Schweiz. The bartender was not pleased with the prospect of Slats hanging around. It always meant trouble, but paying customers got service if they acted in a civil manner. Alan ordered beer and Slats ordered a shot of whiskey. The bartender poured the drinks and they paid promptly. Slats eyed Obediah playing Solitaire. Alan picked up his beer and walked over to Obediah's table. "You interested in some five card stud?" he asked.

"I wouldn't mind, but we need more'n two people to play," Obediah replied.

"Slats would play, maybe Emile would sit in," Alan said. He looked inquiringly at Emile. Emile shook his head no.

Doug Watsik entered the Pastime and Obediah greeted him. "Good mornin' Doug, you interested in a few hands of five card stud, drinks on me?" he inquired.

"Never turn down an offer like that," Doug said. He sat at the table and Obediah dealt out the cards from the deck.

The bartender took drink orders. When he returned, Obediah paid for the round for all four men. The poker game went on till nearly noon, when Slats said he needed to head for Cairo. He and Alan cashed out, rose and left the Pastime.

"I was surprised how Slats played cards. Watching all the hands, playing carefully, even buying a round of drinks mid-morning," the bartender commented.

Obediah was disappointed when the game broke up, but then realized the time and folded and promptly left too.

Obediah returned to the lumber yard expecting to have his wagon loaded with his morning orders, only to find the wagon empty and his mules bleating their malcontent. Their blowing and snuffling told of their discomfort and their muzzles were coated with film from thirst. Obediah's eyes stretched tight across his brow, then furrowed with anger when he discovered his mules. He stormed into the office demanding to know what the trouble could be.

"I told you this morning we had other orders here, Obediah," Emile insisted.

"You didn't have any trouble taking my order or ringing up a big sale with my money. The least you could'a done was put my mules in your pen ; and give them some water," Obediah stormed.

"You're welcome to do that yourself. Me and my men are busy. You're full of orders about what you need done, but my men don't work for you," Emile persisted.

Obediah was nettled. This day had not gone as he wanted, and he resented not being given the service he'd already paid for. Somehow he knew Emile wouldn't have even taken his order without payment.

"Would it have been a big deal to send somebody to tell me so I could at least take care of my mules? You was at the Pastime your own self, yet you never peeped that this order wasn't getting done," Obediah steamed.

"Obediah, we'll get to you as soon as we can," Emile replied. He began to think Obediah was going to ask for his money back. He'd made a bad judgment call he was sure he was going to regret.

Obediah unhitched his mules and led them to the stock tank, then unhooked feed bags and gave all of them some oats. He promptly turned them into the pen and walked back to his wagon. As he walked along the cribs of lumber, he called to two of the men and told them he needed his order filled. They pulled the order and proceeded to work on it.

Emile barged up taking in the scene. He looked straight at Obediah and then quickly looked away. He resigned himself, knowing Obediah's true nature. He gave up in despair and walked away. Obediah watched him go; gloat washed across his face.

Obediah led his mules up and harnessed them again, climbed aboard and flicked the reins. The midafternoon sun beat down hard. He'd have to hurry to get this unloaded before dark. He stopped briefly to pick up Mary's groceries at Bybee's Grocery and Mercantile. He bought a slab of bologna, made a sandwich, and took some sugar cubes to treat the mules. The mules brayed their discontent as they bore the load, then headed East toward Shady Grazelands. He rode along slowly, savoring the spicy meat on hard rye.

The day came out better than he thought. He'd showed Emile Skulla a thing or two. Maybe he'd go to Grant Station in the future. This should be the last of the finishing lumber for the house. He wouldn't need too much more lumber to finish up the house. He wished Hessie would move home, but he knew he was daydreaming on that. Things had always been strained with her, but the other day she'd been different, like she maybe woulda' been if her Ma hadn't died. Them girls and Greta Sikes had been a wonder for Hessie.

Obediah clucked to his mules, their big heads swinging from side to side full of empty thoughts as they trotted along. The wagon rolled briskly down the gravel road, puffs of dust accompanied the mules hooves. The flat land was lush and green. The setting sun signaled the wild critters to their nests with evening meals of grubs, worms and field mice, gulped into persisting hungry mouths of their young.

The mules made gentle gurgling sounds sated with the water and oats eaten quickly in the silence of their lonely vigil outside the lumberyard. Shadows deepened as the wagon moved along. Slats Mahoney and his brother rode silently a few miles behind Obediah where they would not be observed.

Obediah came to the crossroads that led to Shady Grazeland. He turned the mules with a strong pull of the reins, worrying the load along to turn slowly at the corner of the road to his land. Evening shadows fell among the firs that lined the roadside. He stopped briefly to light the lanterns on the wagon listening to the sounds of the evening. He heard the whinny of a horse a short distance away. As he climbed aboard, he dismissed the sound; he decided it was in a pasture nearby.

He approached Sweet Creek, glad his journey was nearly at an end. Suddenly, he felt a jolt when something hit him. At first he thought a board had escaped and hit his back, but when he felt the spot, blood poured out. He strained on the mules' reins, which caused them to halt. The second shot he heard clearly, as it pinged past his skull. The next shot spun him out of his seat and across the front of his wagon. The mules bolted and began to run. As the wagon crossed the Sweet Creek bridge, two bullets hit the front mule and it lunged sightless through the rails. Obediah heard the wood shift as it fell in a crooked pattern from the rack. It splintered as it shifted with a cracking sound. It fell forward over him. Finally he couldn't see anything anymore. He heard his pursuer dismount, moving about the wreckage. Then there was another shot and blackness fell. The rush of the wagon spiraling down into the water, the scream of the mules, all melted into the darkness.

Chapter 16

The Gilded Age of Politics The Grange movement dissolved into the Farmer's Alliance giving the farmer's a power hold in politics. The Alliance sponsored ambitious social and educational programs, and welcomed farm men and women. Women were redeemed from their traditional role and elevated some of them into politics. In 1890, Mary Elizabeth Lease, a Kansan, advised farmers to "raise less corn and more hell." Lease joined the Alliance as well as the Knights of Labor, and soon applied her gifts as a speaker to the cause of free silver. A tall, proud and imposing woman, Lease drew attentive audiences. "The people are at bay." She warned in 1894. "Let the blood hounds of money beware."

Death in the Afternoon

The day of the Wood River frolic began like many others. The sun rose glistening as it peeked over the horizon, a tempting sight of gold shimmering as it crested the plains of Nebraska. Moisture from morning dew sat on the garden in distilled drops where ladybugs and dragon flies sipped peacefully on the plant leaves.

Pearl and I rose early to get ready and Hannah came into the kitchen, her face full of sleep and questions.

"I thought I heard you up already. Mercy, I'll have to hurry to get ready if you're about to leave."

"Take your time. We still need to fix a place for the food baskets." Pearl said.

"Pa got up a hunk of ice to put in one of the storage kegs to keep our food cold until we have lunch," I said.

"I put a cake in the pantry yesterday. Don't let me forget it," Hannah said.

"Wouldn't think of letting you forget your cake," Pearl said, his face breaking into a wide grin.

Presently all three of us were outside packing food and checking every little last minute detail. The surrey was polished to perfection. Pearl had added coal oil lamps on the back in case we were late getting home.

The family bid us goodbye. Maudie and Ethel looked wistfully after the surrey as we left the yard. I thought to myself, I have to do something about my sisters heading for spinsterhood unless someone comes along that would suite everyone. They had little clocks ticking away inside them. Little timepieces like coins meant to be spent on domestic things like marriage and babies. Thinking on it was a consuming activity knowing the individuals involved. My mind didn't want to go there, especially not today.

When we arrived at the Sikes's household, everyone came out to see the new carriage.

Wildfire

"Where'd you get this outfit, Jesse?" Pete Sikes inquired.

"From the Blacksmith in Cairo. It's one of those outfits that can sit ten to twelve people. They're usually for sightseeing but light enough for two horses to pull. You can hitch it up with a span of horses if you need to," I continued.

"Never seen one before. What time you and Pearl get home yesterday?" Hans inquired. "You say you were in town all day?"

"Not nearly all day; it took us an hour back and forth. Another two-three hours to make a deal with the blacksmith. Then home again to get the surrey cleaned up, so's it'd be ready for today," I said.

"The two of you together all day or separated some doing other things?" Pete continued.

"Mostly together. Why you askin' all these questions, Sheriff Sikes?" Pearl asked.

"Well, it seems you two were out and about and unaccounted for the whole blamed day. Ain't that right?" Pete continued. Pete Sikes looked at his Pa and then quickly looked away. A knowing kind of look, resigning himself to tried knowledge of human behavior. Pearl and I couldn't fathom what all the questions were about. It stuck in my mind for days afterward.

Hans Sikes walked around the surrey looking it over carefully. Hannah had met him last winter and had heard how difficult he could be. "You enjoying a ride in this contraption, young lady?" He asked.

"Well, yes, I guess I am. Pearl worked so hard cleaning it up, I'd be hard put not to enjoy riding in it," Hannah replied. Hannah had chosen a pale green floor length dress with a bonnet made of the same material. Even Hans Sikes could not ignore what a lovely woman sat aboard the surrey. The look on her face let you see inside, into the private places of her heart. Hannah was in love and she radiated happiness. There was something amazing about her and it was not lost on Hans Sikes.

At last Rose appeared in her Sunday best. She wore a pale green dress also, and her green eyes surrounded by black lashes matched nicely with what she wore. Her appearance was not wasted on me, and my look told the story. Perhaps I had found my own special lady. Time would tell. I helped her into the carriage, my hands touching her soft skin as I crawled up beside her. The surrey shaded the hot summer sun, and the fringes around the top swayed gently in the breeze.

"I say, that breeze is mighty nice overhead. The sun won't go down for hours and we'll be in the shade the whole time," she said.

"Glad you like the carriage, Rose. Pearl worked so hard to make it nice and comfy. We'll surely enjoy this ride through the country today. Perhaps we'll even visit the river where the runaway took place. You do remember the run away, don't you?" I inquired.

Rose blushed. The memory of me grabbing her around the middle and hauling her to the river bank was apparent. She dropped her eyes and said, "How would I ever forget. You were forthright in making me feel safe that day. Papa, remember when Jesse straightened that coachman out, the day I came back from Grant Station early this year?"

Wildfire

Hans looked at his daughter, "I remember the incident when you were coach wrecked on the Loup River in March. I'd almost forgotten about it." Pete Sikes looked inquiringly at his Pa. "Oh, don't concern yourself, Pete. Rosa came home by coach; the driver got inebriated and the horses ran off. Rosa like to expired, before she got home. I'm sure it wasn't anything serious, but she thought so."

The men started back for the house. Pete Sikes continued on inquiring about this near disaster his sister was involved in. Rose gave a sigh of relief driving away. It would be good for her to leave the house for awhile.

When we arrived in Wood River, the campground was a mass of activity. Tents were pitched this year, as last year rain had ruined some of the activities left in the open. We found the food tent decorated with red, white and blue bunting.

Alphonse Lockhorn was in charge of the food tent, and he bustled about with a huge white apron tied around his ample middle. "Howdy folks, I'm cooking weenies and burgers today. You can put your food over on the long table there. We just got the barbeque pit started, but the meat will be ready by dinner time."

"I brought potato salad, but we have it on ice so we'll wait with that. I have an apple pie," Rose added.

"I brought a cake and some dill pickles. The deviled eggs I'll want to keep on ice for awhile," Hannah informed him.

Pearl and I stood watching the whole thing. "Alphonse, I guess there's horseshoes and a few card games around about," Pearl inquired. "Ain't that right?"

"There shore is and more besides. There's cold beer over in that last tent. At least right now there is. If Corrie Veder has her way, it won't be for long," Alphonse added. A frown fell across his face touched with anger that played there.

"Pearl and I noted this. Knowing Corrie, you may have a problem," I agreed. "She isn't too anxious to serve liquor to anyone these days."

Hannah and Rose pulled them away after placing food on the long table. They strolled along the middle of the campground. A calliope played merrily while children rode by on the merry-go-round. Further down the campground was the Granger Hall, and a bandstand with three or four musicians were setting up tripods to hold their music. Delwood Conroy signaled to me to come over. "You got your fiddle with you today, Jesse?" he asked.

"Never thought of it. In all the excitement, I didn't think to bring it. I'd love to play with you," I lamented.

"Otis Burry is going to join us today. He might have one you could borrow. Come back when you hear us start playing," Delwood said. The Granger hall was big enough for a fifty-square-foot dance floor. We moved outside once more.

"You got your dancin' shoes on, Hannah? I'll probably be able to show you a few nice steps," Pearl said.

"Oh, I think I can follow your lead well enough, Pearl Lux. You say the word and I'll be right there."

The look on Pearl's face was worth a million words right at that moment. Happiness seeped through every contour of his face. It was not wasted on Hannah, her face turned up to his. The look there a caress in itself.

By noon, half the county seemed to have arrived for the Wood River frolic. Pearl and I had unhitched our horses and tethered them 'neath shade trees. Other men were carrying food baskets for their girlfriends and wives. The turmoil was a pleasant exchange of neighbors, seeing each other for the first time this spring. Mothers controlled their children as well as they could; warning them to stay clear of the river with threats of discipline if they disobeyed.

Pearl looked around at the crowd. "I'd not thought so many folks would be here today." He carried Hannah's cake holder on one arm and guided her through the crowd with the other.

"Don't drop my cake, Pearl," Hannah teased.

"I'd have to go home and bake another if I did," was his reply.

The food tables were already brimming full, but Hannah found a place for her special cake; and Rose followed with the apple pie.

"We'll need to come back when it's time to eat and put the potato salad and deviled eggs out. Let's set the cooler here in the shade, Jesse." Rose said.

We started back along the way, watching the calliope and the children. The Ferris wheel was full, and nearby the local farmers were trying their luck whacking the huge machine with a large mallet to prove how strong they were. Occasionally, the bell would ring because someone had hit it hard enough. The barker would yell, "Give that gentleman his choice of prizes."

When we walked back to the bandstand, Otis Burry halloed to me. "Come on over and pick a few with us, Jesse."

I beamed and shouted, "Be right there. Rose, would you mind if I play a few tunes with the boys here?"

"I'd love to hear you play, Jesse." Rose replied. There was a look of amazement on her face. She had not known I was a musician. I vaulted up on the bandstand while Otis handed me his specialty, a red violin. As the music started, people began to collect. Before long couples gathered on the dance floor and the caller began a Virginia Reel. Hannah, Rose and Pearl walked out on the floor. Horace Lockhorn joined Rose and they danced off in the pattern of the reel. Next came a doh-see doh number called especially for Corrie Veder. This went on for five or six square dances. At last, Rose and Hannah collapsed on a bench in the shade. Pearl wore a smile that came straight from his heart. I saw all this and took up the notes of "Back Home Again in Indiana."

"Hannah, it's time for you to have the treat of your life and join me in a waltz."

Hannah rose and stepped lightly into Pearl's arms. Resting her hand on his shoulder while his encircled her waist, they move out on the dance floor. People collected and watched as the handsome young man cradled his sweetheart in his arms and danced away. The dance floor was nearly deserted as they danced. Rose listened intently as I played the beautiful melody, pouring my heart out on the strings with the musical talent of a man possessed. My fingers found the notes so sweet and clear, they rang out through the crisp summer air. It was wonderful joining these folks playing their favorite songs. People stood listening to my rendition as I played the song through. The band joined in at the chorus. Pearl and Hannah swung around the floor as if no one else existed but them.

At last the sun shown directly down like a glistening golden disk on the campground as the dinner bell rang. Everyone returned to the food tents while women handed out plates and silverware.

I moved quickly from the bandstand through the crowd to Rose. As we joined Hannah and Pearl, they opened the cooler, brought out their food and placed it on the long table. We moved to the line and proceeded to fill our plates. Rose produced a blanket that had been thrown over the cooler. We sat down and ate in silence. "I suppose that cake will disappear before we ever get back to that table," Pearl whined.

"Let me see what I can do. The pies and cakes weren't cut when we went through the line," Hannah insisted.

She came back with a plate piled with cake and pie. Rose went to the ice cream kegs and came back with bowls heaped high with vanilla ice cream. I whooped "Alright!" as Pearl and I helped ourselves to the pie topped with ice cream and then finished it off with cake. We savored these last moments eating quietly. Rose's pie was apple mixed with bits of rhubarb with a crumby crust that melted in your mouth.

"I think I've just died and gone to heaven, Rose. You've got me wound around your little finger. Say whatever you might wish for and I'll do it."

"Now don't be gettin' carried away over there, Jesse, old buddy. You might not be able to follow through on that promise," Pearl smirked. A smile stretched wide across his face, his eyes electric with the mirth there.

"Oh, I'll do whatever she asks." I insisted.

"Well, we'll see about that," Pearl chuckled.

Once dinner was over the tables were cleared and bingo cards were brought out. Rose and I, and Pearl and Hannah sat across the table from each other. As the bingo numbers were called the excitement grew until Rose's card needed only one number. The caller shouted "B4" and Rose screamed "Bingo!" in unison with two other folks. They split the prize of five dollars three ways. The game went on and Pearl's card needed one number. The caller said "G21" and Pearl yelled "Bingo." This time there were two winners and they split five dollars. Hannah and I won later on, so the four of us shared nearly ten dollars when we left the frolic.

The sun began to set and the air was cooler as we returned to the surrey. Pearl and I hitched up the team and led them to a water trough at the end of the park. It was time to turn for home. The horses nickered softly, glad to be moving about from their solitary vigil.

"It was quite a party they provided today. Is it always that way?" I asked.

"Nearly always. Usually there are more fire crackers, but last year the Syrie boy got a finger blown off. So they forbid fireworks this year," Rose replied. "It was a mess and they couldn't find a doctor to care for him. I was afraid he was going to bleed out before we could get it taken care of. Pete refused to come this year because of that."

"He decided to stay away? Why would he do that?" Pearl asked.

"People thought he was supposed to make it all go away. He was there with the boy the entire time. Addie Syrie, the boy's Mom, fainted right off and Andy, his Pa, was off drinking whiskey under the trees and had passed out. Pete thought it better if he just wasn't here this year."

"Can't say I blame him. I don't think anybody got hurt this year, do you?" I asked.

"I'd thought some of those children would get injured the way they run around and roughhouse. Even some of the little girls were pretty reckless," Hannah said.

"Nobody got hurt on the dance floor—not one," Pearl teased. "See how nice that dancin' was I promised you?"

"Yes, I did and I liked the dancin' very much," Hannah replied looking at Pearl coyly.

We waved to friends and neighbors as we made our way to the trees and packed up our picnic baskets, then turned our horses toward home. As we sped along the road, dust swirled behind the surrey. The cover and fringe swayed nicely in the breeze and cooled and shaded us as we rode along. At last, we came to the county road by the river winding through the flat land, finally reaching Buffalo county.

"That's Obediah Riddle's place over there. Right on Sweet Creek. See that little house here? That's where Hessie was born, and her Mama died there birthin' her. Obediah decided to build across the road in that stand of cedar trees to get out of that house. He was never the same after Delia Riddle died."

"That's a pretty sad story, Rose. How do you know so much about them?" Hannah asked.

"Hessie lives with us. She helps Mama with housework. Maggie and I like to work in the garden and fields, so Mama needed somebody and found out Hessie was looking to leave home. That's when she came to us."

We sped along the county road and turned the corner south along a stand of cottonwood trees. A train sounded its mournful whistle that echoed across the miles from Cairo. When we came to the bridge over Sweet Creek Pearl said, "I'll need to light the lamps soon."

I pulled the horses' reins and began to slow when we realized someone had run off the bridge. Pearl lit the lamps and proceeded ahead to see what had happened. As he raised the lantern, a voice cried out, "Help!" We hurried down the slope of the river bank. A lumber wagon had toppled over, and a man was pinned beneath the lumber just above the water.

"We better see what's happened here before we move anything," I insisted.

We tried to move lumber, but it shifted dangerously. The man was wedged beneath the burden of the load. The mules were pulling, struggling to get up, but each time they tugged the lumber shifted worse.

"Better unhitch the mules before they pull the whole mess over him," Pearl said as he reached for the harnesses. He unhitched the mules, lifted the harness from the one that was dead, and led the rest up on the road. They shivered in the evening light. They were scared and Pearl soothed them with comforting words to calm them while he led them away and tied them to the rails of the bridge.

"Who are you?" I asked the man.

The slow halting answer came back, "Obediah Riddle. I'm hurt bad. I been gut shot and them sidewinders drove me off the bridge."

"Best get a doctor here. Do you think Rose could find one at this hour?" Pearl asked.

"She should know where to go. Maybe Hannah can help. She was along last winter when we picked Doc Dickinson up in Cairo."

As I worked with the loose timber, Pearl went back to the surrey. "Do you think you two could drive to Cairo and get Doc? Do you remember where he lived, Hannah? You were there last winter when we picked him up at his house."

"Yes, I remember. Who is it Pearl?"

"It's Obediah Riddle and he's hurt awful bad."

"He was having trouble last week. Some guys tried to run him off then. He didn't know who they were though," Rose replied.

"You mean he's been having trouble?"

"Yes, and he was really shook up. He came to my folks and told my Pa what happened."

"How far are we from Cairo?" Pearl asked.

"Probably two or three miles. It won't take long to get there," Rose replied.

"I'll light the lanterns for you. I hate sending you alone. There's a pistol under the seat. If anybody tries anything, give them the buggy whip and use the gun. Don't take no chances, ask questions later," Pearl insisted.

Rose turned the surrey around, flicked the reins, and the two women sped away. I managed to pull lumber off Obediah, and Pearl and I carried him up to the road. Pearl set the lantern up and we attempted to see Obediah's wounds. He was bruised and cut where the lumber had fallen on him. The stomach wound seeped in a bloody trail that poured on the ground as we moved along. Pearl fashioned a tourniquet out of his bandana. "You got a undershirt you can spare, Jesse?" he asked. He tied the bandana around Obediah's middle with a compress made of my undershirt.

As we worked, Obediah whispered, "Somebody's comin'. I can hear the horse. Maybe more than one. Dowse the lantern."

We huddled in the shadows as a horseback rider approached and slowed. Whoever it was walked around the wreckage, and examined the mules tied to the bridge. The mules shied away from him smelling danger. "You down there. You hear me?" a voice shouted. We realized at once it was Slats Mahoney.

"That's one of them come back. I bet they're all here," Obediah whispered.

"Make yourself known! Who are you?" I shouted.

"None of yer damn business. I just come back to finish the job here. Guess I didn't do the job right the first time. Where the hell are ya anyway." He pulled his gun and shot, but it went over our heads.

"Right over here," Pearl pulled his gun and fired. The bullet struck flesh and Slats screamed.

"You bastard, you've shot me! Now I'm comin for ya'!" He shot several bullets that went wild.

Pearl raised his gun. The barrel tipped slightly with the speed of the bullet. The sound roared as the gun flashed and exploded in the silence of the night. In the flash of fire I saw Slats Mahoney reel and plunge head first into the stream.

"Didja' kill him mister?" came Obediah's hoarse whisper.

"I'm afraid so. He wasn't about to quit the first time," Pearl replied. His voice shook with emotion. I knew he hated what had happened, but he had no choice. The sky had changed to a rosy hue shining through ragged clouds. Heat lightning flashed in the distance as the wind picked up and churned the gathering clouds like pink cotton candy. An early moon rose. I lit the lanterns again and examined Obediah. "This man would not've had a chance if we hadn't come this way."

Violence has a chain reaction on all its recipients. It fires a volley that ricochets through the nerves of every person it visits upon. It seemed ages before the women returned, Doctor Dickinson followed close behind with his buckboard.

"We got another injured man, Doc. Slats Mahoney come back to be sure he finished Obediah off. Pearl shot him and he fell over the side of the bridge. He's down there in the water. Good thing Pearl's a good shot or you might've had a bunch of dead men when you returned. "

"Well, let's have a look here and see what can be done." He examined Obediah and it was plain he was not encouraged by what he found. Obediah was weak from loss of blood.

"Did you bring this load clear from Ravenna today?" Doc asked.

We had to lean close as Obediah spoke, he was so weak. "Yes, played cards with Slats and one of his buddies early mornin' at the Pastime. They knowed I recognized them. Won money too then cashed out and left. Played for couple hours. Didn't think no more on it. They acted cocky. I know these two were the ones run me off the road last week. Made my mules run away," Obediah lisped softly.

Doc held Obediah's hand, taking his pulse. "You women got a blanket back there someplace?" he asked.

"There's a couple blankets and a small pillow," Hannah said. She and Rose placed Obediah's head on a pillow then covered him with the blankets. He was cold and in shock; he began to shiver.

"Obediah, is there anything you want to tell us? Anything we need to know?" Doc asked. His voice shook as he said this.

"Tell Hessie she'll have a house to finish. She's my only living kin. See she gets a fair deal. I 'ner was much of a pa, tell her. I'm right sorry about that." Obediah was quiet at last.

Doc took out his watch and continued to hold Obediah's hand. "Well folks, he's gone. It's a shame we got people like that one layin' yonder in the ditch. If you'll help me we'll put Obediah in my buckboard. I'll take him to the mortician in Cairo. You best get these women home before they have the militia out lookin' for you. If Pearl needs anyone to speak for him, call on me. We'll have to load the other man soon as I check on him."

Pearl and I held the lanterns as we approached the still form in the creek. As we suspected Slats Mahoney lay prone in the water.

"Well, you took as good as you handed out, you gol' durn varmint. Ain't never been worth a damn. Causing nothin' but misery from the first breath you took.," Doc Dickinson said. He closed Slats Mahoney's eyes and the three of us climbed back up the bank of the stream. Carefully, we placed the bodies side by side in the flatbed of Doc's buckboard. All of us watched as he rode off toward town.

"You gonna be okay, Pearl?" Rose asked. "You did the world a favor getting rid of him."

"Even so, we're all keeping an eye out now for Pearl," Hannah whimpered.

Pearl put his arms around her. "Nothin' is gonna' happen 'cause I gotta dance again with you. Many, many times," Pearl consoled her.

Tears poured down Hannah's face as the two climbed in the back of the surrey where Pearl held Hannah close. Rose and I took the front seat. "We'll come back tomorrow and clean this up," I said. "Those mules will be fine till we get back here early tomorrow."

We sped off into the cool summer night. The horses moved at a good clip, and before long we would arrive at the Sikes's farm. We had a task to perform and Hessie Riddle headed up the list. Was Hessie Riddle psychic? No one would ever doubt again that Hepsabaugh Riddle had an ear for the unknown, and an eye for the unseen.

Chapter 17

Charles Dana Gibson created the image of the "new woman" in his drawings for Life Magazine in 1890. Tall, spirited, athletic, and chastely sexual, the Gibson girl's clothing was constructive shedding bustles, hoop skirts, and hourglass corsets. Shirtwaists and other natural styles did not hide but enhanced the female form. Women's styles began to take on a more public character. The department store, among the new urban institutions catering to women, became a temple for the emerging roles of the New American woman as consumers. Reflections of a feminist, 1893.

Hessie Riddle

It's hard growing up female. When I was five or six, small and insignificant, with my withered hand, I was cursed with an eternally sorrowful Pa, who never seemed to see my needs. Becoming a teen was even worse. As my bones grew about as long as they ever would, we finally got a permanent housekeeper. She did not arrive before my monthly bleeding began, and I went into hysterics not knowing what it was all about. The look on Pa's face didn't help matters as it frightened him more than me. There was that brief moment between knowing and not knowing what had happened. We both found that regular events were taking an irregular turn. My fear abated as Pa began to explain. Try as he might, he could not form the words with his lips. What he said was, "I'll get someone who can help you. Just calm down."

That evening small clean cloths appeared with rubber elastic and pins that confounded me even further to figure it all out. Pa brought Mary home the next day and simply said, "Mary's gonna' live here from now on and take care of you and the house."

He had some kind of blinders on and I was plain and simple invisible until this revelation he had that I was alive and he had responsibility. Leave it to Pa to figure he'd fixed things. Just nail boards in place. That would keep everything in, nice and safe.

Those times, I'd melt down into tears, no real reason, as unpredictable emotions slithered through me like an eel sending me slamming to my bedroom. Moods left me depressed and sent me into places I couldn't understand not until I was much older at least. Childhood had left me as briefly as Spring, it was all over.

The day Mary came, my legs were long enough to reach the bottom rung of the kitchen stool I'd sat on since I was two years old. It sits there in the corner of the kitchen like it's being punished now. The time before was like freedom, before my legs got this long. A small time that seemed like seconds now, it was so brief. I wish I'd never grown this big, why couldn't I just stay small so I wouldn't ever have the memories that exist in this house. The ones that make Pa and I both sad. Memories were all over the place, flat like a deck of cards, spread out side by side.

There was the day Pa decided to build a new house. Just as soon as he had a frame up and the main floor finished, we moved over there. Two bedrooms, living room, dining room and kitchen. My freedom all got lost somewhere over in that old house with all the pain and sorrow.

Pa looked at me like he couldn't remember me. Is one small person so hard to remember? He studied my face like he don't know me anymore. I wish I'd never grown this tall never. He shook his finger at me when I raged at him. It trembled like I had picked on him, making him the bad guy. Huge, library sized arguments, full of hard edged words and accusations flew between us. My hurried apology was dusty and brittle as that empty house we left behind.

Afterwards, at least I felt more settled in my own mind, could calm myself and be somewhat reasonable. At my first opportunity, I slipped outdoors to the leftover smell of cut grass, heat and sweat; the time to escape to the creek and skinny dip and then dry in the hot sun. Stepping sideways from my own thoughts that scattered and freed me from mental confusion.

At least Mary was receptive to this half child-half woman she'd been assigned to. Mary did things in the kitchen that amazed me. In time I would learn her skills with pot and skillet. While she taught me to clean and spread fresh bedding for the chickens, collected eggs and ready them for our creamery in Ravenna, I learned more than just how things should be done. She gave me some pride.

Her patience brought about my first awareness of who I am. She taught me to milk cows because it exercised my arm, all crippled from childbirth when my Ma died--The reason why Pa was short tempered, why he gave me those strange searching looks of his.

Mary brushed my hair after it was washed, till it shown. It fell shoulder length then and hid my scarred face where the doctor had used forceps to bring me into this life of torment. Mary said, "It isn't bad, and you can learn to wear bangs to hide the scars there on your face." It falls to my shoulders like a heavy shiny curtain, too long now and needing a trimming. Mary braided it in a coil around my head. She said, " It'll keep you cooler like this."

I learned that I "was" smart. Mary would prove out whatever I did by going over things and pointing out not only what I did but what I could do better. Mary made me feel I "was" a person. That I was worthy, that I could learn to do all kinds of things, and that my deformity "was not" the whole me.

When I turned fifteen Greta Sikes came to Pa and asked, "Would Hessie be interested in moving to our farm to work?" At first Pa was full of reservations about how this could have happened. When Pa asked Mary about this she admitted that Greta was a friend of hers. She often talked to her at the stores in Cairo or after church Sundays. Pa was still suspicious about how this all happened. Like I was deserting him trying to get away.

I asked, "Why do you always think the worst of me, Pa? I don't even know the Sike's family."

He whispered an apology and slid out through the door. He's bewildered with what I've become. I figured my days of freedom were really over if I went with Greta Sikes. People seem to like her; but her husband is another matter. Pa says he commands respect. Go ahead and command it, I'm staying right out of his way. Yes sir, just keep to myself.

A few weeks later Mary bundled up my few clothes, extra socks and undergarments--those pantaloon things that cut at the waist and feel hot in summer sun. It would seem a body should be free of all these restraints when weather is so hot clothes get soaked with perspiration.

Mrs. Sikes put me in the bedroom with Rose and Maggie. They look nothing alike and differ in their ways so much it's a shock when you finally figure it out. Maggie, between her fits of temper and her whining, can be a trial. I learned quickly as I overheard her tattling to Hans Sikes about some trivial matter that she'd trumped up because I differed with her. Oh she's slick. So my first opportunity, I slapped her face. "Go tell your Pa that and you'll be in the kitchen doing my work instead of being outside like you'd rather do. Your Ma will send me home." Later, I heard Rose point this out to her too. Maggie sat with her face stretched tight in a scowl.

Several nights after that I began having nightmares. The kind you'd wake up from all soaked with perspiration and shaking like a leaf. At first I thought this to be nonsense, but then I found things happened that I dreamed about. I was channeling some things. I saw Pa's mules bolt over the side of our bridge. I saw Pa surrounded by a river of blood. I heard his cries of

Wildfire

pain. Afterward, I'd calm down and slip into a deep sleep, velvety and soft, not the flimsy stuff before my dream began. Chatter in the kitchen effected the whole family. Maggie would complain about disturbed sleep or some such thing. She wanted everyone to know how she had so much to contend with.

Things got real testy with Mr. Sikes after that. I believe he was afraid of what I would reveal. I had one gut wrenching nightmare. I dreamed of these little boys running around in my hands, their feet so tiny they were like pinpricks meandering wildly until they fell silent. They disappeared into my palm like droplets of blood and were no longer visible. When I woke and searched my hands, Rose asked, "What are you looking for Hessie? Do your hands hurt?"

I'd frightened both Maggie and Rose; I knew I had to explain. When I told them about those little boys a shiver ran through all of us as to what it might mean. Maggie turned pale as her bed sheets. Rose's big eyes were wide and darkened with fear.

Afterward Greta had her Sewing Bee and one of her guests mentioned the Howe boys. It seemed they had their throats severed by a field hand, and they ran helter skelter around the corn field till they bled out. The hired man had run off before the Howes found their boys all bloody and dead in their cornfield.

Greta and Hans had tried for many years to buy that acreage near my Pa's place, across Sweet Creek. I knew those little boys because Pa sent me over there with a basket of food. Their Ma was poorly and never had another child. Although she tried many times, now her only two living children would have a headstone in the cemetery near their garden, just like all the rest of those babies she lost.

Rose told Maggie and me that Jesse Peers had outbid her Pa at their auction. The Howe's had loaded up their belongings and left Nebraska. Hans Sikes had his first reason to dislike Jesse Peers, when that happened. I asked Rose why Jesse would want that piece of land, and she looked at me like I was out of my head for sure. "It seems them two little boys that died there would forever linger especially since they were rundown and cut in that cornfield," I said. Maggie got upset and glared in my face. Her eyes snapped with scorn. She said I should be ashamed even talking about such things and threatened to tell her Ma.

I said, "Go ahead, seems like a quick way for me to be shed of this place."

Rose pulled me close to her as we walked along the garden path. "Hessie, please don't leave here, especially now."

It seems ages ago that this revelation visited upon me, when my life changed from my dreams so much I can hardly recognize who I am. Hard enough to realize Sheriff Sikes is set to arrest Pearl Lux for the death of that miscreant, Slats Mahoney, who shot my father in cold blood.

The Mahoney's were hard put to accept their brother's death, but even more than that threats against Sikes had made him skulk about, a frightened man. Even with the offer of help from several families, he continues to do nothing.

Hans Sikes demanded his son Pete turn in his badge. Moreover, he's sending our precious Rose off to

Wildfire

Colorado to live in the home of Annie Runge until this matter has been settled. This house has been eternally in turmoil I'd like to be shed of. Greta Sikes has been unable to bring about any kind of compromise on this matter with her husband though she has tried hard enough.

About the most pleasant time I've seen in my time here was when Jesse Peers came to invite Rose to the Woodriver Frolic. My, didn't we try our best to please Hans Sikes so he'd be agreeable. Even then he had a problem accepting the best the women had to offer. Overlooked all the work Maggie, Rose and I went to in the kitchen to prepare the food he liked best. Never said thank you or show any sign he appreciated what we did.

Sorrow has gathered me in a firm grasp. I must let it go like the fluff on a mature dandelion, let it blow away with the next breeze. It is hard though and grabs at my thoughts. I feel fragile as the hummers that feed on the blooms in Greta's garden. My heart beats nearly as fast as those delicate wings.

Chapter 18

A Violent Culture Although often exaggerated in films and television shows, the western frontier during the second half of the nineteenth century was indeed a violent time. Guns, rifles, and knives were prevalent, and people readily used them to resolve their disputes. The brutal requirement for self-preservation on the frontier or in the mining communities led to a change in the long-standing premise of English common law that required a person to flee or retreat in the face of a violent threat. In 1876, a court rules that a "true man" was no longer obligated "to fly" from an assailant— As the famous frontier Marshal James Butler ["Wild Bill"] Hickok explained, "Meet anyone face to face with whom you disagree, and if you meet him face to face and took the same risk as he did, you could get away with almost anything [including killing] as long as the bullet was in the front." America , "The New Frontier, A violent culture." (Chap.18), p.670

A Day To Remember

Jesse drove the horses down the winding country road, and across the Sweet Creek that fled like a brilliant ribbon neath the crowning moon. He looked up the mighty stream of water that poured rich gifts of silt and loam to its banks that enriched the land. Sweet Creek traveled beside the road a man could travel to anywhere he had a mind to.

Rose sat quietly at his side gazing at the passing maples, oaks, cedars, and cottonwoods. They had turned a brilliant green and scattered leaves like rusted shillings on the ground. Lightning bugs drifted along the valley in billows of icy crystalline lights. The landscape now a soft grey as they flew along, their coach bells tinkled beneath the lantern lights on the surrey.

For a moment, they felt peaceful and mindless, postponing the inevitable. At the Sikes home, the yard and roadway were ablaze with lantern light. The household stirred as Rose became aware of the alarming scene before them. Heat lightning cracked and disappeared in the distance. Jesse put his arm around Rose's shoulders to comfort her. Her eyes were electric with apprehension and worry as a hint of fear lingered there.

"Don't worry Rose. We'll explain what's happened. We were doing the right thing here. Your Pa can't fault us with that," Jesse insisted.

"I hope you're right Jesse. Just know that whatever takes place, I had a great day with all of you. Sometime, will you play some music for me?" she asked.

"Be my pleasure, Rose. Just say the word and I'll do just that," Jesse's face lit with a smile.

He pulled the surrey to the front door as Pearl stepped down and collected the food carriers Rose brought. Hans Sikes followed by Greta burst out the front door, followed by Maggie and Hessie Riddle. Hans was angry with potent eyes that scolded them. "Just what have you folks been up to that took nearly all night?"

"Now Papa, I can explain if you'll just listen," Rose said.

"You go straight to your room young lady. Don't come out till I tell you to," he shouted.

Greta confronted her husband. "Hans be reasonable, and let her explain!"

"No need to get upset with Rose. We came along the road and found Obediah Riddle wounded by a gunshot," Hessie gasped at Jesse's words, trying to fathom what had happened.

"Make your story good, young man," Hans sneered.

"You doubt my word? Ask Pearl or check with Doctor Dickinson, who came out to help us," Jesse insisted.

Greta motioned to the girls. "Hessie, you and Rose come inside. We need to get this story straight."

"That's right, Hessie, we need to talk. Please, come inside. Good evening, Jesse. You too, Hannah and Pearl," Rose spoke softly, dreading the task. The three women gathered moving as one shadow up the front walk into the house and out of sight.

The silence was a golden coin to be parceled out carefully. Pearl offered his explanation first. "I understand Obediah was run down last week when he came to your farm. We figure the same bunch followed him from Ravenna today, rousted his team, chased him down and shot him. His wagon load of timber tumbled over on him. He was pinned underneath it before we came along. He suffered a gunshot in his belly and died just about the time Doc Dickinson got there. Doc just left us a little while ago. We left Obediah's mules tied to the Sweet Creek bridge. We need to go back in the morning and care for them."

"You expect me to believe all this? You two think you can keep my daughter out half the night, cook up this story and make me believe it? You get your ornery hide out of my yard, right now," he ordered.

A wail raised from Hessie's eternal soul sounded from inside the house, a message to the world of a wounding that Hessie released into a single breath. Letting the world know of her torment, the pain of being hurt so deeply came in a string of vowels. Her last contact with the world had been cancelled by some scoundrel she didn't even know, would never see, could never repay.

Somehow Hans Sikes realized that what Jesse and Pearl swore to was truth. He was gripped by a sudden panic, his face molten like he was about to have a seizure, unaware that the unwanted guests had suddenly left. Jesse and Pearl entered the surrey, clucked to the team and evaporated down the road into a circle of light that twinkled along in the darkness till it disappeared.

"Never knowed a man to be so block headed he confused himself," Pearl muttered.

"I've heard he was a strange one, but a man almost has to experience some such thing to believe it. How are you doing there, Pearl? This wasn't altogether the way you planned to spend this day," Jesse soothed.

Pearl studied his hands for some hidden message there. "Can't change what happened. It bodes eternally that I have this unwritten duty to take care of everybody. All's I want is a quiet corner of the world to spend with this pretty woman. That ain't askin' too much, do ya think?"

Jesse looked in Pearl's face. Anything he said would not take the pain away. "I'd say that's about right and you're entitled."

Hannah folded into Pearl's arms and cuddled there. There was nothing between the two now, their separateness drifted together like a piece of music. Her lips only a whisper away, her breathe so close he could breathe it. The night was cool and still and untroubled. Moths sought comfort around the carriage lamps for warmth. The steady clop of the horses' hooves played a crescendo to the descending darkness.

The Sikes household would be awake for hours on this day. Hessie felt damaged she was hurt so bad. Moreover, she was concerned that her dear Rose had to experience her father's death. This disturbed her. Greta's attempts to comfort her were futile. She felt this awful pain, a surge of energy that raced through her. Wailing only made matters worse so she inhaled her breath and let it go slowly to keep control of herself. At last spent, she fell asleep sobbing in her private snare of pain, shut up in a dark hole of unconscious sleep.

When Hessie woke, she watched the sun come up rim on rim, till it lit the morning sky. It boiled up brightly, lighting the trees that raised their limbs to the sky. Poison sumac and elder vines twined around the trunks in scarlet scarves. The wind became confused

Wildfire

and blew dust whirlwinds around the prairie grass. Breath spiraled from her mouth in a cloud of steam, her sign to the world that she was very much alive. She gazed up at the warm billows that floated away and swore her vengeance. Whoever had done this terrible thing would pay and she would see to it. Her words were a silent stream of thought in a string of vile promises.

Greta Sikes called from the kitchen. "Maggie! Rose! You and Hessie come in here."

The three women came into the dining room. Hessie's face told the terrible toll the events of the past few days had taken.--circles under her eyes, nervous movements, her hair swept into a tight net and her dark gingham dress was caught at the waist in a stark white apron. Her eyes moved nervously around the room from one face to another. Rose moved to Hessie's side and extended her hands as they sat in the small settee.

Greta took cups and saucers out of the china cabinet. "Sometimes events follow in such a way we all feel vulnerable. We're only human, there's only so much we can do. Even though we'd put up a terrible struggle, sometimes we lose."

Anger curled up tightly in Hessie's gut. "Slats Mahoney is dead! Pearl made fast work out of that devil disguised as a human. Pearl shot him. Slats came back when they were trying to get the blood stopped from Obediah's wounds. I don't think he realized anyone was there. That happened while Hannah and I went to get Dr. Dickinson," Rose said. "Slats came back to wipe Obediah out. He thought he hadn't got him the first time. In the dark, he shot five or six more times but didn't hit anything. It gave a clear view for

Pearl. He shot him in the arm and thought that would stop him. But Slats kept on coming. Only took one bullet to pick him off." Rose went to the kitchen for the coffee pot and returned. "He wasn't proud of what happened You could see in his face how awful he felt." She clasped Hessie in her arms. Greta moved beside her and extended her arms around both women.

"Hessie was forewarned about danger three nights before we went to the frolic in Wood River. I'm sorry we were so late, Mama, but we couldn't come away from there any sooner than we did. We made every minute count." Rose poured coffee in the waiting cups.

Greta looked at Rose. "Where's Obediah's Body?"

Rose passed her mother a cup. "Dr. Dickinson took him back to Cairo to the morgue."

"Well, he's the County Coroner, so that's all fine and good. I'm thinking Pearl and Jesse may be in trouble when the Mahoney's come looking for Slats. You might want to think about where the two of them might go for awhile until this gets straightened out," Greta added.

"I will ponder on that. I'd not thought I'd be tested on a day that was planned for pleasure," Rose lamented.

Pete Sikes walked into the dining room. "Best figure on going somewhere safe until this blows over or we see that justice is served. We've had a powerful lot of problems from this Mahoney bunch."

Sunlight poured into the room. It was brilliant gold and heat lightning forked into the green velvet of the farm fields outside. Rose's thoughts bunched privately like worms in a bait can. Brave people keep the fire in their guts out of their heads and lead sane lives. What we are dealing with is a group that boiled like a cauldron of insanity all the time, she thought. Her concern for Pearl, for that matter all of them, was paramount. They would forever be startled by any unforeseen action until the remaining Mahoneys were dead or imprisoned. It left her feeling apprehensive and regret, strangers to her peaceful country way of life.

The day of Obediah's funeral was a typical summer day. Dew sparkled on the leaves of the garden plants in glistening jewels where hummingbirds and goldfinches sipped nectar and fussed among the plants. Pearl must soon ride off saddle back toward the Medicine Bow country and the home of Lone Buffalo where he would be safe until it was time for his return.

By mid-morning, everyone was dressed and ready for church. When the Sikes arrived at the church, hardly anyone was there. As they pulled up and tied the horses at a hitching rail, Emory and Sara Ann Peers held food and cake pans, while Maudie and Ethel climbed from the Peers' surrey. The girls carried the food to the church hall, their faces tight with grief and sorrow.

The Sikes brought several covered casseroles and cakes and pies for the potluck at the church hall after the service. When all this was accomplished, neighbors and friends began to arrive. Rose escorted Hessie Riddle, who was so distraught one doubted if she should be there. Maggie and Rose moved along with her to the pew. Pete and Johnny followed down the aisle of the church. Pete wore his gun belt and brandished his sheriff's badge. Dr. Dickinson, his wife and children greeted everyone as they entered the church and found their pew.

Hessie Riddle was having such a struggle it tore at her. Her strength to face this seemed to come from inside. Occasionally, a gut wrenching sob would issue from her, but she fought to get through the final fateful event. She needed to participate in her father's farewell. Jesse found Rose and moved forward with them as Maggie squeezed in beside them. Rose's eyes were full of pity and defused anger boiled there. A strange sensation whispered across the room. A premonition of things to come no one wanted to face.

Jesse was moved to the core as he watched Rose comfort Hessie. He reacted without reservation, anticipating Rose's every move or emotion as it happened. He found himself in an abyss of shock and wonder. He cherished this woman of the plains. Hardly more than a girl; she was so mature and poised. Her depth for caring surprised him as she comforted Hessie. Her words and gestures leaking strength and determination Hessie seemed to absorb and need.

The service was quiet and orderly. Obediah's life had not been exemplary, but it was based on honesty and the strength everyone in this land recognized and respected. A tenacity claimed him until someone had murdered him in cold blood. There was something demeaning in his death as if he'd been humiliated publicly and something needed to be done about it. Thinking on this is a consuming activity and one Jesse did not want to dwell on today. In the near future, though, he would need to act on his conscience to do the right thing.

Wildfire

Hessie burst out crying at some of the statements about Obediah in the service. Huge out bursts of sobs required both Rose and Jesse to calm her.

At last the service was over, and friends and neighbors were invited to join in the meal served by the women of the parish. They moved slowly out of the church, feeling relief that this point had been reached. The families walked in silence to the church cemetery. The small Cairo resting place where nearly everyone there, at one time or another, placed a loved one during their tenacious struggle prairie families all experienced. This was another of the tragedies the pioneer families suffered in creating a place in the future for themselves in the plains. The somber group gathered around the grave side, while the pall bearers bore Obediah's casket to his final resting place. The minister began with the 23rd Psalm. "Yeah though I walk through the valley of death, I fear not for the Lord is with me. He is my shepherd--"

As the casket lowered slowly into the earth, Hessie cast roses into the grave upon the casket. She cried as if her soul was about to burst through her skin. Her eyes were wide open and so brilliant they jittered in their sockets. There was an aura about her, some strange presence that developed as she stood at the grave side. As Rose gazed upward into the clear blue sky, a raven rested on the church steeple. A shudder passed through Rose as she stood with her arm around Hessie. As the service ended, everyone turned toward the church hall where lunch awaited. Obediah Riddle passed from this life.

Chapter 19

In 1891, large ranchers organized a "lynching bee" to eliminate rustlers and hired gunmen to do their bidding. In 1892, two dozen mercenaries with an equal number of ranchers, dubbed themselves "regulators" and set out to wipe out the rustlers. After killing two men, the vigilantes fled north, only to be surrounded by a handful of small ranchers. The arrival of federal cavalry prevented a massacre. The cattlemen turned to bounty hunters, who murdered rustlers. The bounty hunters were very often convicted and hanged. <u>America</u>, "The New West," (Chap.18), p.667

The Summer Of Regret

The summer in the plains is torrid at times, and as I stand among the cornstalks, they grow each day giving to the expression "hearing the corn grow." Maudie, Ethel and I walk once a day to the garden with our skirts drawn up front between our knees, and gathered into a neat waistband. It gives extra pockets to stow vegetables to be carried to the house for our meals served at noon. The abundant noon meal is the time the men rest briefly and go again to the fields.

My mind is heavy with worry a good deal these days, when I ponder as whether Pearl and I will ever have a peaceful life or will we spend our lives out running the law. Sheriff Sikes was here yesterday to talk to Pearl and Jesse about the murder of Hessie's Pa, Obediah Riddle. In my heart I know Pearl did the only thing he could, when he shot down Slats Mahoney out on Sweet Creek the day of the Woodriver Frolic. Sheriff Sikes listened to Pearl intently, but didn't relieve anyone's mind with his pronouncement that Pearl should not flee Nebraska until the whole story comes out. I was furious Sheriff Sikes could ask all these questions, in a seemingly practiced, smooth manner. He sounds dangerous. He's done this dozens of times before. We tried to answer in a like manner, but I think we created a web of information that could be interpreted any way Sheriff Sikes chooses to do so. He changed our lives in one conversation. The Mahoney's reacted to the news Slats was dead with a unified vow of revenge. It would seem Pearl would be best served to flee, regardless of Sike's admonition not to.

My heart lies heavy in my bosom, loaded down with the uncertain knowledge that my head tells me could be nonsense. To ponder on what could be is fool hardy and not worth the anguish I feel. Sweat pours down my face and throat in rivulets like tears, taunting and tickling over me. It startled me, the intimacy it produced. It felt good to be out here working hard, breathing in tandem ridding me of my tension. The occasional brisk breeze whirling over us, feels fresh blasting around our bodies, discarding our careful arrangement of hair and dresses drawn up in folded pleats and tied round our waists.

The carrots, onions, and potatoes, shook clean of the moist dirt, disappeared into our skirts and will soon find their way to our cooking pots. No doubt by now Ms. Peers has killed and cleaned enough chickens to sate the hunger of the men, who arrive sweaty and tired from the fields.

Alfalfa scythed straight from the field and stacked for the livestock creates enough work for more people than the head count available here at the farm. Soon new men will appear down the ribbon of road that folds over the hills and flatland, allowing the Peers to harvest their crops in the fields around us.

The first ears of succulent corn are ready for the boiling pot now, their husks strewn to the cows and horses in the pens. I think with melancholy daydreams of Pearl and his continued effort to bring a few feral horses in from the plains to train and sell to the farmers. His horses are needed and coveted by the people who have heard of his work training horses. Farmers, especially, like the ponies their families purchase to ride and care for.

At dinner time, everyone filed into the dining room, the windows thrown wide to pull in any breeze that might whirl through to give some relief from the heat. Everyone sat with heads bowed while Emory Peers said a brief blessing. He grabbed a bandana from his overall pocket and sopped sweat from his brow and neck. "This weather is enough to parch a man's brain. A shower would be a huge relief right now to the land and all of us as well. Sara Ann, bring us coffee and sandwiches this afternoon in the field."

"Gladly. We'll bring round a wagon with food mid-afternoon," she acknowledged.

"Use the new dun mare I brought in last week," Pearl said.

"The new one? Do you think that wise?" Ethel asked.

"That's right," Pearl replied. "Never saw such a beautiful horse. Unusual coloring with burnished straw that looks black till she walks about. Then you see the mix of straw color with the black hair. She turns a gold Grey. Prettiest horse I ever saw. Black legs and mane that tapers down the back of all four legs. Never saw such markings. She takes no nonsense from the other horses. Those great black eyes flash with fire when she interacts with the other horses. Big Red sidled up and she let him know right off she wasn't tolerating any foolishness from him. She'd drop a foal to own bred to a black stud."

The excitement in his voice lightened my heart and lifted my spirit. We tend to be worried so much lately. Violence has taken an uncommon amount of turns in this household. It's time we made the effort to bring some relief from all this sadness that plagues us. I look upon my Pearl, my precious loving Pearl. How could anyone entertain thoughts of Pearl doing anything but good.

Jesse's next remark brought out a firestorm of opinions. He looked down at his rough cotton homespun shirt, a trail of sweat evaporating 'neath his underarms. "This place is a mighty lot of work for all of us. But Pearl, if you feel you need to leave here till things turn around, you shouldn't give it another thought. You and Hannah could leave here and ride off toward Medicine Bow where B. J. could be found. He'd put you up till the whole mess blew over.

Emory and Sara Ann nodded in agreement, vowing their support if Pearl decided to leave. It had never occurred to me they would feel this way. I found an explosion of glee on it's way through my senses in a chain reaction of joy. At the same time, I was nearly certain Pearl would stay right here and face whatever was to be.

After dinner the men collected around the pump, watching fresh water gin into the stock tank. Del Cole and Ephraim Hobbs were the first to see Lone Buffalo ride up on a pinto stallion. They greeted him by clasping hands, and pounding him on the back. Pearl spied the stallion and hurried toward Lone Buffalo. Jesse had not seen the animal and walked quickly forward, eyeballing Lone Buffalo's mount.

"Where did you get that pinto, Lone Buffalo?" Jesse asked.

"We captured him up in Medicine Bow country this spring when Pearl rode up there," Buffalo replied.

"Early Dawn must be doing fine if she let you ride her horse," Pearl commented.

The look on Lone Buffalo's face was a mixture of worry and pride. His eyes stretched tight across his face as he spoke. "Early Dawn has had her baby and that takes up most of her time," he replied.

The men chorused congratulations to Lone Buffalo on his new baby. His smile crested broad across his face.

"What brings you down here, Lone Buffalo?" Jesse inquired.

Mrs. Peers walked out in the yard wondering what all the noise was about. She stood listening intently to what Lone Buffalo was saying.

"We know your mama's skill with medicine. We don't have women around anymore that have skills with birthing and babies. They left and move to other places. Early Dawn is nearly worn out, we wondered if Mrs. Peers have something for baby who cries so much. Early Dawn is up day and night with him. She say horse need exercise to ride here, ask if Mrs. Peers had anything to help."

"Does the baby cry especially after feeding? Isn't comfortable no matter what you do? Then doubles up with a cramp and pain in his belly?" Mrs. Peers inquired with concern.

"Yes, that so. We afraid Early Dawn doing something wrong with him," Buffalo lamented. "She afraid baby die."

"I'll give you some ginger powder to mix with some gruel, cornmeal or oatmeal ground fine. If after awhile this doesn't work, then your baby needs to have plain goat's milk. That's all for awhile. I'll give you instructions how much powder to use. Only a little bit will do lots of good," Mrs. Peers added. "If that doesn't work, I'll come up, but this should work fine." Mrs. Peers gathered up some fine powder and an ointment she'd made from goose grease. Once again she gave Lone Buffalo careful instructions. His face began to relax as she talked describing what he should do.

"Cynci said you good with doctoring. She not know about this though," Buffalo said.

"How are Cynci and B J.?" Mrs. Peers asked.

"Doing as good as anyone. Government in our affairs. Cynci messing with Yellow Calf, and B. J. always watching, eyes snapping with anger."

"Cynci must be up to her old tricks," Mrs. Peers lamented. "I'd hoped she'd change some and settle down. B. J. is a good man."

Jesse faced this mother, "She's always at the bottom of something that's amiss. Look at Maudie and Ethel."

"They didn't exactly make Cynci a priority around here either. We'd have her and B. J. right here, if my girls weren't riled so easy." She replied.

"Well, if things don't change, we are afraid B. J. will be leaving and probably without much notice to anyone," Lone Buffalo added.

"You tell them we sent our best to them," Mrs. Peers added.

"I'll do that. I have to get back so we can see if this works," he said.

"Here's a basket of food and the other things you can take along. Better feed and water that horse while you eat a bite," Mrs. Peers handed him a bundle of things.

Lone Buffalo followed her into the kitchen while Pearl looked over the pinto stallion. Pride brimmed from his face as the horse sensed he knew Pearl. He patted the horse down and looked at his hooves before leading him to the watering trough. The pinto whinnied softly and nuzzled Pearl's arm as they walked along.

We would learn months later that the powder mixed in with some gruel had worked. Lone Buffalo's mother had made a concoction and now the child was big enough to crawl, was sleeping and eating soft foods, and had some baby teeth. Buffalo talked of his infant with pride during his next visit with us.

Pearl recalled how Early Dawn had been given that pinto stallion in early spring. It was with some regret he had allowed the horse to stay with her. The mare and colt brought from Medicine Bow that were so winter starved, now cantered around the homestead with Maudie and Ethel aboard. They called her Brindle because of her strange markings.

Lone Buffalo brought sad news. Cynci and B. J. had gone on to Idaho after B. J. fought with Yellow Calf. At the bottom of the dispute was the dusky cunning squaw Cynci. Shunned and despised by the family, Cynci left with him to meander through the mountains to find a new home.

Mrs. Peer's face filled with regret, tears lingering there at the news. Especially since Sheriff Sikes last visit indicated Pearl may be charged with murder and tried for the death of Slats Mahoney.

As the sun disappeared over the rim of the horizon and the Little Dipper bent its handle toward the eastern sky, I wandered to the garden with my thoughts in conflict. How could this be, that someone who protected Jesse and the nearly dead, Obediah, from being killed? How could he be in so much trouble. How could he be charged with murder? I know in my heart Sheriff Sikes is a yellow as a pole cat.

Chapter 20

Alfalfa Big Crop: Special Dispatch to The World Herald: Miller NE—May 22. Buffalo County is having plenty of rain and crops could not look better for this time of year. Rye is heading out and in some places Waist high. Corn is a good stand but cut worms are working some. Alfalfa will be a big crop.

Hessie's Mission

Heat flashes crackled at the edges of Sweet Creek as lightning bugs skated along the surface, ripples that ran to the shore disappeared into the pussy willows and cattails along the edge. Catfish swam with their ugly heads just above water, devouring everything on the surface of the creek. They siphoned off tadpoles and water bugs as they floated along the ripples of the low tide. Summer passed over in one giant step.

Hessie Riddle opened her eyes to a new day, and then remembered what day it was. Washing would soon fly from the wash lines in the back of the house, getting Rose ready to leave for Colorado. Hessie pushed off her sleep covers and rubbed sand from her eyes, found her robe and ambled to the kitchen from the bedroom she shared with Rose and Maggie. As she tiptoed into the kitchen, she saw the kitchen door close softly, and she smelled the rich aroma of fresh coffee and coffee cake. Greta had been up early.

She opened the kitchen door with a finger tracing the edge opening slightly like the scar of a wound. Hesitating only a minute as she observed Hans and Greta Sikes, Pete and Johnny, their sons, seated around the table in conversation. She withdrew her finger carefully from the thin seam she had opened. No one observed the door as it moved and closed quietly. She saw the family evaporate into a thin ray of light. Hessie knew this must be a grave moment for the people around the table. They were intent on their conversation.

"You say you got a warrant for Pearl's arrest? How can that be?" Greta asked.

"No, I said it's on the judge's desk down in Kearney; but it'll be here at least by tomorrow. Then I will arrest Pearl," Pete answered. "There's a group out at the Mahoney's claiming they want justice for Slats. A group of mercenaries from other counties around Nebraska, got organized to deal with rustlers and thieving going on. The problem is most of them aren't above the crime they are said to prevent. Pearl will be the safest right there in Cairo's jail till all this blows over."

"Greta, I told you Jesse Peers was up to no good. What did I say? And not long ago either. No good would come of those two," Hans remarked.

"You know your accusations are unfounded. The only reason you dislike Jesse is Rose never was serious about anyone else before. Admit it!" Greta insisted. "Hannah Ahrens seems like a nice woman and Rose likes her very much also."

"There's something amiss with those four, I say. You mark my word on that," Hans replied.

"Well, that's neither our affair nor your responsibility. The thing that concerns me is Rose could very well be with them when this bunch rides up and shoots it out with Pearl," Pete insisted.

"Rose damn well better leave and the sooner the better, I say," Hans persisted.

"We'll get her ready and she'll be safe on the train on her way to Denver. But we really need to decide what else needs to be done to keep everyone safe. When you have a vigilante group riding around, you need a back up of some kind," Pete said.

"I say we get some of the farmers together and warn them so's no one else gets hurt. Get them organized so all of us don't get shot at and burned out," Johnny added.

"Now that's the smartest thing I've heard said today," Hans said.

Hessie fled silently up the steps and nudged Rose awake. "They're gonna arrest Pearl just as soon as Sheriff Pete can get the papers from the judge in Kearney," Hessie cried. Their eyes met in a clash of fear and alarm.

Rose put a finger to her lips and cautioned Hessie not to waken Maggie. Together they fled into the hallway. "You need to go and warn Pearl what's happened. Take Sukie out of the pasture and ride along Sweet Creek. The Peers homestead is the first place on the West side of the Creek. You'll pass three other homesteads along the way. They are the ones on the East side of Sweet Creek. It'll take about an hour to get there. If they ask about you downstairs, I'll think of something till you get back. Tell Jesse I have to go into Cairo today to do some shopping. Tell him I'll look for him at the Mercantile around four o'clock this afternoon. Sukie knows the way so you shouldn't worry you'll get lost."

Hessie shrugged off her nighty and robes. She pulled her homespun dress over her head and ran a brush through her straight hair. Rose continued giving her directions, "Tell Pearl to leave cause the jail isn't any safer than any old barn. They could shoot it full of holes or even burn it down. Tell Jesse that Pearl has to leave right away! Explain about the warrant they have out for his arrest. Try to come right back unless you just can't do it. Ms. Peers will no doubt want to feed and take care of you, but you mustn't tary."

Hessie clutched her shawl and hurried downstairs, crept carefully through the kitchen and down the garden path.   Greta peered briefly out the window as Hessie fled toward the chicken coop. Chickens and ducks fled before her hurried steps all the way to the barn   At the entrance of the barn she smelled the sweetness of the newly cut alfalfa and the subtle waft of fresh grain. She snatched a bridle off the wall along with a handful of oats and hurried to the pasture gate. Hessie placed her fingers to her lips and whistled and Sukie came briskly through the tall grass to her. She thumbed the handful of oats into Sukie's mouth as she stroked her muzzle. Once the bridle was in place, she put the heavy shawl over Sukie's back and hefted herself bareback aboard the mare. Her cotton skirts tucked under her bottom cushioned her boney rear end until she settled into a sitting pattern. Long stockings covered her legs and her feet were tucked into her scuffed boots. Her skirt was placed neatly into her waist band where it would not flutter or fly in her face. The sun moved slowly above the violet hills, amid the quiet, flowing new fields of radiant wheat.

Hessie rode steadily as the sun rose higher in the sky. The horse and rider galloped along as one molded shadow of floating movement. She cast a long glance at the road behind her and saw nothing but dust and brush where the path was worn along the Creek. Before long she came to the first homestead where she observed a pasture that led up to the creek. The second homestead sat back somewhat further, and the house was the first thing that came into view. The third homestead was much bigger, and men were already in the field pitching hay into a haystack and onto a hay rack. They observed her riding along and waved. They whooped at Hessie galloping by, her skirts hitched above her thighs. She rode on like a freight train bound for a certain destination. Since she neither knew or cared what they thought she ignored them and kicked Sukie into a gallop. The horse was warm and inviting, the feeling of freedom she felt was as rich as the blood in Sukie's veins. A little further were signs of another homestead; the split rail around it marked the boundaries. As she trotted up on Sukie, Pearl was in the yard with Little Blue working an Appaloosa mare. Little Blue would hold and pull as Pearl roped the Appaloosa and began to walk. He was teaching the Appaloosa to hold and pull. Little Blue would hold her ground until Pearl signaled for Little Blue to loosen the tether rope. Both horses would trot around in unison together. He spotted Hessie riding along the Creek.

"What you doin' out ridin' all by yourself, Hessie? Ain't you a sight for sore eyes. I'd not thought to tell you to take such a trip just to go visiting," he laughed.

"It ain't no laughin' matter I'm about, Pearl Lux. Rose's brother Sheriff Sikes is all set to arrest the likes of you and throw your sorry self in jail. Miss Rose sent me to tell you to get high tailin' it out of here and not be seen till this whole mess with Slats Mahoney blows over. There's a vigilante group just rarin' to move in on you and settle up this whole thing. The Sikes are talking about getting up a bunch of farmers to counter this nasty business. Only Sikes thinks you'd be better off in jail. Miss Rose says it ain't safe and you need to get out of here till it all blows over," Hessie said. Out of breath and upset as she was, she savored the moment, excitement rising in ripples through her. Pearl came up beside her to lift her off the horse and tried to calm her down.

"Never knew such a mess would come of trying to save my own hide. What are we comin' too anyway that folks ride off in the night and kill each other. It confounds me that this kind of justice could even exist," Pearl lamented. "You come on in and let Mrs. Peers get you a cool drink and rest a bit while we figure this all out."

"Nothn' to figure. Rose wants me back just as soon as my hide can get back to the farm. She don't want anyone to know I come over here," Hessie cried.

"Will you just come in and explain? I'm afraid they'll think I've lost my mind if I go running in the house and say what you just told me. Please, Hessie, for just one minute. Then you can high tail it out of here just as fast as you come," Pearl pleaded.

When Hessie thought about it, she decided it best to go in and explain . She wasn't too happy with once again sharing this story, but common sense told her she had to. Together they walked into the kitchen of the farmhouse. Sara Ann Peers was surprised at the sight of the two of them hurrying into the house.

"My goodness, Hessie, what on earth has happened?" Sara Ann asked.

"Sheriff Sikes is going to arrest Pearl and throw him in jail just as soon as he gets a warrant from Kearney. It'll happen sometime today, so tomorrow at the latest he will be out here after Pearl. Rose says the jail is no fit place to protect anybody. Seems there's a vigilante group up at the Mahoney's fixin' to take matters into

Wildfire

their own hands. Lord knows what all they'll think of before this is over. Rose said to tell Pearl to get out of here just as fast as he possibly can." Hessie burst into tears

Sara Ann stepped forward and held Hessie until she composed herself. Jesse, Hannah, Maudie and Ethel had all come into the kitchen wondering what the noise was about. Pearl explained to Jesse why Hessie was here and what had happened. Jesse listened intently. Hannah slipped into a kitchen chair while Maudie and Ethel brought out coffee left from breakfast and set out cups. Ethel brought out a pan of apple cake and set out plates and forks. Emory Peers and the hired men: Eban, Joe, and Ephraim followed.

"There's a vigilante group all set to move in on me over this Slats Mahoney shooting. It's a bunch of ruffians. The Sikes want to form a group of farmers to get rid of this bunch," Pearl explained. "Hessie says I should leave cause the Sheriff has a warrant for my arrest."

"Rose said to tell you the jail ain't safe. They could burn it down even. She thinks Pearl should go before Sheriff Sikes gets this warrant. He thought by tomorrow he'd have it," Hessie went on. "Rose wants me to tell Jesse she needs some things from the Mercantile store and she'll be there around four o'clock this afternoon. She wants Jesse to meet her there."

"I'll try to find out who the men are that are forming this group to roundup these vigilantes. Rose is right Pearl. You need to head out. Maybe you and Joe could ride up to Lone Buffalo's. He could hide you until this is over," Jesse said. "Tell Rose I'll be there at four o'clock to see her before she leaves."

Emory Peers motioned, "Best get ready and leave right away. Sara Ann and the girls can fix up a back pack and have you ready in no time,"

Hannah sat quietly listening while Emory spoke. Her eyes reflected concern, her face tight with sadness. Tears fell from nowhere; her emotions slithered through her slick as an eel. She fought the panic feeling as it crawled up through her thoughts and held her fast. "I'm afraid for Pearl. There are so many things that can happen. I'll help with the clothes he'll need. Mrs. Peers will do the rest." A break in her voice caused Pearl to move to her side. The two walked to the bedroom where Pearl and Jesse slept. Silently, he clasped her in his arms and kissed her. Her head rested on his chest as he bent and kissed her tenderly. "When this is over and settled, you and I are going to get married and move where my reputation has not been smeared with threats and murder. Will you marry me, Hannah? Promise me now and we'll get married just as soon as this thing is taken care of," Pearl said.

"Yes, Pearl. I think I've been so lucky to have you in my life. Right from the time you carried me from the St. Pious Church yard to Mattie's, I knew you'd be special."

"Do you remember that? I thought you'd not remember such. I'm so glad I'd gone to the church that day to check on you. It frightens me to think what if I had not." He kissed her again lightly on the cheek and hugged her close. His emotions flew off like a kite with a broken string. He tugged the ring from his little finger and put it on Hannah's left hand. "Just till I can find a better one for you," he promised. "Let's say Thanksgiving time we'll plan for a wedding. Unless things clear up before hand."

"I'd like that. Ms. Peers and the girls will help. Just you stay safe and come back as soon as you can," Hannah added. Quietly, they packed Pearl's clothes and put them in his possible's bag. Their hands met and held as they placed things there. As they returned to the kitchen, Hessie repeated what she had overheard from the Sike's kitchen.

"Even though he means well, Pete Sikes is a coward. He's run away from all this trouble. He blamed Pearl and Jesse for the time Slats rousted Ephraim and Joe over at the Whistle Stop last winter. He has his own way of looking at things. I gotta get home before Hans discovers I'm gone." Hessie rose and fled out the door with Jesse close behind. He boosted her up on Sukie and she rode off toward the creek. Sukie cantered along the stream. Hessie could smell the outdoors she loved best. The left over smell of cut grass, heat and sweat. It reminded her of days at Pa's, swimming in the creek. Her thoughts scattered away from her, testing her. Finally, she became more settled in her mind. August had never seemed this strange before.

By afternoon, Pearl and Joe Lone Bear rode off, Pearl on Big Red and Joe on the Appaloosa mare. Big Red whinnied and stamped about, sensing the excitement of the family crowded around to send them off. Pearl swept Hannah up in his arms and whispered, "Tell Ms. Peers just as soon as you can get her alone. We'll try to keep in touch somehow. I love you, Hannah."

Hannah kissed him once more and whispered, "I love you, Pearl." The two men rode off at a gallop toward the North Platte Fork and Lone Buffalo's home. Their swift clear cut forms soon merged into the dust of their horses. At last all that appeared was their heads above the tall grass that bordered their path.

"Well, we'd better get to work. We'll be shorthanded for a few days. I expect to have threshers come through soon so we need to get ready. Sara Ann, maybe you and the girls can pitch hay for the cows and milk. Help out that way. Hate to think we'll go hungry," he chuckled. "Very soon, men will come over that ribbon of road through the flatlands. We need to prepare for them."

"We'll do what we can, but this bunch works on its stomach. You'll leave us alone for a few hours each day to make meals I suppose." She smiled as she said it. She knew they would agree with her.

"What can I do to help, Ms. Peers There must be some field work I can do," Hannah pleaded.

"You aren't big enough or strong enough to pitch hay or wrangle a team. I'm thinking you'll do the best for us right in the kitchen doing some cooking," Ms. Peers had this look on her face, between knowing and not knowing. As she looked in Hannah's face something there hinted of a secret between Hannah and Pearl, a nagging suspicion of something that was about to happen.

Hessie dug her heels into Sukie's sides and trotted along the Sweet Creek until she spied the outbuildings of the Sikes homestead. Gently she slid to the ground and rubbed Sukie down with her shawl. When she removed the bridle, Sukie trotted to the stock tank.

Hessie walked quickly to the garden plot and picked tomatoes, cucumbers and green peppers that she placed in her folded skirt. She walked slowly through the kitchen door just as Rose hurried down the hall. A look of relief fell over Rose's face seeing Hessie safely back home again. They unloaded Hessie's garden vegetables quietly, studying each other with piercing eyes. Each one braced against what might happen next.

"Maggie is upstairs making beds and cleaning up. Mama asked for you. She must've seen you go down the path to the chicken coop. What happened over at the Peers?" Rose asked.

"Pearl rode off with Joe Lone Bear. Don't know where they planned to go. "

"Help me hang out this basket of clothes. I put the hand washed things out earlier. We'll need to iron blouses and get stuff packed. Maggie brought my suitcase from the attic. I need my wardrobe brought down. Mama said Johnny or August would set it out here so we can pack," Rose replied.

Rose's lingerie on the line was nearly dry. She hoisted the basket of wet wash up on her hip. Hessie set up the ironing board and clamped a hot iron from the back of the cook stove to the iron handle. The flat irons were kept on the stove for ironing, and wrapped in towels during cold winter night, they warmed the beds upstairs. By afternoon the blouses, skirts, nightgowns, and underwear were ironed and put away. Clothes hung in pristine rows in the wardrobe trunk accompanied by slippers, and an extra pair of shoes, the stockings rolled and pulled into a ball inside the lips of the elastic tops. Silence fell over them like a steel quilt smothering them as the two women struggled to control their sadness.

Greta handed Rose a letter. "Take this to Annie. Here is money to purchase things you'll need for the long trek to Colorado on the train. Maggie and Hessie can help me with the cooking for this evening's meal. Hessie, you look so tired. Why don't you rest for a bit while Rose goes into town. She will be back in time for supper."

"I'd just as soon stay busy, Ms. Sikes, if you don't mind." She didn't plan to miss anything that happened in the household for the rest of the day.

"Peter will take you to Cairo, Rose. That way we'll feel like you are safe. When you're done shopping, go over and get him at the County building and he'll bring you home," Greta said.

Pete Sikes came into the parlor where the women sat. "You ready Rose?"

"Gracious Peter, you must really be worried if you're wearing guns even around the house," Rose said.

"Until this mess is cleaned up with the Mahoneys, I'll be wearing these all the time," Pete stated.

"No need to protect poor Hessie. They can't do anything more to her," Rose insisted. Pete looked down ashamed of himself. Rose hadn't realized the affect her remark would make.

Pete helped Rose into the buggy and snapped the horse's reins. The sun beat down mercilessly on the pair seated inside the buggy. It rose in glistening waves from the ground. The wind was confused and blew buffalo grass in spirals along the road. It would be

Wildfire

hours before the sun would sink behind the sand hills and give them some relief.

As they trotted into the cobweb of streets of Cairo, the church bell tolled the hour as faint as the drip of a faucet. The horses sensed the difference of their surroundings as they came near the blacksmith shop. Pete pulled the buggy up before the Mercantile Store and helped Rose down. Brother and sister searched each others face for some degree of understanding, some common ground and found nothing. A blank slate to be filled in at some later time, when it was too late.

Rose adjusted her bonnet and clutched her shopping bag. As Pete clucked to the horses, Rose searched the street for a familiar face and saw no one. When she entered the store, she moved directly toward the dry goods department.

"Miss Sikes, what can I help you with today?" Lou Razitski asked.

"I'm looking for some fabric to make a dress. I need a pattern and some lace to trim it."

"There are the pattern books right there. The fabric is along the back wall. When you figure out what you need, I'll help you cut the fabric. Don't like to fuss too much, the ladies don't like it," he stated.

"I'd appreciate that, Lou." Rose looked at the pattern books intently. She cast a glance around the store to see if anyone had come in. She found exactly what she wanted and began the search for fabric. She selected a white silk and a lace trim. As she carried her selections to the cutting table Lou came forward to help her.

Jesse entered the front door of the Mercantile Store and looked around, searching for Rose. She saw him and rushed to him. He hugged her briefly. "It's so good to see you. Are you all packed, ready to leave?" he asked.

"Almost. Mama gave me the money to choose some fabric, so Lou is helping me with my selection."

"White fabric? For yourself?" Jesse inquired.

"Yes, for me. If I'm gone a long time, this will take some time to make. Give me two of those packets of seed pearls too, Lou, and four yards of the wide lace and a packet of tissue paper. I need a tablet and some ink also. That should be about it," Rose said.

"You'll need to be careful with this fabric. It frays some and it stains easily. Do some basting and here is some binding tape for your seams. You have to have that with silk," Lou insisted.

Jesse led Rose over to the pastry cupboard and fished cookies out of a cookie jar. Rose poured them each a cup of lemonade from the cooler and carried them to a small table in the corner of the store. Dust motes floated in the rays of light that poured down from the windows above the corner. The young lovers were oblivious to their surroundings. They looked only at each other. For a moment, Jesse sat and savored the occasion. "I don't suppose we'll meet this way again. When Hessie told me you'd be here today, I couldn't believe my ears. Will you write to me, Rose?"

"I plan to and I hope you'll answer my letters. I know this is a busy time for your family. With Pearl gone and until the harvesters come, it'll be even busier. I hoped you'd come today anyway." Rose's voice was tinged with sorrow.

"I had to. You'll be gone and I will miss you. All these months when you've come over for music lessons have been the happiest ones of my life. Happier than I'd been ever."

"Why Jesse Peers, are you saying you're in love with me? I declare, you do surprise a person. Whenever did you decide you cared about me? It's almost too much for me." Rose hid a smile behind her gloved hand. It was not wasted on Jesse and he clasped her hand carefully.

"Rose Sikes, you confound the likes of me no end. You send your conspirator and confident flying to my home to save Pearl. Yet you treat the whole thing lightly, as if you did nothing. Yes, I'm in love with you. There it is. You've pulled it out of me and confounded me again. I must remember you are Greta Sikes' daughter. My heart will never be my own again. I will answer every letter you write, and think of you because I must stay here and work. You must come back to me. If not, I will come for you. I hear your father will not permit it, though," Jesse lamented.

"Oh shaw, Pa will just have to. Mama will see to it. I will talk to her, maybe not at this moment but soon. Annie and Bernie will speak on my behalf, I'm sure," Rose said.

"Here is your pattern, fabric and trimming Miss Sikes. I'll make up a slip for you and wrap them up," Lou said as he moved to the cash register.

Jesse and Rose spoke softly to each other. At last, Jesse stood and kissed Rose on the cheek. He held her for only a moment then grasped his hat and gave Lou a silver dollar on his way out. "That should take care of the refreshments. Keep the change, Lou."

"Thank you , Mr. Peers. Appreciate your business. Tell your Ma I got that peach calico she was inquiring about," Lou added.

"I'll do that," Jesse replied. "Rose, have a good trip." He gazed at her once more, one last look that would sustain him for months to come. He strode swiftly out the door. Jesse peered up at the sun and hurried to the blacksmith shop where he had stabled Wildfire. Henry Mueller, the blacksmith, had a perplexed look on his face.

"Wildfire just kicked the slats out of his stall right after I run him in there. You need to have that damned horse gelded. Maybe that'd calm him down. He looked at me and showed them teeth. I thumped him between his ears cause he wouldn't settle down. He proceeded to take out the dam wall of his stall."

Jesse looked from the Smithy to Wildfire, who calmly chewed some oats. "What's up with you fella? You got a bee in your bonnet?" Jesse paid Henry and reached for his saddle. As he saddled Wildfire, the horse spotted the Smithy and whinnied his discontent. Wildfire reared up on his hind legs as Jesse mounted up. The horse sprung from a squat position with an explosion of energy. Jesse could hear the Blacksmith shout, "Crazy dam horse Never seen anything like him." Jesse galloped out of town, leaving a trail of dust behind.

At the Mercantile Store, Lou Rezitsky put Rose's purchases in a bag. "Nice young man that Jesse Peers. Not many men as upstanding and fair as the Peers," Lou commented.

"Yes, I know. We need good people like the Peers around this country. There's enough of the bad ones around," Rose commented.

"That's bad business with Obediah Riddle getting killed. There's a war brewing around abouts. The Syries, Butlers and the Reedys have sworn revenge, and are organizing a posse to go out and get the Mahoneys. It'll be a nasty business if they do."

You say the Syries, Butlers and the Reedys too? Lord goodness, it's almost to much for me to think of," Rose cried.

Lou realized he'd upset her and fluttered around getting her purchases packed. "I'm mighty sorry I shared that with you Rose. Wasn't my intentions to upset you so," Lou apologized.

Rose paid him for the fabric and accessories and hurried out of the store. She went straight to the County building to find Peter. Rose entered the County building where the jail was just as Pete Sikes was unlocking a jail cell. "Now Sam, stay sober. Else I'll be seeing you right here again. You go home to your Mrs. Straight away, you hear?" he exclaimed.

"I never woulda' been here in the first place, if I hadn't talked to Leslie Syrie. Seemed to me you'd be interested when the folks around here are planning a neck stretching party. Instead you arrested me. That's what I get for thinkin' law enforcement protects the citizens of this town," Sam whined.

"What made you think any of these folks are fixing to stretch somebody's neck? All this trouble causes people to take the law into their own hands. They can't do it, and you can tell them that for me," Pete insisted.

Sam looked belligerently at Pete's face and then shook his head. As he walked out of the jail he cautioned, "Don't say I didn't warn you about it. "

"It's true you know. Even Lou over at the Mercantile Store is talking about the farmers getting together," Rose insisted.

"They can't take the law into their own hands! Are you ready to go home?" he asked sullenly. With that the conversation stopped and Rose knew Peter Sikes was not going to discuss it again.

They walked to the blacksmith shop together to get the buggy. Pete caught up the horses and hitched them to the buggy. He helped Rose into the seat. Silence fell as heavy as the humid air they moved in.

It was stifling. Not one person stirred. The town seemed deserted. It was an exceptional day when the citizens of Cairo were not out on the street. The flag hung limply from the pole in the courthouse square. The lonely town did not share its secrets any better than Pete Sikes. Rose's heart settled uneasily in her breast. Her mind flew in many directions concerning this latest piece of news. The townsfolk were taking matters out of Sheriff Sikes' hands. Fear danced with her as an unwanted guest. She knew she must be still, be calm, and savor her meeting with Jesse until they would meet again.

Chapter 21

The Granger Movement: (1867-1893) The founding of the Granger Movement was designed to aid the isolation of the farming community. It started as a social and educational response to the problem and to encourage cooperatives that were farmer owned. The ideal was to free farmer's from the obstacles of the marketplace. The Grangers soon became politically influenced and the goal was state regulation of taxes and tariffs. "The Granger Laws" provided ground for court challenges. This evolved into the Farmer's Alliance. The goals were principally the same as the Granger's. They sought collective relief from laws and tariffs. Its powerful attraction was its sense of community resembling in some instances to a "revival" or "Pentecostal" movement. The Alliance realized political importance as well and Nebraska saw the birth of the Populist Party (1892) whereby it controlled both houses of the Nebraska legislature. America. "The Farm Problem and Agrarian Protest Movements, The New West," (Chap.21), pp.774-776

Donna R. McGrew

Rose Goes to Colorado

Soon it will be September when the yard shouts with leaves at every step. The vegetables and flowers that survived the summer will be dead and dormant until they become food for another season of gardening. Greta sat at her writing desk, the sun dipped behind a cloud and turned the hydrangeas and daisies a soft gold shade touched with lavender. It was a pleasure to look out on the garden.

"Dearest Annie,
I take pen in hand as I sit here in the library to tell you of our plight with Rose. Your father is most displeased with her. His eyes have a most saddened look, a flat cruel sadness that lives inside him. He cannot let it go, but ponders on what the best course of action will be. The farmland drains the sap from his bones. He becomes older and more foreign to me by the day. My words went through Rose's brain as rainwater through dry earth. I learned early on she could not be deterred from a most rash and daring course of action. I have always cradled this family with warmth, a treasure robust and strong that whispers its love. Now I am torn between daughter and father, of which I am too fond to be rational. Sometimes I think that what I know and reality are two different matters entirely. That is why Rose must move to Colorado for as long as possible and distance herself from Jesse Peers, or I fear

for both my husband and daughter. I wrote you earlier about Pearl Lux, Hannah Ahrens, Jesse and Rose coming home from the Wood River frolic. Pearl shot Slats Mahoney and mortally wounded this sculling mass of vermin, who eternally finds new and different ways to amuse himself. Now the Mahoneys have sworn vengeance against Pearl, and your brother Peter is struggling to keep peace amongst everyone in the community. The small homesteaders are becoming organized and we have a major conflict brewing between these two groups.

So you see the sooner Rose is not the pivotal figure in all this the better. She may grieve a bit, as she has claimed her undying affection for Jesse Peers.

It is my fondest desire that you and Willie avail yourselves to help her through this by encouraging her in endeavors that will entertain and educate her. I instructed her to buy enough fabric to do a dress suitable for church and festive occasions. Rose has promised me, after considerable wheedling, that she will indeed try to occupy her mind on other matters than this malicious vengeance going on here in the plains.

I remain your loving mother, Greta Sikes

The family gathered in the dining room as they did every day after breakfast. Even the men are here today as Rose will soon disappear up that rickety steel path of railroad tracks. Peter's eyes were pinched and his face drawn tight. There seemed to be a mixture of feelings reflected there this morning.

"Peter, you look tired, as if you'd not rested well," Greta said.

"Nothing that couldn't be fixed with the fast action of some sod busters who could restore peace to this prairie and its residents," Pete replied.

"There seems to be enough for these folks to occupy themselves without your help, I say. What do you say about that?" Hans asked.

"Suddenly you're full of opinions. You claim you want my advice, but you're fast giving me yours," Pete snapped. Hans looked away—guilty and troubled.

"We better lay tracks on that road if we are to get Rose to the depot on time." Maggie's voice was loud and troubled. "I've never heard so much bickering among you all. One would think you'd stop palavering and take action. Let's get our buggy on the road." She will be happy when Rose is gone and she can reclaim everyone for herself.

The family flowed down the front steps like water rushing down a spillway and evaporated into the buggy. Hans turned the carriage south toward Cairo. Rose glanced at her mother, stark threatening looks exchanged between them. It frightened her. Rose gazed covetously about the homestead and the garden as they drove away. She knew that she would miss all this when she was gone.

"Rose, did you find fabric and patterns yesterday to work on while Annie can help you?" Greta asked. "You have the letter I wrote this morning for Annie?"

Rose stood her ground. "Yes, mama. I chose a nice silk fabric I've never worked with before. Trimming, buttons, thread, everything else I needed. The letter is in my handbag."

The family settled into the carriage, everyone holding their own private thoughts. The smell of fresh-cut alfalfa, the early morning richness that floats on the air, an ambrosia to one's soul. Cows peered through the fence, their mouths chewing their cuds constantly, their tails lashed their backsides where huge pies of manure splattered the ground. How beautiful the animals were against the fields of corn and wheat. A cow bawled for her recently weaned calf.

The boys were out early this morning cutting hay and doing chores. Hessie will start dinner by 11 o'clock this morning, as the men will be in tired and hot today. It is doubtful having Hessie here was a good idea. She insulted Peter during the past few days. She doesn't think he's doing anything about Obediah's murder. In trying to do his job, he angered people on both sides of this problem. Wherever Hessie is there is a conspiracy. Maggie complains about her, but Maggie is another matter entirely.

"Hans, when is the train supposed to arrive at the depot?" Greta asked.

"It's supposed to be here at 10 o'clock, but if there are lots of passengers coming from Omaha and Lincoln and on to Cheyenne, they'll likely be late." His answer was clipped as if saying anything was an effort.

As they pulled into town, The Limited gave a shrill whistle like nails raking a blackboard. Hans flicked the reins and the horses trotted off at a faster pace. People were already on the train platform. The family drew up before the station, rushed through the maize of people gathered to meet the train, and went directly to the ticket window.

"I need a ticket for my daughter Rose. She's going to Grand Junction Colorado today," Hans said.

Ross Still smiled in recognition. "One way or round trip, Mr. Sikes? You'd save a little buying round trip.".

Hans hesitated for only a minute. "One way. We'll not worry about the return trip."

Rose walked over to Greta. "Mama, Annie and Willie will likely bring me home unless it's mid-winter."

"Now Rose, you'd better put such out of your mind until this matter is cleared up with the homesteaders," Greta said.

Ross Still overheard our conversation. A questioning look crossed his face. He gazed from Hans to Peter, sizing up the two men. Peter's responsibility was as heavy as the Colts that hung from his holster

Maggie and Peter brought Rose's luggage. Maggie pouted. As usual she's unhappy when she's not the center of attention. Rose should be the best off because of her easier demeanor, but with Hessie stirring things up no one knows what's going to happen. This issue must be resolved. If Hessie and Maggie don't get along better, there's only one way to resolve matters. However it turns out, Maggie won't like the outcome. If Hessie stays, Maggie will pout; if Hessie leaves, Maggie will have one tantrum after another.

"Come girls. We must get Rose aboard the train. Now darlin', try not to be a burden for Annie. She can use help with her boarding house. You can be lots of help to her," Greta pleaded.

"Maybe she'll find a railroader for herself, Mama," Maggie teased. Rose pulled Maggie's hair as she hugged her goodbye. "I'll take Rose aboard the train. Peter and I can get her settled, Mama," Maggie insisted. "Come along , Rose. We'll help you find your seat and make you comfy. Try to cheer up a bit dearie. Men don't like a scowling face, you know."

"Oh Maggie. Behave yourself. You shouldn't say such things. You should be the one going to Colorado. Then you could flirt with all the trainmen and find one for yourself," Rose threatened.

From the train platform Greta watched from where she stood. Peter found Rose's seat as they wandered up the long aisle of the passenger car. He helped her get settled and stowed her overnight bag away.

"Goodbye, sister dear. Don't work too hard," Maggie said.

Peter gave his sister a brotherly goodbye kiss. He strode up the long aisle to the doorway of the train. Maggie was close at his side. They hurried along the platform as the train pulled out. Greta gazed lovingly at her daughter as she waved goodbye. Everyone waved frantically at the passenger car as it disappeared down the train tracks.

As they gathered at the carriage, Greta glanced at Hans. The anxious look left his face drained and stagnant now. He'd been about as talkative as a thief to a judge ever since he'd left home today. It didn't mean a thing though, even though we were hopeful he'd try to be more understanding, not so cantankerous and nasty.

Soon the carriage was on a long stretch of prairie road. The horses August had hitched to the buggy today were a sturdy lot. They were stumpy heavy dun horses with heads as big as hams. Their feet, the size of Dutch ovens, plodded along the road stirring up a whirlwind of dust.

Maggie looked wistfully out on the countryside. The cottonwoods and sycamores were a brilliant green, their leaves glittering in the blustery hot summer breeze. Maggie's face was sweaty and angry, even now--a moon phase perhaps, or just a cranky mood caught up in a fit of despondency.

At the homestead, the horse and buggy of Emory Peers sat in the yard neath the Sycamore trees. Emory and Jesse climbed from their buggy and came forward. Hans sat back, a look of surprise on his face.

"Mornin' Mr. and Mrs. Sikes, Sheriff Sikes, Maggie. Good day to you," Jesse said.

"Good mornin' sir," Hans said. The tone of his voice was an insult. "What has brought you away from your fields on such a day?" he demanded.

"We've come to inform you, we plan to attend a meeting of the Farmers Alliance hereabouts at the Grange Hall in Wood River. We want to organize and prepare for what might come of this affair over the death of Obediah Riddle. Surely you've heard that the folks are preparing to rid themselves of these vigilantes who set out to gun down anyone opposing them," Jesse Peers stated.

"I'd not heard of such, but I believe it's in your best interest to prepare for a time when these people organize and come against you," Pete Sikes said.

"We want to know if you are interested and would join us?" Emory Peers looked directly at Peter.

"Perhaps you did not know of the warrant for Pearl Lux's arrest. I would have been on my way to your place by now, but we took my sister, Rose, to Cairo to catch a train this morning," Pete Sikes shifted his gun belt.

"You're wasting your time. Pearl isn't here and hasn't been for some time now," Jesse adjusted his buggy whip.

"Don't get yourselves in trouble by harboring him. I have a warrant here to serve on him. He needs to turn himself in and put an end to all this trouble," Sheriff Sikes walked restlessly about.

"No need to upset yourself, but Pearl is not at our home or anywhere near," Emory insisted. "Come and see for yourself if you must, but he's not here anymore."

"Perhaps he's gone back to Indiana. Would you know where he could be found?" Sheriff Sikes moved toward Jesse and Emory.

"Perhaps. Why waste your time on Pearl when there are more important matters to concern yourself with," Emory Peers rubbed his forehead as if to erase troubling thoughts that lingered there.

Jesse's statement that Pearl was gone and his commitment to the Farmer's Alliance, made it very clear what the Farmer's intentions were. Peter didn't add anything to convince anyone otherwise. It seemed Jesse and Emory were being truthful. A sense of relief came over Greta. If the Farmer's Alliance was involved, they'd see an end to this problem. The thin watercolor image no longer defined their lives but a very clear black and white picture clarified from all this talk. Would Sheriff Sikes listen?

"Can't we go inside out of this blistering sun and wind for a cool drink of water?" Greta moved toward the house.

"That's kind of you, Mrs. Sikes. We just stopped to tell you there's to be a meeting to get the Farmers Alliance around here organized. We have other places to visit and folks to inform of what's happened," Jesse said as he climbed aboard his buggy.

He stood so tall, blonde and strong. No wonder Rose was taken with him. His voice and his presence commanded a person's respect. Hans was in a state of shock. He was totally unprepared for this turn of events so soon. Rose was far ahead of everyone. She did more than take music lessons this winter and spring. She set the background for a life here with Jesse on the plains. Jesse Peers would be a man to reckon with very soon.

Jesse flicked the reins at his horses. They were gone in a heartbeat up the long road between our farms and around the acres of land where other neighbors lived.

Greta hurried into the house as Hessie busied herself drying the dinner dishes. The kitchen was a disarray of dirty and clean dishes. The look on Hessie's face told more than anything else. She had not missed one word of what had happened in the yard. In days to come she could be found in the strangest places, listening intently to someone or something. It's a bit frightening when someone with this inner voice lingers near. Greta was prompted to ask, "What are you doing, Hessie?" but refrained from the temptation. She had enough on her mind without listening to Hessie's stories as well. Maggie's tattling and Hessie's complaints cause them to be at odds with each other. Someone must deal with this before it gets worse.

It was unbearably hot for August. This month brought threshers and their machines down the long ribbon of road over the distant hill to our farm. Their lives were a blur of waking and working, the time disappearing into another day. It's been weeks since Rose left and Greta had not dealt with Hessie. Maggie got the idea, perhaps from Hans, that if she does not improve, Hessie will leave soon. She's made a great effort to conceal her feelings, however, which eased the tension quite a bit for now.

August brought news from town when he delivered the grain and corn to the elevator. It seems a group of farmers gathered at the Grange Hall in Wood River. There is a rumor we will be invaded by this vigilante group. There will be an open conflict. This group of gunmen cling together with a common cause. Some are gunslingers; others are known outlaws. Apparently, the Mahoneys have paid them to come here. Once winter was upon us perhaps the strife would stop.

Peter spent more time in town and ceased his pursuit of Pearl Lux. Rustling yearling calves has become a consuming activity of this group; snapping up twenty or thirty calves that would be the fall auction profits for these farmers. This caused an alarming number of complaints to Peter. Not a day goes by that someone comes to him with a problem. He is on edge that something more tragic will occur. He fears it will not be long before these farmers will catch a thief and make an example.

Today is the last of the threshing crew. They disappear tomorrow up the road into the countryside to finish someone else's harvest. The nights at least have become cooler. However, these were the hottest days of the year. The sun broke through clouds of mist, and swarms of mosquitoes searched for a place to land. August built smudge fires to take care of the worst, but it made the heat even more unbearable.

Peter rode down the long road with two bags tied to his saddle, his holster hung heavily and an old shot borer rifle thrust beneath his leg. He grows more gaunt by the day. Since early spring he's become a shadow. Naturally tall and lanky, he looks spare as a skeleton now. An unseemly thing for his mother to withstand. Her heart ached for him and she wished he was rid of this assignment. He wanted something brought about that would get the culprits imprisoned, but he feared someone would be run down on the open plains and shot. He wanted a confession signed, and the thieves jailed--his sign to the world he'd done a respectable job.

He dismounted and led the horse to the pen, then took the money bags and set them inside the house. "Maggie, you and Hessie keep a strong eye on these bags till the settlement is over and these men are paid," he instructed.

The men gathered to clean up in our washroom; Maggie and Hessie stood with towels and inspected the washing. Maggie paid lots of attention to young

Calvin, flirting with him, then bossing him around. One moment she was all smiles and sweetness, the next making some disdainful comment. Maggie was free with her tongue. "Your face is dirtier than your hands." Or "Step outside and shake out your shirt; it's full of dust from the threshing machine." Today, Maggie was particularly hard on Calvin, as he eyed her up and down. Maggie seemed undaunted by his behavior. As the men sat around the dining room table, there was a look of relief on the young fellow's face when he cleared Maggie's inspection process. All was forgotten as the large bowls of chicken and dumplings were brought in by Hessie. Greta followed with mashed potatoes and gravy, while Maggie came with bowls of fresh sliced tomatoes and slabs of homemade bread. Greta baked peach pies today for this final meal. No breakfast would be provided tomorrow, as these folks will want to leave early. This final day is always difficult because everyone has grown accustomed to these folks, and this marked the passage of another harvest.

As supper ended, Hans and Peter walked to the grape arbor with the great bags of money. Peter took hold of the tally papers. He held the whole mess of detailed accounting before him. Hans had this blank reserved expression on his face. He looked over the men crowded under the arbor with an air of expectancy. "You men line up in the garden. Dad and I will pay out whatever is owed."

These men with their gnarled hands and sunburned faces looked on the Sikes with some contempt. Their callused hands and tattered clothes attested to their hard work, earning every penny they would be paid today. Hans made no secret that he would not cheat anyone. That does not keep these folks from their own suspicions. Peter serves a purpose at a time such as this, as they tend not to argue. The sun dipped behind the distant violet-tinted sand hills far away from the barren fields harvested clean of every shoot of wheat and stalk of corn. The fields stood fallow and stark naked, now ready for this final passage of the summer. The last dime was parceled out and each form marked with whatever sign a man claimed to identify himself. We learned painfully early never to allow payment of any kind in advance.

Hessie and Maggie washed and dried the last supper dishes. Tomorrow morning would be brief with food. Some would wander away yet tonight toward the lights of town, throwing good money at bad practices. Then they will be out looking for another repeat of this vagrant life they'd chosen.

The morning brought a mixture of clouds and sunshine. The sun rose a sliver above the horizon, as Greta peered out at the backyard. The threshers stirred from the bunkhouse where they slept. They meandered about coming and going from the house, drinking coffee and eating leftover food. Hessie had the kitchen under control.

Maggie walked to the hen house with a basket to collect yesterday's eggs. As Greta watched, young Calvin entered the fenced area and walked to the hen house. She was too startled to grasp what was happening until she heard Maggie scream. She called Hans who had also heard Maggie. As he grabbed at his clothes and pulled his overalls over his shoulders, he snatched a pistol from the bedside stand. The two competed for space as they ran together out of the house, through the garden, and into the shelter of the hen house. Maggie sprawled beside the brood hen nests, her clothing in disarray, her face a mass of bloody bruises. Her look of confusion and dismay was unbearable. Calvin glared as he hovered over her. His hand gripped her leg as he fell over her. Hans grasped Calvin's head and threw him sideways onto the floor. The gun exploded point blank in Calvin's face. Blood splattered everywhere as the body twisted on the floor. Maggie was semi-conscious and white as a sheet, not comprehending what had just happened.

"Maggie, look at me! Do you know me? Here dear, cover yourself and come with me. Come quickly dear! Maggie can you hear me?" As Greta helped her out of the hen house, Hans suddenly realized what he had done. He knelt beside Calvin and felt for a pulse, but there was nothing. Hans' eyes had this vacant far away look as shock set in. Maggie shook convulsively as Greta caught her in her arms to balance her. Johnny and August both ran to the garden when they heard the crack of the pistol. Once again everyone was embroiled in a violent aftermath where the ricochet would re-vibrate over and over again. Would this madness ever stop.

Calvin lay in a mass of blood, and brains oozed out of a hole the size of a fist on the side of his face. He convulsed as his spirit fled from his body. His mouth gaped in a final maw of surprise as he lay there. Blood sprayed everywhere--the walls, the straw, the nests. A mass of feathers flew about as the hens clamored to get away from the horror. Hans stood over Calvin trying to comprehend what he'd done. He was incoherent as his sons gathered round and helped him into the house.

August agreed to ride into Cairo for the doctor. When he returned, Peter came along with Doctor Dickinson. The doctor examined the corpse of Calvin. Calvin's trousers were around his ankles, and his sunburned back contrasted sharply with his pale buttocks.

"Well, I can't make this situation go away, but what has visited upon you folks today will take a long time to remedy. Hans chose a closure that no one would deny him. Even with our lawlessness, a man is allowed to protect his family. He is not required to overlook such matters." The doctor's face was grave as he said this.

"August, you and John help me load this rascal into my buckboard. Peter, you need to get a report from everyone here and file it. God bless, Ms. Sikes. Try not to be too hard on yourselves. I believe the repercussions will arrive soon enough. Just be ready should anything more happen." Dr. Dickinson moved toward his buckboard.

As the boys loaded up the dead man, Hans and Greta stood in Maggie's bedroom. What could they tell a fifteen year old of the ways of men such as this one? She had touched off a firestorm during the past week with her actions They would know instantly from the reactions of the threshers as they learned what had happened. The threshers left, glancing cautiously sideways at the family. No one gave eye contact, no one knew what might come of this. The consequences of this tragedy would follow. Whether they were responsible or not, word spread quickly of such an incident. They may not find work they wanted here in the plains as the story spread.

Peter talked with Doctor Dickinson, the load on his shoulders even heavier now. Somehow he got through the day. The glitter in Hessie's eyes told Greta this was only the beginning. She walked about all day listening to someone or something no one could see or hear. It made Greta's scalp crawl. Hans would not go near her. He and the boys cleaned every shotgun, pistol and handgun in the farmhouse. Then they waited.

Jesse Peers rode into our yard. He came to the door and rapped the knocker just as he had other times he came to visit us but everyone knew this visit was different. "Mornin' Mr. And Mrs. Sikes. Sheriff Sikes, August and John. I've come to tell you, we have found a trail up by the Syrie farmhouse. They lost twenty calves from their pasture, taken sometime yesterday, probably about night fall . One of the calves was injured. They tried to make it look like wild animals did it. We witnessed Mastiffs the size of young horses over at their homestead trained to kill anything in front of them. The Alliance is gathering in Cairo this afternoon and will ride to the Mahoney farm for a showdown. Perhaps you'd like to join us. We'll understand if you don't, but we'll be most appreciative if you were to say you would."

"I need to think on this," Hans said as he paced around nervously.

"You say the Alliance is going out there? How many would that be?" August asked.

"Forty-fifty men. Enough to roust them out or burn them out. We're prepared for anything," Jesse said.

August and John agreed to join them, but they left it up to Hans to let them go. Greta assumed Jesse Peers knew nothing of their troubles here.

Maggie had not improved, stayed entirely to herself. She looked shamed and embarrassed about what happened. She had nothing to say, even when asked a question. Greta feared she would never recover from this attack. Hans shooting Calvin would forever haunt her. Hans was afraid and commiserated that he should be with the other farmers, driving out the Mahoneys to bring an end to that struggle.

It had been five days since Maggie's attack, but things have not changed with her. Greta urged her to go outside today, but when she saw the hen house and garden, she ran sobbing into the house. Doctor Dickinson came back to visit. He examined Maggie's injuries and found nothing broken but her spirit. He left a sedative to help her sleep, and he told us there was not much else he could do. She was young and would forget, but the people here would not.

Peter came at dinner time. He gave us news of the Alliance. Hessie had been a blessing during this time. She listened spellbound how the farmers set up a volley of gunfire to bring the Mahoneys down. At last her face reflected a composure which was new for the poor soul.

"They've set up a fortress above the Mahoney's house on a shale cliff. Jesse seemed to know exactly where to position them, so they could watch anyone at the farmhouse. Some of the field hands that came with the threshing machines were seen buying liquor from the Mahoney's still. If any of them stayed, it was not apparent," Peter told us.

Each day brought news. Ed Reedy came by today to say, "Everyone is about to come home. Jesse, August and Lloyd Syrie left the group late one night to sneak up near the ranch house. The first man to use the outhouse was Robb Mahoney. They came up behind and knocked him out, then drug him up on the ledge and demanded he make his men surrender. He told them to go to hell. They refused to let him get away with that, threatened him, and finally strung a rope up on an apple tree in the orchard. He told them those men weren't about to give up. We demanded justice, and Jesse flicked the roan stallion's rump and Robb hung there twistin' and jerkin, convulsed in midair till he quit kickin'. He pissed all over hisself as he swung there. The horse galloped off to get away from the place. Jesse watched the spectacle, then turned and walked away. It surprised us Jesse would react, but he's set to end this problem. Besides he was there when Obediah got murdered, so he don't have a lot of sympathy for them Mahoneys. He don't need to harbor any remorse or regret over what he done neither."

"It wasn't long and the rest were out looking for Robb. I guess Jesse knowed that, though. The crack of pistols and shotguns followed, and both sides reacted. It was awful! The noise and people getting shot. It was a regular war. When the smoke cleared and all was quiet, we had some wounded men, but so did the Mahoney bunch. When it turned quiet, we fashioned a fire brand like the Indians do and shot flaming arrows onto the roof. The ones that didn't surrender died from the smoke and flames. One lone mastiff ran from the house, his fur singed, he ran to Robb's feet and looked up at his master. He had them wild eyes lookin' around crazy like, then lowered his head and ran into the prairie. I don't never want to experience such a thing again," he said.

Hessie stood transfixed while this tale unfolded, tears the size of quarters poured down her cheeks. She's cried so much lately. At least she knows her father was avenged, but it won't bring him back.

Hans has been more relaxed since August and Johnny returned. Now that the harvest is over and his part finished, Johnny will go back to town to work. Greta and Hessie made a nice supper of potato salad and ham sandwiches, along with a huge pitcher of lemonade. The cold food was a change from our usual hot meals. Hans refused to talk even when spoken to during supper.

Peter finally spoke up. "I've given the county my notice. I'll work a short time, but November elections will no doubt bring in new law enforcement. What we need is a crack shot; someone with the nerves and iron gut of a gun fighter. Talk among the Alliance is they'll run Pearl Lux for sheriff. The clout and power of the Farmer's Alliance indeed makes it possible to bring such as Pearl back and elect him."

You could hear a pin drop in that room. Maggie sat transfixed. Her face had begun to heal, but the black and blue turned an ugly yellow and green. Her eyes are still smoky and dark. Hessie has been so kind to her, but there is still that evil glitter there. It is unsettling.

This morning this letter was received from Annie in Colorado.

14 September 1885

Dear Mama and Papa,
Your letter has been read and re-read many times as we are so concerned about what all has happened at the close of harvest time. We both extend our sincerest best wishes that all of you can heal and put this horrible time behind you. Perhaps with the winter holidays coming we can plan a visit to see my family. We would feel more at ease in our own minds that you are well. Rose has been terribly homesick, but because of Maggie, she feels her presence would only add to your strife. It is her sincerest wish not to trouble you at this time.

I feel it my responsibility, however, to share this news with you. Rose brought yards of white silk fabric along with lace veiling and seed pearls to trim it. It is apparent this is fast becoming a most beautiful wedding dress. And whether you agree or not, Rose intends to marry Jesse Peers with or without your approval.

This is upsetting to Willie and me, as we know nothing of Jesse Peers. We hope he is worthy of the devotion of my lovely sister. If not, you should be warned.

Otherwise, Rose has been a great help to me and is quite a wonder at organizing my kitchen into a proper galley to feed our roomers. She works timelessly without a single complaint.

We are most indebted to her for her patience with us.
 I remain,
 Your Devoted Daughter, Annie

It seems Jesse Peers is destined to enter our lives and be here forever. Greta has been very supportive of him. Hans was another matter. As the days wear on, Greta saw such a change in him. Since Maggie's attack and the killing of Calvin, Hans was a different man. It had changed him; but Greta expected any day he would rise up in protest about Jesse Peers. The Peers are a respected, upstanding family and would be a wonderful alliance for the Sikes. Rose has chosen well. Greta would try to bring about some agreement with Hans in the days to come.

Chapter 22

From 1854-1929, 250,000 children traveled on the Orphan Trains from places far east to the mid-western states. As many as 40 children at a time were transported to train stations and public buildings where eligible adopting parents met them. Poor and impoverished children in abundance lived throughout the United States and many found prospective good homes. Very few of these children were considered depraved or criminalized. Many poor families allowed their children to go on the Children's Trains because they could not afford to support them. Many kept in touch with their offspring even after they were adopted out. Those that were not fortunate enough to find binding relationships with families to care for them often shuttled about in a meager existence. A few were fortunate enough to reside in caring communities where the Children's Aid Society attempted to help them.

Hannah Ahrens

My first breath was drawn April 10,1861, when my mother gave birth in a ten-bed maternity ward in St. Louis. I slipped out into the midwife's hands weighing a slight six pounds eight ounces, measuring 15 inches, a small birth weight compared to most babies born at that time. The confinement left no trail of amazement or memorable remembrance as far as the nuns who attended the women there were concerned. There was a no nonsense kind of attitude about the event. When I was a meager five days old, my mother and my father, Benny, slipped quietly out of the maternity ward, and the city as well, to avoid paying the bill. The nuns do remember this however. Benny Ahrens married my mother in a fit of remorse and greed, convinced she could provide him with everything he needed.

Even in the budding of youth, Benny would not be considered handsome. His eyes had the cunning of a weasel, his stature frail. His movements always quick, hurrying toward something, somewhere. Hurrying in a maize of turns and searches running in circles, finding nothing and more of the same. Like everyone on earth never concluding we are alone. It's ourselves we need to live with. His father-in-law did not approve of him and disowned his daughter. Benny was angered to the point of beating her. One of the events that would eventually cause her to flee in fear of her life. She left him one August morning when I was three, never to be heard from again. Since there is no proof otherwise, I am left to assume she escaped, able bodied and glad to be rid of her miscreant spouse. No record exists beyond the time she fled the maternity ward. Her path was either well hidden or suspiciously without a trace. Now as I look for that small forlorn person from the past, I have wondered ever after, did I look like her? What was she like? Did she ever think of me? I pondered on this after

Wildfire

I was grown, when I'd been married a dozen years with a house full of children. After I'd known the love and trust of a good husband, after I had birthed and cared for my own babies that I held wondering how anyone could leave a babe. These precious souls are born so innocent and needful.

Benny, left with a toddler, prevailed again upon his in-laws to help with me. He was told to find himself assistance elsewhere. I do recall his endless whining about their neglect never owning the part he played. Benny began his long pursuit of neglect and abuse, primarily because he didn't know any better. We lived in flop houses and flea-infested hotel rooms until about the age of five when we fled to Valparaiso, Indiana. For a short time we lived in a tent city at the edge of town where I shared a curtained off area of Benny's tent. We had an abundance of company. People like ourselves in a disgraceful existence. This was the time of the Civil War, so we shared our lives with deserters, freed slaves, and poor white folks.

My life changed some for the better about the age of four. Although anything may have been better than the way things were. I was still the constant nagging responsibility of Benny, who used me for his own ill gotten gain whenever possible. The more pitiful we looked, the better he liked it. I never called him father because he didn't deserve this respect and because he did not want me to. He continued to mistreat and abuse me until one day Pearl Lux came into my life.

Pearl was a little older than me. I knew immediately the secrets residing there in his eyes, he too had known a childhood very much like mine. You looked into his eyes and knew the person gazing back at you understood the destructive forces at work were too much to bear. At times the conscious so overwhelmed it closed down from sheer need to avoid the pain. I don't know when I began to love Pearl Lux, but it surely was very soon after he came to our humble hovel. I discovered the kindness of the only person who had ever shown any concern for me. I had a strong remembrance of that face of meanness.

Pearl would come by when Benny was away and leave a bag of food and clothes. I learned quickly to devour or hide whatever he brought. If something was left where Benny could see it, what he didn't consume he sold. The clothes were grabbed up early, as they were worth pocket money that Benny needed to gamble. He was still ousted from most of the pool halls and bars because he had the idea nobody knew he was cheating. He would come in bloody and bruised, contaminated with the stuff he put into his body, losing his last bit of connection with the plane he lived on.

For a long time, I believed I'd done something wrong. Maybe I hadn't shown him what the kindness of Pearl's heart had left in my possession. As I grew older I realized it wasn't possible to determine Benny Ahren's treacherous moods or how far he would go, especially when he was high.

One time Pearl brought a doll. A pretty golden haired baby doll that had a fine white gown, a hood, diapers and a blanket. The next time Pearl came by he inquired, "Did you like the baby doll?"

I said "I don't have it any longer. Benny tuk it somewheres, I never seen it again." A look of shock came over Pearl's face, followed by a furious flash of anger.

Benny managed to keep me out of sight at times because his fist and his temper had damaged me enough to leave marks. He would threaten, "I'll give ya' worse if you talk to anyone until I say you can." Soon after the doll disappeared, Pearl's Uncle Ambrose came and got me. I mean he bodily picked me up and carried me. We moved into Mattie Kelly's Boarding house.

I began to improve because I was under Mattie's watchful eyes. Mattie didn't try to hide her contempt of Benny and he returned it liberally. He changed after he learned Mattie would back up threats by having Sheriff Tate pay him a visit. Before long my skin became tinged with the pink of good health and clothes appeared that remained on my back. It was the early years of puberty. At this time I started school and learned to read and write. Pearl and I both had Ada Hornby as a teacher, and she was almost as mean as Benny. Her cane came out regularly and it was the first time I witnessed the discipline of other students and Pearl Lux in particular.

These were not good years for Pearl Lux, as he was at odds with some of the other students as well. Flop Reedy was the bully of the school. I learned never to cross Flop or I'd be in for more trouble, not only from him but some mischief he framed me into with Ada Hornby. Pearl wasn't so lucky in this respect and was sent home repeatedly for some infraction Ms. Hornby calculated he had done. Everyone knew it was Flop, but how could we prove anything. And if we complained, Flop took it up after school. One day Pearl beat the tar out of Flop Reedy right in the schoolroom. We all stood around and cheered him on too. It made us all feel good.

I missed Pearl terribly when he quit school. My subtle love affair with Pearl was over. I was busy with grammar and spelling and began to read authors like Robert Louis Stevenson, Louisa May Alcott, and Jane Austin. I consumed books with a voracious appetite. I found an outlet for my solitary life by reading. Benny was getting thrown out of the best places in town and came in tipsy and bragging about something he had done. The bills he stuffed into his vest pockets bore witness to his most recent chicanery.

Then Benny failed to pay our rent. He didn't bother for six months, in fact, and Mattie took it up with him. She threw us out. Afterward, I heard Father O'Houlihan chide Mattie over what she had done. Both of them had a heavy Irish brogue that I could hear clearly as they argued.

Father insisted, "You've done a bad thing as Hannah would be nowhere of any consequence, and I'm afraid for what might become of the likes of her."

Mattie allowed, "I'd not thought this through, but good Lord willing, Father yerrself had some ideas of yer own as to what might be done." Father stormed out muttering to himself and returned later to encounter Benny and me gathering up our meager trove. It was then he offered, "Benny, the rooms at the back of the parsonage are empty. I'll do my best to have them altered so they might be used and efficiently turned into a bedroom and kitchen." And that was how we moved. Benny always had a deal going on with someone. I don't know if people were concerned for me, or disgusted with him, anyway, it led to yet another part of the drama.

Benny liked to go to Ambrose Lux's farm and play poker. One day after a poker game, a storm came up. Benny, being a nitwit, rode off out of Ambrose's into a heavy thunderstorm. That's just how he was--never learned a thing, just kept on doing the same thing over and over. Never learned from his mistakes. Maybe we all do. Not intentionally, but more like he couldn't even help himself. Spent his whole life doing things as if he already knew who he was. Clouds boiled over the sun in huge cumulus fluffs, dark at the edges, shot through with purple that day. The sun leaking through in spots before it disappeared. As he neared the town, lightning struck, and he lay prone and unconscious in the rain.

I expected Benny to return for supper and when he didn't I began to wonder what happened. Jim Reeves happened by the parsonage and I was there with Father at the time. Jim tended bar at Fitz's tavern in downtown Valparaiso. Benny liked to hang out there occasionally. The conversation turned to Benny and Jim said, "He was at Ambrose's before the storm set in. Benny's horse come into the stable alone." This led to speculating on what had become of Benny. Jim offered, " I'll drive you out there in a buckboard to search for Benny." Jim didn't seem surprised to find Benny laid out in a ditch right near the road, pale as an albino, struck dumb with the force of nature.

Benny lay in a coma for a few days. After he recovered he believed he'd been entered into with some kind of spirit. Instead of being chastened, he was convinced he was empowered like some special being. He found himself lying in bed at the back of the parsonage. Our new home was three large rooms. Father had a partition built off the kitchen where I could have a bed and dresser to myself and a door to close upon the world. In my heart, I was so jubilant I praised the Lord for landing me there. I had a window that looked out on the backyard of the church on a lovely garden, and trees where the birds sang the whole day long. The magnificent grass grew taller than my head where chipmunks and ground squirrels languished in the afternoon sun.

About this time Benny became convinced he was being watched. A "friend" had made Benny's acquaintance with Cocaine and Benny was an avid learner. This sent Benny into a fit of suspicion that no good ever came from. He suspected everyone, even me. Benny accused me of spying on him and telling tales that weren't true. I was to know a kind of torment worse than ever before. When he was high on Cocaine he wasn't lucid, and when he was off it and down, he was unbearable looking for another hit. I grew to fear him and would run out into the woods and hide. One day he caught up with me. He struck my back and flung me down. He pummeled me hurting himself as well, till I didn't know whose blood was spilled. He stopped only short of beating me too death. This time he'd gone too far.

Benny ran off down the river back of the parsonage. I wandered around dazed and bleeding. I stumbled into the cemetery plot next to the church. I rested there on the cool pillar of stone, trying to stay lucid and awake. The next thing I knew, Pearl Lux was carrying me on horseback to Mattie Kelly's. I thought surely I had died that day, sitting on that horse's back. Pearl with his arms around me felt so safe and secure. In a dream state, I tried to tell Pearl what had happened.

I stayed at Mattie's and it was a long time before I began to feel better. The bruises etched in my skin seemed to stay forever. The trauma in my brain would never go away. My body healed, but Father O'Houlihan came nearly every day to check on me. He began to talk to me and asked questions about what I remembered. Father inquired carefully about what had happened. He wanted me to delve into my past and to express some of the feelings I'd had early on about Benny and his tantrums. I told him Benny didn't have tantrums. "It was more like he's possessed. I don't have much of a memory about my early childhood. There were periods all along that are huge blanks." A tantalizing hint, an odor, the squeak of leather, but those unfamiliar surges would not come, no matter how I tried. The trauma beat in me like blood in my veins, those ticking moments of my survival. Father said, "That's the way the mind dealt with such matters. It simply blocked them out because they are too painful to remember." My imagination did its share of betrayal, falling into a fit of despair in some abyss of fear and doubt.

Then one day Father came and talked to me at length. Like he was trying to decide something. I listened intently wishing he'd say whatever was bothering. Finally, he said, "Benny's dead, someone murdered him out back of the rooms you live in." I saw in my mind that beautiful tall grass I had loved to walk in during the days there. The way it always seemed to heal me. And then it hit me, he was gone. It drained from me like a beaver dam drains a swamp and turns it into rich farm soil. Now Benny was dead right out there in that garden that I thought was so beautiful, driving out of me with an excitement edged with fear. Fear poured out like a rupture leaving me deliciously clean. People were more guarded than ever around me. Pearl visited me and for the first time I spoke with him. It was as if I couldn't make the break through to talk to Pearl. The thing was inside me like a burst vial that leaked through me telling me, I was bad and not worthy. He came often during those days. I wanted to say everything that was in my heart, but I couldn't. I realized then that I would love Pearl forever, even if he didn't love me back.

Unfortunately, Pearl was accused of murdering Benny. Sheriff Tate wouldn't even consider anyone else till Sadie Hawkins, the spitfire of the boarding house, set Tate straight. She reminded him Benny's earlier acquaintances were now in jail and Pearl wouldn't hurt anyone. Tate made a beeline to the telegraph office to wire the prison in Joliet. Some of Benny's cohorts were incarcerated there, and sure enough, one of them had escaped. It seemed Benny had turned state's evidence against one of them which earned his "partner" a lifetime sentence in exchange for his own leniency. An axe had ended Benny's life. It was as if he knew all along he'd end up like this. We all believed Benny would end up like this.

Life became a little simpler after Benny's death. No longer a threat to me, I actually began to make sense out of what had happened. One day I asked to help Mattie and Sadie out at the boarding house. Jesse Peers arrived in Valparaiso and often stopped in. He was crazy about Mattie Kelly. I never saw the likes of how they carried on. At times it seemed they did not care who knew what they were doing. Mattie and Jesse would be cuddling in the backrooms of the Boarding House. They even took a trip to St. Louis together. Sadie was by turns accepting and resentful of Jesse. He was so nice looking, I was in agreement with Mattie. Sadie didn't think she could trust Jesse, or any man I might add. Jesse talked about taking a herd of milk cows to Nebraska for his daddy who was homesteading out there. He planned on taking a group of people and a bunch of Conestoga wagons across the plains and herd these cows out there.

One day, Jesse came and asked if I would like to go along. Pearl, B. J. Rivera, and the family of Joe Lone Bear was going too. They were all friends of Jesse Peers. I told him I wasn't sure, that I'd have to let him know. It was too much for me to fathom. Being alone in the world, and now being asked to leave all this for Lord knows what in an unsettled part of the country. It was a powerful preponderance for my tender years on this earth. It entailed risk, more than I'd ever thought. Like spading new earth and sowing seeds, the risk was great. A mistake or a failure could even raise demons from the past. I knew somehow it could set me free. This essential act allowed me to fill my lungs with breath and give me a future.

Mattie pulled me aside and talked about whether I should go. She made me feel it wasn't important for me to go along, but if I wanted she'd understand. Whatever I decided I'd always have a place with her. These were the most comforting words to hear from all her conversation.

Late in the long soft dusk of a summer afternoon before the cool blue of autumn, I made up my mind to go along to Nebraska. And from the first it seemed like a sound idea. It was quite a crowd with all of us riding horseback or driving a team aboard one of the wagons. My meager belongings didn't add much to the bulk carried across the plains. I saw Pearl every day, during meals, through storms, and pleasant times. I saw how hard he worked to make everyone feel safe. When it comes to knowing exactly what to do, Pearl could always be depended on. I may be partial here, but it was a pleasure being around this man.

I helped the women cook and wash clothes. Occasionally, I'd sit up front on one of the wagons. I couldn't rein the horses because I wasn't strong enough. Joe Lone Bear's wife, Sweet Water, could drive those teams like a veteran. There was a sweet and soft understanding between her and Joe. You could see it whenever they were together. Her body was short and stocky, thick in waist and trunk from years of hard work with muscles like steel. I was happy just sitting there beside her. Early mornings were the best. There was always grouse and quail that tasted like chicken when cooked right. Sweet Water set traps to snare these birds. We'd get busy lighting fires and putting food to cook. Events through the long journey will remain with me to the end of my days.

The Red Cliff Indians that met us in Wisconsin was an unexpected event. These were Sweet Water's kin come to visit her and Joe. This unexpected meeting made me begin to look differently at the trees, brush and beyond with a new knowledge. Perhaps we were watched constantly. Not long after we met Sauk warriors, a sorry lot with a slave in tow whom they sold to Jesse Peers. Cynci, a settler's daughter, was taken as a baby and sold to the Sauks sometime in that miserable life of hers. Shortly after, we met with traders that had been bushwhacked probably by the likes of the Sauk Indians we encountered. Finally, we came near Nebraska and Jesse and Pearl rode with these traders to Omaha. Before Pearl and Jesse returned we came upon a Pony Express rider who was near death. He'd been tortured by renegade Indians and left to die. This caused tremendous concern among us especially for the woman Cynci. as she thought the poor man was possessed. Sweet Water was able to make the man comfortable until he died. We buried him on the Nebraska prairie and took his possible's bag along to return to the Express office.

The rest of this story unfolded with Jesse's parents, Emory and his wonderful wife, Sara Ann. To my mind she was as near to a mother I would ever experience. Not even Mattie had a presence like Jesse's Mother. Her nurturing enhanced all our lives. Now when I find myself involved in another dilemma because Pearl was forced to shoot Slats Mahoney, we've had the support of these good people. Pearl has fled to Johnson County in Wyoming territory where he works for a rancher. Already he has found someone that would take us in. Emory Peers communicated with this rancher that we needed a safe haven until we could return to the Nebraska homestead of the Peers family.

This took Pearl to the Teton Mountains, a distant blue with altitude much higher than Nebraska. Mountains that stood out blue and white in the vigorous mountain air. It's a breath taking place where we see an abundance of deer and elk. Few bison still flourish here although they were near extinction. There is a benevolent relationship between Indians and whites that is amazing, because of the sheer loneliness of ranching. We often barter with the Cheyenne, Shoshone, and Araphoe who are sprinkled among the remote canyons and live as peacefully as the US Government will allow.

Like Lone Buffalo from the Oglala Sioux, these Indians want to live in peace and free of oppression. The rhythm of our lives could lay side by side with theirs like two panes of glass. Our own history and theirs is almost the same, yet different in detail. Both groups wishing to live in peace in a country that is violent where bloodshed is common. We all strive for peace. This is getting ahead of my story.

Chapter 23

The rendevous gatherings were inaugurated in 1825 by Wm. Ashley, driving force behind the Rocky Mountain Fur Co. , to link trappers in the mountains to markets in and supplies from St. Louis and, not incidentally, handsomely line his own pockets. The event turned into an annual blowout .--The very presence of newcomers was quite enough to fire up the athletic, alcoholic, and amatory pride of the veteran mountain men, and they proceeded to demonstrate their skill on beast, bottle, and brown-skin beauty.
THE SUNDAY OREGONIAN, March 6, 2005

Home in the Teton Mountains

In October, Ms. Peers and I fashioned a simple white gown and veil that I will wear on my approaching wedding day. Harvest is over and the trees reflect the friendly tones of autumn. Emory Peers forged two silver wedding rings for the event taking pains to make them fit. We prepared a wedding feast anticipating Pearl's brief return when he would spirit me away someplace safe until this Slats Mahoney affair either goes away or justice prevails.

Ms. Peers worked swiftly pinning the hem of my dress and making fitting adjustments. "Hannah, you are so fidgety today. I swear I'll stick you yet. It's been awhile since I've seen a bride as nervous as you are."

"Lord, I can hardly stand it. Preparation for this day has nearly done me in. I hardly slept last night thinking about all my plans. Each time a horse whinnies, I think Pearl may have arrived." I walked out to the barn a dozen times, expecting Pearl to ride in. Sitting on a rail fence, hands folded in my lap, knees pinched close, I looked wistfully at the skinny shimmering coil of road that ran off into the sand hills west where he'd approach from.

Inside, the women had little trinkets for me. Maudie brought me her pearl earrings and Ethel handed me a blue hanky to tuck into my bodice. "Somethin' old, somethin' new, somethin' borrowed, somethn' blue. It's so exciting. Mama has asked Rose and Hessie to come over just like any other day. They're the only ones that know, though." Maudie pinned the hanky into my pocket.

Ethel looked thoughtfully at the flowers in vases around the living room where we'd have the minister perform our vows. The chicanery afoot was too much for her as well as me. "Law enforcement was known to show up around the county and we didn't want any slip up now. Papa decided it was safe to have Reverend Hypaul do your ceremony." Ethel shared this bit of information covertly with us.

Everyone bustled around cleaning and pressing clothes. The very best was taken out and aired or carefully hand washed, ready for the event. The air of expectation flooded through the house.

When Pearl and Lone Buffalo rode in accompanied by Buffalo's wife Early Dawn, we exchanged silent smiles and rushed to greet him. Pearl dismounted from his horse and gathered me into his arms. I thought I would burst, I was so happy. He looked down at me with this apparent jangle of emotions and bent down and kissed me, his eyes hooded with a bliss I'd not seen there before. Seeing this, I matched his emotions and a tremble ran through me. Sara Ann and Emory smiled broadly seeing us together. In the din of noise, the farmyard aflutter with animal sounds, the people in the house a cacophony of pleasant greetings spoke legions of the happiness we all felt.

"Is everything ready? Your stuff all packed and ready to leave? Did you ask Ms. Peers to help?" Pearl erupted with an excitement he was trying very hard to conceal. His anticipation was apparent.

"Heavens, take it easy. Let me look at you," I insisted. "You are so tan. Yes, I'm all ready to leave right after you marry me, Pearl Lux. Ms. Peers has worked herself into a fine case of nerves. Says she hasn't done this for awhile. Maudie and Ethel even baked us a cake. We're going to have a celebration."

Jesse hurried in from the yard and grabbed Pearl in a bear hug. "Rose will be here soon. She and Hessie are the only guests besides Reverend Hypaul. Mama has prepared a feast for all of us for this celebration."

Emory rushed in followed by Hank and Ephraim, Joe Lone Bear, Morning Star and Ishtapa, each looking expectant. "Ain't never been to a weddin' before," Hank

Simon lamented. They were scrubbed up and dressed in their best clothes.

Soon we heard the tinkle of Sukie's harness as Del Cole shouted, "Rose and Hessie are here!" He grabbed up Sukie's reins while the women bustled into the house. The next few hours were a delightful blur of confusion and joy.

Emory Peers folded my hand inside his strong arm and escorted me down the long hallway into the living room. He had a proud contented smile upon his tanned wrinkled face. The calm peaceful man centered exactly in this place, his shoes owning every step he took and the ground they stepped upon. He walked me into the living room and placed my hand in Pearl's. Maudie sat at the spinet playing Lohengren's wedding March. I admit I hadn't the foggiest notion what I was doing. There was not a clear path from here to there, but an ever widening circle pouring forth into new paths and new ways. This was not one event but many, many things all joining in one fluid motion. I was the happiest woman alive. After our vows spoken quietly to each other Reverend Hypaul announced, "Pearl, you may kiss your bride." I thought my heart would burst with happiness right there. Everyone began to relax as they filed into the dining room. Pearl and I remained briefly in the living room while he held me in a hard embrace and kissed me. Slowly I began to realize I was a wife, Pearl Lux was mine after all this time. We would at last become close as the ceremony had said "as one."

The dinner was a grand celebration with an eight layer cake that Maudie and Ethel had managed to bake and decorate. All the women helped serve the dinner of roast pork and apple sauce. The mashed potatoes sat steaming in a large bowl. Gravy and vegetables were served from bowls heated in the warming oven. Ephraim and Del had churned ice cream in a hand turned freezer. Jesse brought out his violin and Maudie and Ethel joined him on a spinet and the old viola. We sat in the living room eating wedding cake. Rose sat with Ms. Peers and Hessie enjoying every minute of this wedding celebration. Rose watched intently as Jesse said, "I promised I'd play a song for Rose. Today I'm playing a song I call 'Rose's Ballad.'"

Jesse settled the bow onto the strings of the fiddle and the sharp, pure clarity of his song had a startling harmonic sound. The tune was slow and rhythmic with considerable range. It caused a somber reaction in all of us. A yearning melody searching in long bow strokes found a sweetness as easy as drawing a breath. Maudie and Ethel joined in at the chorus with chords and harmony matching Jesse's search for volume and cleanness. There was a profound silence when the song came to an end, and the little trio ceased, a look of satisfaction on their faces. I had not seen the two women so happy in a long time.

This was the final event that would climax all that had happened. Before long, Rose too would leave and live in Colorado with her sister. By evening, we loaded our pack animals for the long trek through strange land. I wondered when I would again see all these fine folks. Ms. Peer had been the closest I would ever come to a mother. A motherless child is a sorrowful event. Leaving me alone in a careless world was a cruel and unjust way to begin my days on this earth. I forgive my mother because I know she didn't have a choice. I felt certain our future would be vastly different than the life either of us had known so far. As long as Pearl or I drew a breath in our bodies, we would make a difference. We hated to leave but the time had come to bid everyone farewell.

We followed Buffalo's lead through the trail along the North Loup River. Leaves crunched under the horse's hooves, crisp from the evening chill. The night was cool and trees had long gone through the glow of fall. At last we advanced through the bare far margins of mountain country with the hanging drift of smoke gray skies of the Tetons. Trees and grass grew in leisurely patterns of buffalo grass slopes intermixed with fir trees. Our huge shadows loomed behind us in the moonlight. An eerie reflection followed us as we galloped along against the trail cut into the shale and hills. We traveled mostly at night, finding some hidden spot before dawn where we would have the cover of trees or a hidden cave. Caves worked the best where we built a fire and cooked some of our food and boiled coffee. Afterward we would fold into a mindless sleep until dusk of that day arrived.

Pearl had brought Little Blue, the sassy cutting horse this time He rode Big Red, his favorite saddle horse. I rode a roan stallion called Whiskey that showed temperament at times. Pearl would ride up and grab the horse's bridle and stroke his muzzle as he talked to him. He would lean close and talk quietly to Whiskey then breathe into the stallion's nose. It seemed to calm the spirited horse. We brought the mustard-colored Arabian Pearl had captured in Wyoming two years ago.

She and her two year old were with us without a trace of the pathetic condition she was in at that time. Her coat shone a rich golden yellow now without a sign of the cruelty she experienced at the hands of Yellow Calf. It was a grey dusk with clouds that rolled an underbelly in the wind. It was warm with faint brief light smeared across the sky as the sun dropped low in the pines.

Mid-afternoon of the fifth day, saddle weary and tired to the core, we arrived at the ranch house of Howard Sweet and his wife Amilee. They greeted us warmly and helped us unload our pack animals. We could look out on a vast landscape of wilderness and meadowland. The shale hills speckled with timber gave way to generous pastureland that bordered the water source of the property. Hundreds of cattle fed peacefully there. Sweet's apparent pride was obvious as all of us walked along the garden and buildings around the cabin. Pearl liked the sparsely populated land of the mountains. After visiting with the couple and eating a scant meal, Amilee showed us our bedroom at the corner of the log cabin. Buffalo and Early Dawn slept in the bunkhouse.

I flung new cotton sheets I'd embroidered on the bed and covered them with a log cabin quilt. A feather tick laid on a chest in case it was cold during the night. Pearl and I stood close, with our arms around each other. We looked out through the drizzle of sleet coming down from the gathering storm. Flashes of lightning unleashed across the sky above a sea of grass. The sky streamed above with clouds the likes of mares' tails in the wind. The lamp wick flickered and needed trimming to even out the flame. The room weaving in shadow seemed to crawl the walls and spread away over the ceiling. Pearl became quiet with some personal thoughts. "I'll go check the horses while you get ready for bed."

He'd read my mind as I pulled out my cotton robe and gown. They unfolded across the bed like a white tent. The women at the Peer's household held whispered conversations over this gift to me. Maudie and Ethel had hand sewn blue lace and ribbon at the neckline of my gown. I have no idea how they managed all this, but I do know Rose shuttled back and forth carrying a large travel case. A happy task since Jesse was always there to carry the case in and out to her buggy.

When Pearl returned, I was buried between the cotton sheets trying to look serene which was nearly impossible by now. Pearl chuckled at the sight of me peering out of the huge bed. He blew out the lamp, sat upon the bed while he undressed. Pearl had some problem finding me among those sheets in that huge nightgown. He muttered to himself as he reached through layers on the bed and found my arms, my lips. There was language there without words, he was silent as he opened his arms and his heart and all the secrets he held for me We sated ourselves between knowing and not knowing. How sweet to call Pearl my husband.

Eventually we fell into a mindless sleep and did not hear the storm that blew across the mountains and ranch land. A faint brush of light smeared the window as we woke. Early morning found us huffing in the cold bedroom, our breath an icy fume, until we could kindle a fire in a small stove in the room. It crackled pleasantly while we basked in our bed once more. The reflection of the blaze radiated through the room and warmed our bodies as well as our thoughts.

"Did you ever once think you'd be married to the likes of me and live out your life as such?" Pearl had this profound look on his face as if he had discovered something. The truth spiraled in circles of his mind, apparent he was in some new place he'd never been before.

"That's a bit surprising that you never figured I'd lead you on and not suspect what I was about," I feigned innocence. Pearl laughed heartily. I thought never to hear that rich laugh of his again. I hungered for it, for the warmth and strength of his presence—an apparent tenacity, that I recognized immediately.

"If you've changed your mind, it's too late for it. You'll not get away no matter how you plead," I continued.

He collapsed in laughter and hugged me close. "Why didn't you tell those women to make that gown a might fuller. If they had, I'd never have found you last night." It was his turn to banter now. "I hope you'll be content as a cowpoke's wife until I can get you a proper house of your own, my darlin' Hannah."

The next day found us entrenched in our new lives. The excitement of it all disappearing like a brief sorrow. Lone Buffalo and Early Dawn had hardly left us on their journey home, when a snow storm set in. The crankiness of a winter storm set upon us without mercy. The darkened skyline sent clues this was a peculiar run of weather. The gusting measure of wind accompanied by a white out of snow distended blanketing everything as far as one could see. Pearl and the other cowhands spent the next week making sure the cattle were inside the fence. As soon as it was possible, they cleared snow from the yard, barns, and cattle sheds. They rounded up strays and brought calves in lopped over their saddles or pulled them behind them. The calves bellowed their discontent at being roped and towed through snow to shelter. Pearl and Howard spent some time counting cattle. When the last of the lot came into the cattle sheds, one stubborn old heifer butted Howard and dashed past him followed by twenty or so other cows. Howard was all set to go into the ranch house and the whole lot surprised and angered him. Howard is a huge man, over six feet tall. His hands are like Dutch ovens that don't just grab something, they smother things. Your hand disappears into the depth of his warm handshake thinking you'll never get it back. In frustration, he grabbed off his Stetson and threw it down followed by the worst string of profanity we'd ever heard. As we watched, Pearl rode up on Little Blue and bunted Howard's arm which made him worse. He let loose with another string of cuss words that just ripped out of him. Howard threw them out like he had to let them go. Pearl reined Little Blue into the corral, ran close to the lead cow and bit her. She wasn't about to give up her dash for freedom, so Little Blue rode hard at her and knocked her off her feet. The contest was over and Pearl drove the rest obediently back to the sheds. The cow that had led them astray followed. Howard stood with his hat in hand, his mouth agape. "I never saw the likes of that done before."

"Well sir, this is a cutting horse and she is smart as a whip where cow herding is concerned. Won't never let a cow get away with what that heifer just pulled." Pearl looked amused as he thumbed a molasses ball into Little Blue's mouth. Little Blue looked pleased with herself. Happy with the treats and proud of what she'd just done. She'd averted more than one stampede and always knew what to do.

Amilee and I spent our days cooking up vats of food to feed the hungry bunch of men who straggled in out of the cold ready for coffee and rest from the storm. They complained of headaches and strained muscles.

"You've been a big help around the kitchen Hannah. Seems you've done the likes of this many times before." Amilee had this stocky short body built like a bullet, strong and hard as a rock. She was busy peeling potatoes for our evening meal.

"Everyday, even Sunday, Amilee. The Peers had about as many as there are here to feed but five women did the work. How'd you manage alone?"

"Oh, you just do it. We never had anything fancy. Nobody complains when they're hungry. Once in awhile a cake or pudding. Sometimes one of the men would be recuperating, get injured or some such. They'd get well enough to do up something. One guy made a batch of apple sauce and I ended up canning most of it. Howard treated our fruit trees this year, so the apples and cherries were right good."

Amilee looked wistfully at her recipe file, she'd collected in a box she kept in the kitchen. Her hands were callused and pock marked with injuries. I fear she was dreaming on that as by the time meals are prepared there's only time to cook and serve it.

The bunk houses were used for sleeping only not like the Peers' bunk houses which were big enough for a table and chairs as well as a scrub house for washing and personal care. Pearl and I had our own bunk house apart from the wranglers here. We'd stayed in the main ranch house only one night. Buffalo and Early Dawn had slept in our cabin the night they were here.

"Once I've gotten our own belongings settled into the cabin, maybe I can come out sometime and preserve fruit and make jam," I told her.

"Whatever you do will be appreciated and not only by me." A look crept into Amilee's face. Something caught there in the twist of her smile, an expression of anticipation. I doubt Amilee had ever had time to ponder on anything but the immediate meal.

"Must've been rough when someone is injured or gets sick enough to not be able to work," I inquired.

"It happens and oftener than you might think. Thrown from a horse or falls stacking hay in the heat. It seems about every month something goes on that wasn't planned for. Broke bones are a tragedy around here. It creates work for the rest of the crew and is a misfortune for the person it happens to. By fall when the branding and the likes is finished somebody routinely goes to town and isn't worth a tinkers dam when he gets back. Broke and messed up from gambling and fighting. These cowpunchers are transients that move from one ranch to the other. Oh, they get ornery and tell Howard off and he fires them regular, but it doesn't last. They need work and Howard needs help. Things work out."

We laughed at the prospect. This was different than the Peers where we'd had one set of people all the time. Although with Del Cole and Ephraim Hobbs, we'd had our share of problems there too.

November flew by and December and Christmas is a blur now: Everything new and different. We never left the ranch, but once winter set in Amilee showed me her quilting frame and rug loom. Both things help pass winter evenings. Amilee taught me to hand quilt and after repeated attempt and needle pricks that bled all over, I learned to use a thimble. Howard ran traps for muskrat and beaver and tanned the pelts. By spring we'd finished two quilts and a stack of rag rugs. The fur pelts hung in bunches in the shed out by the barn.

In mid-February around the supper table, Howard mentioned a Rendezvous in Fort Washakie. Pearl and I had no experience with a Rendezvous and were anxious to learn all about them. It would be a chance to get to the trading post for supplies. Amilee looked forward to this event.

One evening after Pearl and Howard spent the day working with muskrat pelts, we sat around the fireplace of their cabin. We began to smell this pungent odor. It permeated the place and the warmer the room got the more pungent the odor. Pearl and Howard began to laugh and Amilee went to the kitchen and pumped the reservoir full of water. "I don't know about Hannah, but Howard is not getting in bed with me till he washes off that musk odor." After that baths were always necessary after the two worked in the tanning shed.

The Rendezvous came about in March just as soon as the weather calmed a bit. We loaded up the buggy with our trade goods and set out for Medicine Bow. The wind blew swirls of snow along the ground in white out that we drove through as best we could. There were sun dogs today even though the temperature was warmer. We were bundled in heavy wraps and hats with buffalo robes over everything. Frost formed on eyebrows and mustaches, hair and faces, and ears exposed to the frosty weather made us draw down inside our warm outer clothing. It was a three hour trip starting out early before the sun had hardly cracked to peek over the horizon. Our anticipation was great enough to put haste in everything we did. The buggy lamps were lit and the bells that accompanied our spirited horses heralded our swift journey into daylight.

Fort Washakie was crowded with a mixture of Indians and frontiersmen. The crusty looking men and women were dressed in buckskin and vests of lambs fur, dresses of homespun wool and boots and winter moccasins that reached above the knee. They wore a mixture of dirt, oil, grease and animal aroma. The beaver trappers were particularly smelly. Where they were used to the odor others mainly avoided them. They would lie and brag. Challenge each other in bouts of strength, horse races, foot races, drinking bouts, card games and shooting contests. Cheyenne and Arapaho Indians had horses as well as furs. The Indians were in the thick of things, betting their horses and running their own games of chance. We settled our goods where traders could see the furs, now glossy and rich with the smell of tanning oil. The cold winter made for heavy pelts. The arena used for the Fall Sundance now became the place for traders to set up our ware for trade or sale. The Rocky Mountain Fur Co. was there as well. They would buy furs at a pittance and make a fortune from the furs they bought today.

A barbecue pit had been struck at one side of the arena and hardwood burned bright and hot where roasts of venison and beef carcasses would be turned by hand on a spit. Several chuck wagons had pies, breads, hardtack and stroneground wafers to trade. One wagon displayed a huge vat of cheese with wedges cut ready to sell.

Once we were settled in our spot, Pearl told us, "Howard and I will walk around the circle of wagons. You two want to go along?"

"No, neither of us feel brave enough to move among these folks just yet. We'll stay close to the buggy watchful for some fabric or food we can trade later to take home with us," I said.

By dusk most or our pelts were gone, all of the rag rugs had been traded for cheese, flour and raw sugar. One of the quilts still remained and some of the rancher's wives had been very interested but had nothing Amilee was interested in trading. The two women bartered over the last quilt and finally struck a trade for a large bag of potatoes with a tub and scrub board thrown in. Amilee still wasn't satisfied but the rancher's wife gathered up the quilt, a smug look about her face. The tub was big enough to emerge oneself in but could double for a wash tub with the scrub board fitted nicely at one end. Later Pearl bought that tub and Amilee at last was happy with her bargain. To the end of my days I would remember the luxury of sitting in that bathtub. One of few luxuries I would experience as time passed.

With the close of our business day, Howard said, "We had a room reserved for the night at the hotel in Medicine Bow. I'll pack up those trade goods while Pearl helps you climb aboard to travel back the way we came." The sky was a soft blue black with stars as big a your fist sprinkled across the Milky Way. It was a clear crisp night.

The crowd of country folks scarfed up the last of the barbecued roasts and moved out for home. When we came to the cobweb of a town, only occasional lights could be seen in the darkness. We pulled up at the hotel, everyone gathered up their prizes from the day, and moved into the adjoining rooms. Pearl took the horses and buggy to the livery stable while we prepared for the night. I had traded a rug for a silver hand mirror and a hair clip made of tortoise shell. "I wonder if I'd made a good trade."

Pearl summed it up pretty well by saying, "It depends upon how much you wanted these things. If you were happy with your trade and cherished the things, then no matter what you paid would not be too much."

"How did you become so wise Pearl Lux? How?" Many times afterward I would refer to whatever he had traded or paid too much for. "Was it a good trade?" Sometimes he'd admit he must've been out of his mind. Not often though. Trading got to be a thing we learned to do well.

Early the next morning we returned to the ranch, anxious to put the new purchases away. Not long after we got home Amilee mentioned a conversation she had with one of the rancher's wives while at the Rendezvous. "Mrs. Martins asked if you were Pearl Lux's wife. When I acknowledged that you were, she said she'd heard of Pearl and he had a reputation of being a sharp shooter and a gun fighter. When I said we hired him on as a wrangler, the woman seemed surprised. She thought Pearl was being sought for as a law officer. She said they'd heard over in western Wyoming that a Sheriff had mentioned Pearl and wondered if he would be interested in a job with him. It was a surprise to me as I'd never heard this."

"I don't know what to say. He had problems in Nebraska territory but only because he was trying to protect us against some varmint that was out to kill us all. I can't imagine how anyone knew about Pearl." I tried to be as honest as I could be with Amilee. It wasn't my place to frighten her or reveal anything. I thought that was Pearl's place if it was important to tell the whole story. It surprised me nothing was said about his gifts with horses. Just this larcenous reputation because he'd shot someone in self defense.

It had been awhile since the ice had cracked like a cannon's boom on the Powder. The tell tale signs of the frost that covered the brush along the great river with pristine white began to thaw. I dreamed again of gardens and familiar faces of the Peers family and the folks there.

Awhile after we'd put the quilt frame and the rug loom to rest, in the somber days of March, Lone Buffalo rode in with Jesse and Del Cole. I had this premonition before they ever appeared in sight that something from the future approached. The long plodding gate of Wildfire, Jesse's Gold Coin Arabian, came into view as they galloped toward the ranch house. The horse was always full of energy, busting out ahead of the rest, looking like he might bolt and run. Had those wild crazy eyes that searched ahead of him. They rode swiftly to the gate of the property and slowed their pace very little until they got to the hitching rail and in one motion dismounted. They were in a hurry.

I peered through the shining glass of the kitchen window. The light shimmering in prisms through small bubbles that formed the glass. Pearl and Howard hurried to meet them, an apprehensive look skrimmed on Pearl's face. He greeted the three with a warm hand shake, a clasp of shoulders, eyes a glimmer of suspicion. "Hope you got good news, Jesse."

Jesse turned to him as Howard led them into the cabin. "Good news to some, bad for others. Some of the farmers banned together and rode up to the Mahoney homestead. Maybe 30-40 men in all. We burned the Mahoney's shack to the ground. Dwight, we hung from their gate post. Charges brought by Sheriff Sikes landed on Judge Seivers' desk last week, when some of us were called to testify to see if enough evidence was presented to warrant Pearl's involvement and arrest. Sikes, himself, even testified. It's history now but the judge discharged the complaint, both complainants being deceased. Didn't seem there was anything left to try. Seivers got snotty about all of us taking up his time in a courtroom when other matters needed tending. He went about granting three divorces and signing various warrants none for Pearl Lux though." A smile crept over Jesse's face, relief and happiness shown like an evening star.

Wildfire

The wait was finally over. Pearl rubbed the knees of his work trousers thoughtfully. I knew the depth of the courage and strength held there secret and deep, waiting till he might have to return to Nebraska To go back there, but to what. Fear drained out of both of us, relief like a ruptured balloon.

Just because I have told the story a certain way, it could change. Stories take their own shape, fused with a new twist sometimes that could be more exact. I didn't understand how the tangle of our lives would sort themselves out. Not every bit would be untangled at once. What it takes is time and patience.

As I step back and view all of the story together, gradually a pattern emerged. The story so far was clearly my own. It had brought me to this very moment. The story that would live through me. The final telling wouldn't be all at once but with patience and time, love and caring attention, a certain sequence would revolve in the telling.

About the Author

Donna McGrew is retired and lives in Vancouver, WA. She has published a previous book of which Wildfire is the sequel. ("The Unusual Life of Pearl Lux,") published in 2002. McGrew published an anthology of poetry entitled "One Voice," "Without Chains" a documentary of her travels across the West with her two dogs, and an "Alaska Diary". Her life story is available on the website: www.chess.chsra.wisc.edu/Mistory. She is actively involved in writing groups and a book reading group. She continues to live and enjoy the Northwest.

Copies of "The Unusual Life of Pearl Lux" can be obtained from the author at Email: Donnamcgrew@comcast.net